THIS TIME FOREVER BOOK 1

BUILDING Forever

KELLY JENSEN

Riptide Publishing
PO Box 1537
Burnsville, NC 28714
www.riptidepublishing.com

This is a work of fiction. Names, characters, places, and incidents are either the product of the author's imagination or are used fictitiously. Any resemblance to actual persons living or dead, business establishments, events, or locales is entirely coincidental. All person(s) depicted on the cover are model(s) used for illustrative purposes only.

Building Forever
Copyright © 2018 by Kelly Jensen

Cover art: Natasha Snow, natashasnowdesigns.com
Editors: Sarah Lyons, Carole-ann Galloway
Layout: L.C. Chase, lcchase.com/design.htm

All rights reserved. No part of this book may be reproduced or transmitted in any form or by any means, electronic or mechanical, including photocopying, recording, or by any information storage and retrieval system without the written permission of the publisher, and where permitted by law. Reviewers may quote brief passages in a review. To request permission and all other inquiries, contact Riptide Publishing at the mailing address above, at Riptidepublishing.com, or at marketing@riptidepublishing.com.

ISBN: 978-1-62649-839-6

First edition
October, 2018

Also available in ebook:
ISBN: 978-1-62649-838-9

THIS TIME FOREVER BOOK 1

BUILDING
Forever

KELLY JENSEN

For all the parents who think they're doing it all wrong. You're not.

TABLE OF
Contents

Chapter 1 1
Chapter 2 7
Chapter 3 13
Chapter 4 19
Chapter 5 25
Chapter 6 29
Chapter 7 37
Chapter 8 43
Chapter 9 53
Chapter 10 63
Chapter 11 71
Chapter 12 79
Chapter 13 87
Chapter 14 93
Chapter 15 99
Chapter 16 105
Chapter 17 111
Chapter 18 119
Chapter 19 125
Chapter 20 133
Chapter 21 137
Chapter 22 141

Chapter 23 147
Chapter 24 153
Chapter 25 159
Chapter 26 167
Chapter 27 175
Chapter 28 181
Chapter 29 189
Chapter 30 195
Chapter 31 201
Chapter 32 207
Chapter 33 213
Chapter 34 221
Chapter 35 225
Chapter 36 231
Chapter 37 245
Chapter 38 251
Chapter 39 259
Chapter 40 265
Chapter 41 269

CHAPTER 1

For all he didn't consider himself a religious man, Charlie King had a particular reverence for Cheez-Its. Now and again, he'd worship a single cracker by placing it on his tongue like a communion wafer. As sucking the life out of one little square usually proved unsatisfying, he more often scooped up handfuls and shoved them in the general direction of his mouth. It could be a messy business; he often ended up playing catch with a stray cracker or two, which was exactly what he was doing when Simon Lynley walked into his life.

"Hello?"

Charlie glanced at the open kitchen door and spluttered through a mouthful of cheesy crumbs. Approximate translations might have been *Hello*, *hold on*, and *Holy shit, are those contacts?* His visitor's eyes were an impossible shade of blue. Like the sky on a sunny day. Dark and light at the same time. Golden, but still blue. Celestial.

His wife's eyes had been a greenish sort of brown, and simply one part of the whole that was her face. He could rhapsodize about her face, but then he'd been stupidly in love. Merry could have had a mole sprouting hair at the end of her nose...

Okay, maybe not.

His visitor's eyes were extraordinary, particularly against a vague impression of fair skin framed by black hair, eyebrows, and a shadow of stubble... and Charlie was staring. Possibly gaping. Also, he was thirsty. Blue Eyes' appearance had interrupted his chewing. Charlie grabbed a glass off the rack by the sink, filled it, and washed away the cracker sludge gathering around his molars. Then he figured he should say something.

He indicated the faucet with the empty glass. "Can I get you some water?"

1

Blue Eyes' forehead wrinkled quizzically. "Ah . . . sure."

Charlie handed him a glass of water. A fresh glass, not one sullied with cheesy crumbs. "Is this about the front porch? Listen, I know it looks old and it's probably about ready to fall off the house, but I can't afford to do that and the roof. I need a roof. I don't need a porch."

Blue Eyes gave him a blank look in response. Then Herbert started howling. Well, resumed howling. Charlie hadn't actually registered when he'd stopped. The dog had been competing with the sounds of eighties rock and nail guns all afternoon.

"Is it the dog? I can take him out for a walk if the barking is bothering you guys. Oh, by the way, my daughter has to get out of the driveway—" Charlie checked the digital display on the microwave "—soonish. Sorry, I know we should have parked her car on the street last night, but my friend was blocking the driveway until late." Friday nights with Phil and the Xbox were near tradition. "Then, between walking the dog and checking in on a neighbor who thought she heard something, I totally forgot."

Blue Eyes hadn't taken a drink yet. In fact, he'd paused with the glass raised halfway to his lips. "I'm not one of your contractors."

Right, no Kendricks Roofing logo on his neat polo. No tool belt, no baseball cap. Just a stranger, standing in the middle of Charlie's kitchen, looking at the glass in his hand as if he suspected the water was poisoned.

"Uh . . ." Charlie cleared his throat.

"I'm your new neighbor," Blue Eyes said. "Moving in next door?" He tipped his head toward the door, through which Charlie could see the open gate in the hedge between their properties. Beyond that, the outline of a moving truck in the driveway.

"Huh."

Blue Eyes frowned.

Charlie scrubbed his free hand on the side of his jeans and offered it up. "Sorry, took me a bit by surprise there. I'm Charlie. Welcome to the neighborhood."

"Simon." A warm hand folded around Charlie's, and the touch was as shocking as that first glimpse of his blue, blue, very blue eyes. What the heck?

Charlie let go and rubbed his palm on his jeans again.

Simon watched, a serious little frown marring his brow.

"Sorry, I had Cheez-Its all over my hand, and I didn't want to— Yeah, you already— Or I... Um..."

The brilliance of Simon's eyes had dimmed enough for Charlie to appreciate the rest of him and... Simon was a *really* good-looking guy. Charlie hadn't noticed a guy and thought *Wow* since high school—and that had only been because Billy McHugh, captain of the football team, had been physically perfect, and the envy of every guy at Liberty High.

He was staring again, wasn't he?

"I'm going to get to the front porch soon," Charlie explained, not sure where they'd left the conversation but somehow convinced Simon was there because of the noise, or his cheap-ass choice of roofing tile. "I'd have done the roof myself if my daughter hadn't threatened me with an emancipation suit, whatever that is, if I got up there. She does not want to live in Florida with my folks. Something about frizzy hair and alligators. Not that I'm in the habit of falling off things, but it is kinda high up there. And a long way down."

Simon was staring at *him* now and probably not thinking, *Wow his eyes are so brown.*

"This isn't going how you expected it to, is it?" Charlie said. "It's not too late to shove everything back in the truck and move again. No one wants to live next to the weird guy."

Simon's laugh was sudden and very, very welcome. Charlie inspected the floor rather than the way Simon's eyes crinkled and twinkled. He'd done enough staring for one afternoon. Besides, the back of his neck itched—the sensation almost unfamiliar. He was blushing. Standing in his kitchen with a stranger, staring at his floor, and blushing.

"For all you know, I could be the weird one," Simon said. "I did just let myself into your kitchen, after all."

Charlie glanced up. "Right past my howling attack dog."

"He was busy chewing something that looked like a plastic chair leg."

"I can't have nice things. Not plastic things, anyway. So, where'd you move from?"

Simon was finally taking a sip of his water. Charlie busied himself with refilling his own glass instead of watching Simon's mouth, lips, and the drinking-swallowing thing. He really needed to get out more if he was tempted to watch strangers swallow—and the question of why he might watch, with extreme interest, his *male* neighbor swallow would be tabled until later.

"Morristown," Simon answered.

Huh? Oh, right, where he'd moved from. *Get with the program, Charlie.*

"What brings you across the border?" Moving across the Delaware River into Pennsylvania used to make sense. Lower taxes, less traffic. Now the bills and roads were just as crazy.

Simon's smile faded a little. "Looking for a change of scenery." He turned and put his glass back on the counter. "Anyway, I was checking out the gate in the hedge and when it opened and your door was open and you were standing here, I thought I'd introduce myself." He glanced over his shoulder. "And I left it open, didn't I?"

"'S okay. Herbert is on a chain. He'll strangle himself long before he gets close to the gate."

"Good to know."

"He's managed to push through the hedge when he's off the chain, though. I'll try not to let that happen."

"Hey, it's all good. He seems like a nice dog."

"He is, mostly. Friendly. Had him since Olivia was ten."

"Olivia is your daughter?"

Charlie's smile was involuntary, as it always was when Olivia wandered into the conversation. She had him happily wrapped around her little finger, and he wasn't ashamed to admit it. His days started and ended with his girl. "Yeah. You got kids?"

"No, it's just me."

"That's a big house for one . . . Um, unless you've got a lot of hobbies or like space. A lot of rooms." Moving on, "This is a good neighborhood. Quiet. Well, usually, when Herbert isn't saying hello, and contractors aren't playing music. A few kids, a couple of retirees. The lesbian couple on the corner." Why tell a complete stranger about the supposed sexual orientation of the couple on the corner? "They're very nice. Sue always brings the best salads to cookouts . . . and I'm gonna stop talking now."

Simon was laughing again. "You spend a lot of time alone, don't you?"

"Guilty as charged."

"What do you do?"

"Writer."

"That would explain it. What do you write?"

As if the conversation weren't awkward enough. "Technical writer by day, science fiction author by night."

Simon's eyebrows rose. "Like aliens and stuff?"

"And stuff."

"Cool."

"Do you read?"

"Not much," Simon said. "I used to. Even read some science fiction when I was a kid."

Because grown men didn't read stories about space pirates. Nope.

"I haven't read anything but a trade magazine in years," Simon continued.

"What do you do?"

"Architect."

"Oh yeah? You really don't want to look at my front porch, then."

Simon smiled. "I'll be working with Arthur Beckwith."

"Beckwith and Associates on Main Street? You'll have to tell us who his associates are. We have theories, but no one has ever met any of them. Anyway, I think he redid the place on the corner. They had a sign in their yard for a while after."

"The lesbian couple?" From the sparkle in his eyes, it was clear Simon was messing with Charlie.

"Other corner," Charlie said, grinning. "I thought about using him, but I don't want to do everything at once."

Even though his parents had moved to Florida almost a year ago, the place still felt like their house. Putting on a new roof for now and making plans for the front porch, and maybe the garden, made the house feel more like his.

"One day I might knock out the back wall of the kitchen and put in a nook sorta thing. Like to eat in. Or maybe a sunroom."

Simon smiled again and the whole kitchen felt warmer. "You've definitely got the space for it, and a good aspect."

Charlie's best project to date chose that moment to blow in. "Dad!"

Olivia took after her mother, which meant she was blessed with beauty, poise, and a complete lack of hairy moles. Glossy brown hair she spent two hours doing stuff to every morning, and a pixie-like face. She had Charlie's eyes—more brown than green—long limbs, and a knockout smile. At seventeen going on twenty-seven, she didn't smile enough for his liking, though. Of course, all Charlie remembered about seventeen was not listening to anyone's advice on anything, particularly when it had come to Merry. He should be grateful Liv hadn't lost her head yet.

"I need to go, and there's a truck blocking the driveway," she said.

Right.

Charlie gestured between his new neighbor and his daughter. "Simon, Olivia. Olivia, Simon. Daughter, new neighbor. Back in a second, Simon. I want to ask the guys to move their truck."

"I should head next door, anyway. Make sure my movers are moving."

"Well, nice to meet you. If you need anything, I'm usually around."

With a wave, Simon disappeared, taking his blue eyes and sunshine with him. Charlie probably stared at the empty doorway for too long. He told himself he was practicing a lingering gaze for a scene he wanted to write. Then he glanced over at Olivia.

Her eyes were narrowed. Her jaw moved once, twice, and then gum snapped behind her teeth. "He's hot."

"And way too old for you. Jesus. Don't give your dad a heart attack. I haven't finished doing up the house."

Chuckling, she followed him outside into the late-summer sunshine.

CHAPTER 2

It was hard to say whose company Simon had enjoyed better: Charlie's or that of his house. They both exuded personality. Both obviously had history. It was the house that had called him next door, however.

Something more substantial than history surrounded the fieldstone and timber structure that rambled in true farmhouse tradition. Simon called it *story*. The house spoke of generations of use and abuse. Not that the place looked ready to fall down. Rather, the house showed signs of weathering many storms, within and without, and of standing strong through it all.

It was the sort of house he wanted to live in one day. The sort of house he'd like to dedicate his career to finding and restoring.

From his side of the unruly hedge, only the upper stories were visible. Sunlight glanced off of the half-finished slate roof and weathered siding, brightening the soft gray. The colors complemented the fieldstone chimney, and he wondered if Charlie had chosen them. Charlie, the living component of the house next door—not that houses couldn't live and breathe. They did. Each had a soul, some more unique than others. Charlie . . . He was something else entirely.

Though he couldn't be over forty, he was a lot like his house. Simon had been able to see over the top of his head, which put him at just under six feet, but with a sense of movement. As if he'd recently come from somewhere, or intended to go somewhere. Energy and momentum in human form.

He was a good-looking guy too, with rich-brown hair that might not have seen a comb in near on a decade. The mess suited him. Brown eyes, tanned skin, and lines around his mouth and eyes that spoke of frequent smiles.

That mouth.

Simon closed his eyes. Fantasizing about married men stood pretty much at the top of the stupid list. But, Lordy, that mouth. Charlie's garrulous nature only drew attention to the fact he had generous lips and straight white teeth that he flicked with his tongue now and again. He could have been searching for cracker crumbs, but every time the pink tip had shown, Simon had thought about kissing him. Playing with that tongue, and what it would feel like alongside his own.

"I'd offer a penny for your thoughts, but the look on your face suggests they're worth a lot more."

Simon opened his eyes. Frank stood in front of him, eyebrows raised.

"I was just checking out the house next door," Simon said.

"With your eyes closed."

"Fixing it in memory. It's probably original to the area. I'd like to study it some more."

"Mm-hmm. Did you meet the neighbors?"

"Yeah. A writer and his family." Simon gestured toward the moving truck. "Have they broken anything yet?"

"No, but soon they'll be squaring up for piano versus door."

Simon surveyed the house on his side of the gate, absently checking the width of the front door. This was his home for the next six months—maybe longer. The owner wanted to sell the place, but Simon had no interest in a 1960s-era pile of cream brick. He'd seen some fascinating interpretations of split-level ranch homes, but they didn't appeal to him on a gut level. Hopefully, within six months he'd find something that filled him with wonder and delight. Simon glanced over the hedge again. Something like the place next door would do—preferably with someone like Charlie still in residence.

Married, Simon. And if the wife was anywhere near as beautiful as the daughter, unlikely to look elsewhere. Except he had. Simon could have sworn he'd felt Charlie's gaze at his throat while he was drinking. Then there'd been the long, lingering look when he'd said hello. Charlie had actually gaped, which had been amusing in one sense as cracker crumbs had spilled from his lips, and flattering in another as the source of those crumbs had obviously been forgotten.

Then there'd been all the talking. Simon smiled. He liked men who talked. They made up for his quietness.

Shouts and grunts wafted from the back of the truck. Simon crunched across the gravel drive in time to see the movers struggling with his second-most-precious possession: a grand piano. His heart fluttered anew. Had they already unloaded his drafting table?

"Please don't tilt the piano too much," he said, trying to keep calm.

Even an hour in the moving truck meant he'd have to have the instrument tuned, but excessive jostling would only make it worse.

The only door wide enough to admit the piano was at the back of the house. Simon followed the movers across the lawn and onto the patio, wincing every time the piano hummed and groaned. He'd packed the inside according to a "How To" he'd found on Google, but too much stuffing could be as detrimental as not enough. He breathed a sigh of relief when the movers set the piano down in the middle of the open-plan family room.

"Where did you want it?" Big asked. Simon had dubbed the movers Big and Little in lieu of actually remembering their names.

Pursing his lips, Simon studied the available space.

"How about there?" Frank gestured toward the long expanse of windows looking out over the patio.

The light would reflect nicely off the polished wood of the piano, but the temperature variance might stress the delicate equilibrium of the finely tuned instrument. Besides, it would be nice to put his sofa between the fireplace and the view. Simon turned to the opposite corner, where two walls met in a sort of shaded alcove. Originally he'd planned to install his bookcases there, but perhaps—

"Mister?"

"Over here." Simon indicated the corner.

After having the men turn the piano one hundred and eighty degrees, then back seventy and finally rotating it the other way, Simon was satisfied with the placement. Soon after, the rest of his belongings were in semi-appropriate positions and Little was handing him a clipboard.

"I just need your signature."

Simon felt an odd reluctance to let the movers go. The new house wasn't large, but as Charlie had so helpfully pointed out, it was a lot of space for one person. One person alone. Frank would want to start the drive back to Jersey City soon.

Simon signed the clipboard and handed it back with a cash tip. "Thanks, guys."

He closed the door on his old life and turned around to take in the new. Frank ducked out of the kitchen area with a bottle of wine and two glasses.

"Where did you find all that?"

"Your boxes are labeled with lists, Simon. You're predictably anal in all the ways."

Snorting softly, Simon took the glasses and held them while Frank wrestled the cork from the bottle. He didn't recognize the label, which meant Frank must have brought it with him.

Glancing up, Frank smiled. "I've also got some nibbles in a picnic basket in the car. I'd suggest spreading a rug on the floor and getting all rustic, but my knees are about thirty years beyond such shenanigans."

"I'd thought you might want to get going."

"And leave you all alone in the wilds of Pennsylvania?"

"You're such a giver."

Frank filled the glasses and waved the bottle toward the loose arrangement of furniture between the windows and the stone fireplace. "Go sit and I'll get the food in." He put the bottle on the kitchen island and gathered up his car keys. "And don't touch a single box while I'm gone. You can do that tomorrow."

Simon did as bid, weaving around a stack of boxes to get to the sofa. The light-gray microfiber looked appealing in the afternoon light. If not for Frank, Simon might have taken a nap. But as he sat, he acknowledged the fact that he'd more likely lie there thinking than sleeping. Instead, he surveyed the open-plan space that formed the heart of his new home.

Until he unpacked the boxes piled in every room, the house wouldn't feel like his. It might never feel like his, especially if he didn't stay long. He should make an effort, though. A good part of his motivation to move had been to find his own space—which sounded better than finding his self. This new space echoed with fewer memories of what he'd lost, but each box or familiar piece of furniture served as a subtle reminder.

"You're brooding."

Simon jerked, startled. He hadn't heard Frank return. He looked down at the glasses he still held in his hands, worried he might have spilled some wine, and leaned forward to set them on the table. Frank started laying out a selection of cheese, crackers, dips, olives, sausage, and fruit, all from a gourmet deli in Bethlehem, according to the labels. Trust Frank to have already surveyed the town.

"You grew up somewhere near here, didn't you?" Simon asked.

Frank waved toward the front door. "North. Pocono Mountains. Which is a fact you're supposed to have conveniently forgotten. Now stop thinking about Brian and help me spread out our supper."

The reference to his ex brought with it the usual stab of sadness, but nine months had dulled any sharp points. Simon's sadness was now just that. Purely sad. Not angry, not certain they could work it out, not wrestling with guilt and a need to forgive Brian's sins. Just sad.

"I was thinking more about my new house. My future."

"Know what I like about you?" Frank asked, sitting beside him.

"My anal tendencies?" Simon handed him a glass and lifted the other.

"As if you'd ever let me near that ass of yours."

It was an old joke between old friends. They'd tried once, but the timing had been off, with neither of them in a position to commit. Since, their friendship had deepened to a point where Simon wasn't sure it could ever work between them. He loved Frank—as a friend. As the person who would pack a frivolous picnic basket and keep him company the first day in his new house.

Frank held his glass up. "It's your courage I'm admiring right now. Here you are—a new state, a new job. Brian didn't know you."

"Let's not—"

Frank clinked his glass to Simon's. "To the first day of the rest of your life."

Smiling faintly, Simon sipped his wine.

By the time Frank was shaking the last drops from the bottle, a warm glow had settled over Simon's mood. He felt brave. Comfortable in his decision to start over at forty-six, even though he wasn't exactly starting over—more doing what he'd always wanted to do. Investing in a business that wasn't his and Brian's, but would one day be just his and his *alone*. The word didn't sound so ominous when put that way.

Frank leaned in to rest his head on Simon's shoulder. Their conversation had stalled a little while ago, and neither had rushed to resurrect it.

Simon slipped his arm around the back of Frank's shoulders and pulled him in close. "Thanks for staying. I feel less morose with you here."

"I'm going to count that as a win."

"You want me to make up the couch for you?" They'd shared only a single bottle of wine, but it would be a long drive after a long day.

Frank turned in the half embrace and put his hand on Simon's thigh. "You've a big bed."

Simon looked down at his friend, who'd lifted his face. They were close. Kissably close. The slight fog of wine and fatigue seemed to form a glue, or a field of inertia, and Simon didn't immediately pull back. With the specter of loneliness still lingering in the shadows of the haphazardly furnished living room, he nearly leaned forward. Frank was comfortable, easy. Sex with him could be easy and comfortable. Maybe too comfortable. He needed...

Not that.

Simon saw that when he focused. Saw it in the directness of Frank's gaze, the mood of his light-brown eyes. Frank wanted something Simon couldn't give.

Tucking his arm a little more securely around Frank's shoulders, Simon snuggled in closer and let his head tip to the side so their temples touched, their faces side to side rather than mouth to mouth. It was the gentlest way he could think of saying no.

Tension seemed to stiffen Frank's shoulders briefly before bleeding away. Then he relaxed into Simon's embrace. "It'll be cozy here come winter," he commented absently, his head brushing Simon's as he nodded toward the dark fireplace.

"I might not be here that long."

"We'll have to wait and see, won't we?"

CHAPTER 3

Charlie put his nose to the monitor to see if he could actually count the pixels. Straining his eyes made his head hurt, though, and no new words magically appeared onscreen. Leaning back, he looked at the window behind the monitor. Because the sun had disappeared some hours ago, he caught only a shady outline of himself. But what he saw was Kaze Rider, space pirate: dashing, handsome, daring, smart as the proverbial whatever, and blessed with uncanny luck.

Yeah, Charlie wrote a better self into his books. Or the self he wanted to be in his dreams, because when he was awake, he loved being a writer and he loved being a dad.

Through his ghostly reflection, he could just see the street in front of the house. Supposedly, he was trying to make chapter four work—and for the book to have gone so far off the rails at only chapter four should have told him something. He needed to replot. But watching for Olivia's car seemed more important. She'd missed her curfew twice already over the past couple of weeks. Charlie was beginning to suspect she had a boyfriend, an idea that filled him with nostalgia and concern. He'd married his first girlfriend and then he'd . . . he'd been the one to rob them all of Merry's brightness and vitality. Not every love story ended so badly, but—

Lights finally flashed around the distant corner, cruised down the street, and turned into the driveway. Pushing away from the desk, Charlie made his way through the attic den toward the narrow staircase that led down. If he hurried, he could be in the kitchen before Olivia got inside the house—filling the kettle, rummaging in the fridge, ignoring the piteous cries of four cats who always thought they were starving.

Herbert stirred from his pillow next to the desk and followed him. They met Olivia at the back door.

"I saw you looking through your creepy attic window, Dad. I swear the neighborhood is going to start telling stories about you."

"It's late, Liv. Where have you been?"

She stopped short. He didn't normally go on the attack so early, but this was the *third* time. "I told you," she said. "I was at Rosalie's. We're working on a project together."

"What's the project?"

"You don't believe me?" She dug her phone out of a pocket. "Call her."

"I don't want to talk to Rosalie. I want to know why you've been missing curfew. I'm a reasonable dad, Liv. I don't hassle you about much. I've never had to before now."

"Are you still stuck on chapter four?"

"Don't change the subject!"

Flinching, Olivia picked up one of the cats winding around her ankles, and buried her face in Riddle's soft black fur. Without thinking about it, Charlie reached out to scratch behind Riddle's ears.

He was pretty sure pausing in the middle of an argument amounted to a loss of momentum. At times like these, he really wished he could use such time-honored phrases as: *Listen, we'll keep this one from your mother.* Or: *I won't tell your mom you were out this late, but it can't happen again.* He needed a bad cop to his good cop, and vice versa.

"Liv..."

"So, this guy asked me out on a date."

The small hairs on the back of Charlie's neck rose to attention. He hadn't made this happen by thinking about it, had he? Also, *Holy subject change, Liv.*

"We're going out next Friday night," she continued, either blithely unaware of the tornado sweeping through Charlie's middle, or counting on it to make him stupid and agreeable.

"Okay." He had a week to scroll through her Facebook friends looking for likely candidates. "How do you know this guy?"

"From school."

"School doesn't start back for two weeks."

"He moved here over the summer."

"Were you with him tonight?" Liv had never lied to him before—not about the big stuff. Then again, to his knowledge, she hadn't been with a guy before. Had they had *the talk* enough times?

"No! I told you, I was with Rosalie—"

"Doing a project, right. Liv, school doesn't start for two weeks. How could you have a project?"

Herbert lapped loudly at his empty food bowl before upending it. It spun across the floor. Olivia put Riddle down and pulled out her phone again.

"Liv, I told you I don't want to—"

She showed him the screen. Rendered in miniature was an intricate colonial scene. Water wheels along the river, log cabins, small figures. Charlie took the phone, enlarged the picture to check the detail, and smiled as he recognized his daughter's distinctive style. The figures were wraithlike, but not in a spooky way. Rather, they were suggestions of beings, made from a few strokes of well-placed color. The buildings and creek were the same, but Rosalie's hand was evident as well in the slightly skewed dimensions. The scene made little sense, though. The girls normally drew and painted imaginary landscapes. Surreal stuff. Depressing visions of futures he didn't want to know about. This scene was pastoral and picturesque.

"What is this?" Herbert butted the back of his knees, nearly pushing him off-balance. Charlie handed the phone to Olivia and nudged the dog aside. "Go play with your bowl. We'll go out in a bit."

"It's not quite done," Olivia said. "I was going to show you when we were finished. It's our entry in the Historic Bethlehem Contest. Winners get to paint their mural on the side of the parking garage behind the hotel. Facing the old village."

That would be Hotel Bethlehem, anchoring the bottom corner of Main Street. "This is what you've been working on with Rosalie?"

"Yeah."

"I love it, Liv. I really do."

"I'm sorry I've missed curfew a couple of times. But you know what it's like when you get wrapped up in something. Time goes by."

Charlie exhaled noisily, as if trying to make a statement with breath. Maybe he was. "Who is this guy you want to go out with?"

"The one I *am* going out with, you mean?"

"The one you *are* going out with." He had to trust her judgment, but the idea of her out alone with a walking bag of male hormones freaked him out. Charlie knew all about seventeen. He'd been having sex at seventeen. With Olivia's mother. "I'm sorry I jumped all over you. I just..."

Olivia touched his arm. "Not everyone with a boyfriend gets pregnant by accident, Dad. And not every pregnancy means cancer."

Herbert evidently decided he'd had enough chitchat and started whining.

Clearing his throat, Charlie turned away from the sympathy in his daughter's face. "I gotta take Herbert out."

"It's okay, we can talk tomorrow."

"How about Pancake Place for breakfast?"

"Are you going to make me go hiking afterward?"

Charlie found a quiet chuckle for that. "Not if you don't want to. If it's nice, maybe we could walk somewhere?"

"That's hiking."

"Slow hiking, with sitting in between. We can talk about this guy. And your project. And maybe college?"

"I knew there'd be a catch."

"We need to talk about it soon, Liv."

She kissed his cheek and winced. "You need to shave."

Smiling tiredly, he ignored another subject change. "Night, Duck."

"Night, Dad."

He didn't make the "waddle waddle" sound as she walked away, but he heard it in his head. Could easily picture her at two and three, when she *had* waddled. When guys and college had been visions of another future he hadn't wanted to know about.

Oh, Merry. How was he going to get through this part alone? His little girl wasn't little anymore, and the day was fast approaching—might already be here—when she might repeat what he considered to be his biggest mistake. But could he really stop her? Could he tell her not to live her life to the fullest?

After all, Olivia was *not* a mistake. She was, by far, the best thing he'd ever done with this life.

Olivia went to bed, and Charlie took Herbert for his all-important last walk. One of the cats shadowed them down the street. Probably Joker. Something dead would turn up on the back doorstep in the morning.

CHAPTER 4

The township of Bethlehem sprawled across the map like a coffee stain, clipping Highway 22 to the north and Interstate 78 to the south. The business district, such as it was, nestled in the middle, hidden from both highways by roving suburbia and rambling woods. It was a pretty area, a picturesque town, and unexpectedly lively on a Sunday morning.

Simon watched, amused, as Frank turned his head until his neck cracked, then swiveled back the other way to continue monitoring a cluster of lanky young men crossing Main Street.

"Enjoying yourself?" he asked.

"Just assuaging the sting of your rejection." Frank arched an eyebrow as he picked up his coffee cup. "I'm beginning to get why you moved here."

"It's an eclectic mix of architecture, isn't it? You have that brute of a hotel down on the corner and the juxtaposition of Federation and Victorian styles, which isn't unusual for this corner of the world. It's the historic district I really want to study, though. The Moravian influence."

"Can architects be nerds?"

"Geeks, perhaps."

"I was talking about all the college students roaming around, waiting for an older, steadier hand to show them—"

Simon held up an older, steadier hand. "I'm going to stop you right there."

Frank hid a grin behind his coffee cup. Frank might be fortysomething, but his eyes—and wandering gaze—would always be twentysomething. His focus sharpened again as he glanced up from his cup. Simon resisted the urge to turn and check out the next gorgeous young thing to catch Frank's eye, until someone called his name from behind.

"Simon?"

He turned and smiled quickly as he recognized his new partner, Arthur Beckwith. Slight, a little stooped, but obviously fighting the advancing curve of his spine, Arthur looked exactly like what he was: an older, somewhat distinguished gentleman dressed in a well-tailored suit, perhaps one shade darker than the gray of his hair. His soft-blue tie matched his eyes and the folded handkerchief poking up in a perfect triangle from his left breast pocket.

Standing, Simon offered his hand. "Arthur."

The handshake was light but firm, somewhat like Arthur himself.

Simon made introductions. "Frank, Arthur Beckwith. Arthur, this is my friend Franklin Tern."

Frank shook Arthur's hand and gestured expansively toward their table. "Would you like to join us?"

"Hmm, oh, no, but thank you. I'm on my way to a meeting with Historic Bethlehem."

A blank look replaced the invitation on Frank's face.

"The local historical society," Simon clarified.

"Oh, of course. Simon has been talking architecture at me all morning." What a lie. "He's excited to be here."

I'm not five. Swallowing his peevishness, Simon nodded toward Arthur. "It's nice to see you, Arthur. I hope the meeting goes well."

"You'd be most welcome to come," Arthur said, glancing between Simon and Frank. "We're at the old hotel. We'll be discussing the Christmas City Stroll, I expect. And Winnie has a proposal regarding the Kemerer Museum."

An odd flame kindled inside Simon's chest, and it took him a moment to categorize it. Excitement. This was what he'd come here for. The chance to get involved. To immerse himself in a like-minded community, converse with people who, like him, wanted to preserve the old rather than flatten it to make way for the new. Possibility expanded before him.

Frank was wiping his mouth with a napkin. He put it down and grasped Simon's shoulder. "Go on. It's time I headed back across the border anyway."

"But—"

"Give me a call when you're settled in the house. We'll do something."

Irrationally—or perhaps not—Simon was reluctant to part with Frank. He felt like a kid on the first day of school, watching his mother get ready to walk away. The opportunities of a new town excited him, both personally and professionally. But once Frank left, Simon would be—

Get a grip. He'd been living alone in Morristown for the past few months. He could do this.

Simon pulled Frank into a quick embrace. "Thanks for everything and drive safely."

"Always."

"Wait, how am I going to get home?" Frank had driven them to town for brunch.

"I can drop you off," Arthur said.

Frank and Arthur exchanged a friendly farewell, and then Frank walked one way, Simon and Arthur the other. They arrived at the hotel, and that first day of school feeling returned and dissipated once more as he was met with the welcome of Historic Bethlehem.

Two hours passed in a colorful blur of names, proposals, event planning, and general enthusiasm for subject and project. Simon quite forgot his nerves, asking questions and adding a thought here and there. After the meeting, when he stood back to let the collected men and women file out the hotel conference room, he—with certificates in reservation and broodiness—was smiling. Almost grinning.

One meeting did not make him a part of the community, but his opinions had been listened to—and responded to—with interest and respect.

Had he found his place?

"Thank you for inviting me." Simon allowed another smile for his new business partner.

"Oh, I'm just glad I ran into you, though I'd have invited you along next month certainly. If we're going to make our mark on this town, this is the place to start."

Simon's smile faded. *We*? *Our* mark? Surely Arthur hadn't changed his mind regarding retirement?

Deciding Arthur was using a collective *we*, Simon filed away his niggles and held the door open while they exited the hotel. Outside, rain had transformed the day from light and lively to varying shades of gray. He and Arthur ducked from doorway to doorway on their way to the Walnut Street garage.

"It's been a surprisingly wet summer considering this whole global-warming business," Arthur commented as they stood dripping beside a late-model Volvo. "Do you believe in that?"

"Global warming?"

"Yes, all this about the planet getting hotter. Seems to me we're getting wetter. Four feet of snow in March. Rain all summer. Unbelievable."

"Well..." How in depth to get? "I think 'global warming' is a bit of a misnomer. 'Climate change' might be more accurate."

"I'll say. And all that flooding down South. It's like the end of days. Are you a religious man, Simon?"

"Ah, no. Not really. I'd never disrespect another man's beliefs, though."

Arthur smiled. "What about your friend's religion? Frank."

Anything that promised an afterlife filled with fulsome young men. Not that Frank was easy. He looked far more often than he touched. "I expect his views are similar to mine," Simon said. "Live and let live."

"Just so." Arthur nodded. "I think we're going to get along fine."

Simon's gut tightened slightly. He had invested all of his available assets in Beckwith and Associates. He liked Arthur. Respected what the man had done with his small architectural firm. Arthur had maintained a fair balance between the historic and the necessary—or what clients deemed necessary with building and renovating.

But Simon anticipated the day when he could call the business his own. When he didn't have to answer to a boss or a partner. When he could decide which clients were right for him. Reject projects that didn't make his heart sing.

"Beckwith and Lynley." Arthur's tone was musing. "It has a nice ring to it, doesn't it?"

Simon forced another smile, smaller than the first. Getting along with Arthur until then would make it all easier—no doubt about that. Already, he'd eased Simon's introduction into the local historical society. So the man wandered in conversation a bit. He was entitled. Arthur Beckwith was something of a historic piece of Bethlehem himself.

CHAPTER 5

Wednesday's examination of pixels was interrupted by a call from Shelly, Charlie's agent. "How's chapter twelve coming along?" she asked.

"Well, in theory."

"Chapter six?"

"Might need to fiddle with that one when I get there."

"You're not still on chapter three?"

"Chapter four. Technically. I've typed the words 'chapter' and 'four.'"

"Charlie..."

"I'll meet my deadline. I've always met my deadlines."

"I was hoping you'd have something we could tease at Philcon."

Charlie didn't know his sigh was going to be that loud until it blew back at him through the phone. Maybe Shelly had sighed too?

"Okay, let's talk things through," she said.

They tossed ideas around for about thirty minutes until Shelly fixated on one. "Kaze needs a love interest."

"He has at least one hookup in every book."

"Not a sex interest, a love interest. Someone to ride off into the sunset with at the end of the book. It'd be a great way to cap the series."

"But he needs to be free to ride the wind," Charlie explained.

"How do you feel about writing sex?"

"He has at least one hook—"

"No, I mean giving readers a glimpse of what's going on behind the closed door."

Charlie swallowed.

"You know what would be super awesome?" Sometimes Shelly forgot she was fifty-two. "A spin-off series starring his partner, with Kaze in a lead guest role."

What? No. "I'd still be writing Kaze, though, and I don't want to do that. I want to retire him gracefully, not sadly."

"Science fiction romance is a growing market."

"Shelly."

"Charlie."

"Let's table the sci-fi romance for now. I'll think about it after this book. So . . . a permanent love interest." As usual, while he'd immediately balked at the suggestion, some part of his brain had snatched it up and started working through the possibilities. Someone to ride off into the (windy) sunset with. Hmm. It'd almost worked for James Bond in *Spectre*—except the whole age-difference thing, and the plucking from past obscurity.

Charlie thought over Kaze's hookups. The one from book three popped out to say hi and the back of his neck itched. He was blushing. Again. While on the phone to his agent.

"I've got an idea," he said.

Shelly's smile was evident in her voice. "Send me some pages next week."

Charlie ended the call. He needed to think his idea through, and that meant putting on his running shoes. His calves complained as he stretched, and his lower back tried to convince him that couch surfing was a better form of exercise. Never mind the fact that Sunday's post-pancake nap-a-thon was probably responsible for every twinge back there.

By the time he got to the corner, he felt less like a jar of marbles being shaken too hard. When he got to the end of Bierys Bridge Road, his stride had lengthened and his breath had fallen into a regular rhythm. A sort-of path alongside Monocacy Creek meandered all the way into Bethlehem. He didn't usually run that far, but with as much thinking as he had to do, he needed to put a few miles beneath his shoe soles.

The dense canopy blocked most of the sun, and cool mist rose from the water. Charlie dropped into that space where his legs did one thing, his mind another. He breathed and ran and drifted. The outline of book six floated through his head, a tangled mess. He picked at the snags, one by one, until a couple pulled free. Then his thoughts turned to Olivia and The Boy. Justin. He'd gotten a name on Sunday, but neither a description nor address.

Over the past four days, his imagination had crossed Charles Manson with Donald Trump. Justin probably wasn't a serial killer or the face of American lunacy, but any man left alone with his thoughts for too long got dangerous and maudlin. He dismissed Manson Trump, and tried to imagine a younger face. An innocent face.

And pictured Simon from next door. Damn, if Justin looked like that, he and Olivia were both in trouble.

Pausing, he leaned against a tree to stretch out his calves and hamstrings again. Bent each leg behind him to loosen his thighs a little. His breathing was good. Not shallow, not ragged. Sweat clung to the back of his neck.

Every time he blinked, he saw Simon's face.

Then it clicked. Simon loosely resembled Jory Ondel—or close to how Charlie had imagined him, anyway. Jory was the hookup from book three. Charlie remembered the twist in his stomach when he'd submitted the pages to Shelly. He'd fully expected her to veto the idea, but she hadn't. She'd loved Jory. His subplot had been great.

The idea of bringing Jory back, of expanding his story, was curiously exciting. What Charlie couldn't decide was whether he liked it because of his own curiosity about Simon, or if Jory represented something deeper. Something he'd put aside nearly eighteen years ago upon hearing the words: *I'm pregnant.*

A breeze tickled the sweat at his nape. Charlie pushed off the tree and started running back the way he'd come. By the time he got home, he had a new plan for book six. A plan that rekindled his enthusiasm for Kaze and his retirement.

If only life was as easy to plot.

CHAPTER 6

Simon quickly built a routine. His mornings passed in a quiet and comfortable blur of sketchy plans, elevations, blueprints, and before and after pictures, all from Arthur's files as he waited for the man himself to make an appearance. The office didn't officially open until noon, with hours often extending into the evening for client convenience. Arthur usually appeared around twelve with a selection of sandwiches and coffee.

On Thursday they ate in companionable silence until Arthur pulled a slim fold of glossy paper from his old-fashioned briefcase and stuffed it into Simon's hand. "We've got two months to put together a bid. An entire neighborhood of Beckwith and Lynley designs."

Ignoring the fact "Beckwith and Lynley" was now a thing, Simon glanced down at the cover. It was a prospectus for a planned community called Burnside Province. His gut clenched around his half-digested lunch. This was what he'd fled in New Jersey. He no longer pondered the coincidence of his relationship and his career fizzling at the same time, the former more spectacularly than the latter. While Brian had obviously tired of him, Simon had tired of row upon row of charmless houses only tangentially influenced by local history and architecture styles. Pennsylvania was to be his remaking.

And Arthur was supposed to be making plans to retire, not handing him glossy brochures for planned communities.

Maybe this was his idea of a last project.

You're too nice.

Holding in a sigh, Simon opened the prospectus and started reading. He turned the page. Then another. The hiss of shiny paper against shiny paper was the only sound in the office. Simon glanced up, worried. Arthur had not stopped breathing; he'd simply stopped talking—which was almost as frightening.

He was waiting.

"This is the sort of project I hoped to avoid," Simon said.

Arthur remained silent, damn him, because he knew.

"But," Simon continued, "it looks good on paper." The developer . . . he checked the front cover again. Sierra Mason and her team had done a lot of research into local history. An impressive amount.

Arthur smiled.

Worry still nipped at the edges of Simon's thoughts as he continued to flip through the information. Great disasters often looked good on paper, but Simon sensed a yearning on behalf of the developer to actually create a unique feel. Ms. Mason wanted to do things differently. The proposed lot sizes alone would set the neighborhood apart.

Did he want to make a first project out of something that, on paper, reminded him of everything he'd rather leave behind, though?

Maybe it would be cathartic.

Obviously sensing his thoughts, Arthur tendered a gentle nod. "I understand your reservations, Simon. I know this isn't what you came to Pennsylvania to do. But I do think this is a unique opportunity." There was that word again—this time layered with meaning.

"How long have you had this information?" Simon felt bad for asking, but too many holes had been poked in his trust for him to blithely continue believing others had his best interests in mind.

"It was in last night's mail. Envelope hand addressed."

A small mailing, then. A fishing expedition to see what the local firms could come up with.

"With our combined reputations and vision, we could make a serious go of this," Arthur went on.

Simon put the brochure on the table in front of him and delivered his compromise. "Having a client or two in town at the same time—a current client or new project—would support our bid. Show we're active in the community."

Arthur was nodding again. "Agreed. How are your plans for the website coming along?"

Simon opened his laptop. Now they were talking.

By four in the afternoon, the weight of a full day pulled gently at him. He and Arthur agreed to pick up work on the proposal in the morning. But when he got home, a restless itch traveled up and down his legs... and his head kept turning toward Charlie's house. It wasn't just the fieldstone chimney calling his attention—though vague images of stone houses and farmhouses danced across his thoughts.

How authentic did Ms. Mason want her development to be?

Fieldstone blurred and reformed into Charlie's warm smile. He could use a dose of Charlie's energy about now. It was a dangerous want, but a lifetime's worth of experience with crushes had informed him that they were mostly harmless, and that they usually faded with time—after which he'd often made himself a good friend.

He could use a good friend.

He spent the short walk next door thinking of excuses to visit, only to be disappointed when the doorbell didn't chime, or produce a requisite barking and thunder of footsteps. Simon poked the little button again. Nothing. He raised his hand to knock, but the door opened half a second before his knuckles could tap the wood. Charlie stood in the doorway, blinking in the sunlight. He had a pencil clenched between his teeth, a notebook in one hand, and a tape measure in the other.

Simon let his hand drift back down to his side. "Your doorbell doesn't seem to be working."

As if they'd agreed to test the doorbell together, Charlie tucked the tape measure into a pocket and flipped open the notebook. He plucked the pencil from his teeth and wrote: *fix doorbell*. That done, he looked up with a smile—the same one that had charmed Simon the previous weekend: wide, friendly, effortless, as though the man walked about with his mouth permanently curved, his eyes always sparkling with humor and life.

"Thanks for the reminder," he said. "What's up?"

"I wanted to know who you use for your cable." The perfect excuse. Plausible and simple. "I'd have called, but I don't have your number."

Was it Simon's imagination, or did Charlie flush slightly? Probably the sun on his face. Regardless, Charlie turned to a fresh page of the notebook and started writing. Then he stuffed the pencil back between his teeth and tore out the page.

Simon did *not* imagine the tingle as their fingers touched. Resolutely, he didn't glance up to see if Charlie had registered the small charge.

The list started with a name, *Charlie King*, and included an address, two phone numbers, one marked cell, and an email address.

Simon quirked an eyebrow. "What, no emergency contact?"

Charlie definitely reddened this time. He also gave a wry smile before snatching the page back and scribbling some more. "You're lucky I didn't give you my health insurance information and a list of Liv's allergies." He handed the page back. Under Charlie's email was a second, and the name and number of the cable provider. Simon smiled at the less than professional addresses: liv4ever@valley.net and auntiecassie@valley.net.

"All the cable around here is crap," Charlie said. "So it's pick the pile that stinks the least, you know? It's the wires, they're old. But Valley Net is rolling out fiber in town, so hopefully we'll get it up here soon."

"And Auntie Cassie?"

"Emergency contact." Grinning, Charlie gestured toward the hedge on the other side of his property. "Anything I don't know, Cassie will. She'll probably stop by sometime soon to welcome you to the neighborhood and try to press you into the watch we've never managed to organize."

"Ah, okay. I'll, um, look forward to her visit." Simon started folding the sheet, smoothing each crease as a way to delay the inevitable. He'd asked for assistance, Charlie had rendered it. The meeting was at an end. By the time he'd reduced the list to a tiny square, he couldn't put it off any longer. Simon glanced up—and met Charlie's gaze. It was neither expectant nor impatient. Rather, he maintained his aura of welcome friendliness.

"Are you busy?" Charlie asked. "I was about to measure the porch and start sketching out ideas. I could definitely use your advice or expertise or whatever, if you've got a minute."

"Sure." Simon fought a grin as he slipped the little square into the pocket of his pants.

Charlie followed the movement, then glanced at his own seriously worn jeans. Perhaps comparing the difference in their outfits. Simon had come straight from the office, so he was in navy-blue slacks and a button-down. It'd been a quiet day, so he was still neat and pressed. In comparison, Charlie might have crawled out from beneath a bed, collecting clothes along the way. Normally, Simon would find the tattered and worn clothing somewhat off-putting. The relaxed and comfortable look suited Charlie, though. It added to that feeling of kinetic energy. As if he could burst into motion at any moment, subjecting his clothing to the wear and tear of quick acceleration and sudden stops.

Charlie grinned and shrugged. "Work clothes."

Simon smiled. "Same. So, what do you want to do out here?"

"I figured the first thing to do was check to see what needs doing. I know at least two of the steps need to be replaced."

He followed Charlie around the porch, answering questions and posing his own. After about forty minutes, they determined only the steps, railings, and one post really needed work. The rest of the structure was sound—and doing more would require a complete refit, which would be expensive and unnecessary. It wouldn't add any appreciable value to the house.

"Unless you plan to live here for another ten years," Simon concluded.

Charlie shook his head. "I might sell it when Liv goes to college. It's too much house for us, even now." Herbert chose that moment to start howling from the backyard. Charlie's ever-present smile turned wry. "I'm going to see if the buyer wants a dog too."

"You'd never leave your dog behind."

"Who says I wouldn't?"

"I saw that stack of plastic chairs. You buy them for him, don't you?"

His smile widened quickly, somewhat abashedly. "He's going to choke on one of those damn things, and I'm going to take the guilt to my grave with me."

Simon chuckled. "So how long have you lived here, in this house?"

"Oh . . ." Charlie turned around, perhaps to examine the fading blue paint of the front door. "Forever. It was my parents' place.

Grandparents' before that. Great-grandparents' before them." He turned back. "There've been a few updates since then. Your house is where one of the barns used to be. Cassie's place was built when I was a kid. In fact, I watched all these houses being built. I used to play in them."

"Your parents—"

"Retired to Florida last year. Just before it got stupidly cold."

That did leave a lot of house for a family of three, assuming Olivia didn't have any siblings. A lot of history too. "It's a beautiful property," Simon said. "I can't believe you'd give it up."

"The King family has been selling this place, piece by piece, for decades. This is the last bit." Charlie tucked the tape measure back into a pocket, and tipped his head toward the front door. "Want some ice tea or something? I've got the original plans upstairs somewhere if you'd like to see them."

Simon barely resisted rubbing his hands together. He followed Charlie inside, both of them pausing in the foyer to let their eyes adjust to the dim light.

"I don't really want to give up the last piece." Charlie's voice was more subdued now that they were inside. "But what am I going to do here all by myself when Liv is gone?"

"It's . . . just you?" Where was his wife?

Charlie offered a gentle nod. "Widower." The word had a practiced feel, as though he had repeated it over and over. "Five years." He turned away then, taking a brief frown with him, and led the way toward the back of the house, waving Simon into a dining room halfway along. "Make yourself comfortable while I get the plans."

Expressing his sympathy now, five years too late and after Charlie had already changed the subject, would be awkward. Simon put the urge aside. "I can get the tea if you want."

"Sure. Glasses are in the cupboard next to the sink."

Grateful for the small break—a moment alone—Simon wandered into the kitchen. Did Charlie's bright smiles and talkative nature cover for the empty place at his side? His missing wife? Dead wife. Naturally, Simon's mind conjured further questions. How had she died? How had Charlie coped with grief and a child? None of it was his business, but... he liked Charlie. Quite a lot. His easy manner, his friendliness. Charlie was as different from Brian as night was to day.

Not that he was thinking in those terms. Charlie wasn't gay. Simon had caught the hint of deep loss in Charlie's expression when he said *widower*. For all he seemed to like looking at Simon, he'd obviously adored his wife.

Was he bi, maybe?

Jesus. His wife is dead. Have some class.

Five years, though...

Charlie arrived in the kitchen with rolls of paper tucked under his arms. "Find the tea?" he asked, eyeing Simon's empty hands.

Simon pretended interest in the refrigerator, which was covered in pictures of Olivia and flyers for pizza delivery and area events. "Think the weather will hold for this weekend?" he asked, tapping an advertisement for a local arts and crafts festival while quickly sorting the dates in his head. Yes, it was this weekend. Not last year, or next month. Phew.

Charlie's bright smile reappeared. "I hope so. Olivia's art club has a stall. Hey, you like art and stuff?" Barely pausing for Simon's answering nod, Charlie rolled on. "You should come to the festival. Everyone local will be there. I can introduce you around and tell you which food trucks to avoid."

Oh, Lord. Something was looping around in his gut, and he was suddenly short of breath. *Get a hold of yourself, Lynley.* Simon produced what he hoped was an enthusiastic but not ridiculously pleased smile. "Sure. That'd be great."

CHAPTER 7

"No."

"Aww," Charlie whined. "Come on, Phil. I'd do it for you."

Phil shook his head. "Look, I appreciate what you're going through, but when Bethany starts dating, I want you to take my car keys and hide them. Lock up my guns too."

"No! I'll be your copilot. I'll call out turn-by-turn directions when we're tracking her, and be the one who remembers to bring coffee and donuts."

"You can't tail your daughter on a date. It's crazy stalker territory."

"Sign me up."

"Charlieee." Phil always over extended the last syllable of Charlie's name when he was exasperated—which had happened more often when they were kids. "Can't we drink beer and play *Call of Duty* like we always do? It's Friday night. My one night away from my own house of crazy."

Phil had five kids. Five. Three girls and two boys. To Charlie's mind, it'd make sense if he had four of one and only one of the other, and then he could tell people he'd finally got what he'd wanted when the youngest was born. Instead, Phil liked to joke that they'd have more if Jen didn't cross herself every time he looked at her with a certain glint in his eyes.

Charlie liked Jen. She was good people.

"I don't think I've got any beer," Charlie said.

"I've got some. I'll—"

"I'll come with you. We can stop and pick up a pizza while we're out."

Phil was shaking his head again. "You are so disturbed."

"You're only just figuring this out?"

"You know, if I'd had any other last name . . ." *Kinney* had come right after *King* on the kindergarten roster.

"Your life wouldn't have been the same." Neither would Charlie's, seeing as he'd gone and married Phil's younger sister.

Snorting, Phil nudged Charlie's shoulder and dug keys out of his pocket. "I suppose we could go get some beer. There and back, okay?"

"Yeah, sure." Stalking his daughter probably wasn't the healthiest exercise.

Five minutes later they were rolling down Bierys Bridge Road and Charlie's face had a fixed sort of feel to it, as though the wind had changed, catching him between a grin and a grimace. Around his feet, the detritus of five children rattled and crunched. Inside his chest, his heart was doing flip-flops. His palms were all sweaty. It could have been *his* first date. "He was taking her to dinner and a movie."

"That's nice."

"Dinner first."

"What are they going to see?"

"The new Captain America one."

"Oh, I wanted to see that. Think they'd notice us in the back of the theater?"

Thus Phil proved why he was, had always been, and always would be his best friend, even if they wouldn't actually be going to the movie. Not tonight, anyway.

"Do you think she'll sit in the back so she and Justin can, you know . . ." Charlie made a vague gesture.

Phil glanced over. "Make out?"

"I can't think about my daughter kissing. It makes me want to kill things." Not really. It made him sad in a way he didn't quite understand. "Will she and this boy be kissing on their first date?"

"I hate to be the one to break it to you, Charlie, but she's seventeen. She's probably been kissing boys for a couple years now. And *this* guy? They've been together all summer."

"How do you know that?"

"Because that's how they do it now. A date means it's serious."

Charlie slunk down in the seat a little. Something poked him in the butt. Shifting, he reached back and pulled a disembodied doll leg from between the seat cushions. He dropped it onto the floor. "Times like this, I wish Merry were here. Not that she could do anything more than me, but I'd have her hand to hold. Or squeeze into brittle little bits. That's my baby out there."

Phil patted his hand. "I know. You can break my fingers if you want."

"Thanks."

"Which restaurant were they going to?"

"Thai Thai."

"Classy."

"Hey, he's seventeen. If he was taking her anywhere fancier, I'd be suspicious."

"Let's hit the beer store on Broad, then. *Away* from Main Street."

Charlie bit back the suggestion they get Thai instead of pizza.

After depositing a case of beer he did not need into the back of Phil's truck, Charlie cast a longing look toward the corner of Main Street. "Do you think we cou—"

"No."

"Let me peek around the corner. She's not going to be in the street. I'll just satisfy myself that figures in black aren't rappelling down the front of buildings, getting ready to coordinate some sort of—"

Phil tugged on his sleeve, dragging him toward the building on the corner, and leaned out with him. "No terrorists." He glanced back at Charlie. "Are you going to stop freaking out now?"

Based on the feeling in his gut, "No."

"It's just a date."

"But it's not. She's too young, Phil. She's going to get hurt or... *involved*. If you're right, and this date makes everything official, then she might already be, you know." Doing the thing that came naturally to young people driven by hormones. The thing that weighed so heavily on his soul, because it should be beautiful.

"Hey." Phil put a placating hand on Charlie's shoulder. "Not everyone who—"

Charlie sighed noisily. "I know. Liv already gave me the same speech."

After studying him for a long moment, Phil said, "Let's take a walk. You and me. Not on Main Street."

"We could just go home."

"Hey, we're out now. We'll pick up some Chinese from the place near the laundromat, okay?"

"Sure."

By the time they reached the Chinese place—putting five more blocks between him and Main Street—Charlie did feel calmer. A run would have cleared his head better, but a walk with the solid presence of his best friend at his side was almost as good. They placed their order and ducked back outside to wait. Charlie wandered next door, seeking the mesmerizing line of clothes driers, and stopped. The laundromat was gone. The new store bore the same name, but not quite the same purpose. *Does everything have to change?* The laundromat now sold clothing, and the front window showed a clothesline strung with jeans and T-shirts. The shirts were obviously meant for younger, more fashionable folk, but the jeans he liked. All dark denim and straight. No weird pockets or loops or fake creases across the thighs, and they were clean. He thought about how he'd looked in his old, old, very old jeans in front of Simon yesterday, and cringed inwardly. He should get some new jeans; he was at least a decade overdue.

He pulled Phil into the store.

"What are we doing?"

Charlie walked up to the nearest display and started leafing through the neatly stacked layers of denim. "Distracting me."

"Oh-kay." Phil sauntered toward the T-shirt display.

A blond teenager bounced into existence at Charlie's side. "Hi?"

"Hey."

"Can I help you find a size?" The teenager studied Charlie's hips, crotch, and legs. It was an uncomfortable experience. The back of his neck was just starting to itch when she glanced back up. "Thirty-two by thirty-four?"

Why was everything a question?

After raising his eyebrows in Phil's direction, Charlie followed the girl to a curtained alcove at the rear corner of the shop, accepted two different pairs to try, and pulled on the first. Stepping outside the curtain, he called to Phil, "What do you think?"

"They look like jeans."

"Well, duh."

"Why are you trying on clothes?"

"My old jeans are getting pretty, um, old."

"Liv isn't going to be coming in this direction, is she?"

"No. Banko's is in the other way." Someone had recently reopened the small local theater—and renamed it. Charlie could never remember the new name, though. "I just need new jeans."

Charlie ducked back into the changing room. He studied himself in the mirror and admired the jeans. They made his legs seem longer and all of him more lean. He didn't even have to suck in his gut, though that could have been all the jogging and projects around the house. As he turned to the side to inspect his profile, his thoughts wandered toward Simon again.

Would he notice the new jeans?

Did Charlie want him to?

"Here. I picked out some shirts for your updated wardrobe," Phil called through the curtain.

"Uh-huh."

Phil thrust a handful of material through the gap at the side. Charlie took the shirts and shook the first one out. It had *Cute But Psycho* printed across the front. "Very funny!" A muffled snort sounded from near the front of the shop. The second read: *Sassy Since Birth*.

"I think I see Liv!" Phil called.

Charlie dropped the shirts and scrambled for his own jeans, falling against the wall as he yanked them up his legs—over the pair he already had on. Shit. Tempting as it was to run, getting arrested for shoplifting would stick a wrench in his evening plans. Charlie pulled the new pair off and the old pair on. He pushed through the curtain with his fly half undone and nearly bowled Phil over. A laughing Phil.

"Just foolin'," his new nemesis reported with an evil grin.

"Jesus." Charlie melted back through the curtain and into the wall at the rear of the dressing room. He so wasn't cut out to be the father of a teenager. Then there was this business with the jeans. What was he doing? Why was his life so weird all of a sudden?

"Everything okay in there?" Phil asked from outside the curtain.

Charlie drew it aside. "Yeah. I guess."

"The jeans looked really good. Clean. Um . . . slimming."

"Now you're trying to distract me?"

"Is it working?"

"I dunno."

Phil took the new jeans from Charlie's hand. "C'mon, our food is probably ready."

They paid for the jeans, collected their takeout, and turned back toward the beer store. By the time they got to the truck, Charlie felt drained. Not just empty, but as though he'd spent energy he didn't have. He leaned against the side of the truck and closed his eyes.

"How are you doing?" Phil asked from his side of the truck.

Swallowing, Charlie shook his head.

Phil came around the back and stopped in front of Charlie. "Wherever you're doing in that whacko brain of yours, stop. Okay?" Easier said than done. "Liv's a good kid." Phil delivered an encouraging shoulder squeeze.

"She was always a good kid. Thing is, she's not a kid anymore, is she?"

"Don't make me hug you on Broad Street."

Charlie let go of something that might have been a whimper.

Phil put on a reassuring expression. "They're always gonna be our little girls, man. Always. Even when they're our age and we're too old to even try for Maximum Overdrive."

Charlie waved in the general direction of their heads. "Virtual reality. If we can think it, it will happen."

"That's kinda your problem."

Charlie sighed. He wanted to tell Phil he was scared, but Phil already knew. "Everything's changing," he whispered instead.

He wasn't sure Phil had heard him until his friend patted him on the shoulder. "Let's go home."

Charlie straightened his spine. He had to own this, whatever it was. The good and the bad. The jeans he could return tomorrow. Simon . . . Simon needed more thought. Liv, though, she was his, irrevocably, until the end of time, and he had no regrets there.

None.

But if he could have done things differently— No. Some things just couldn't be changed. You had to own them. Fully.

CHAPTER 8

Charlie seemed a little subdued when he opened the door Saturday morning. It wasn't only the missing smile. He lacked that sense of constrained energy. Maybe he was tired?

"Late night?" Simon asked, immediately regretting it. *Nice, Simon. Why not tell the guy he looks like crap?* Which he didn't. Charlie was still handsome as hell—because lusting after a straight guy put Simon squarely on the highway there—and dressed in something other than "work" clothes. Dark-blue denim showed off legs that were longer than Simon had expected, and a T-shirt defined his muscular shoulders.

Charlie produced a low-wattage version of The Smile. "Stayed up too late trying to achieve Maximum Overdrive. By late, I mean past eleven, which counts as very late when you're over thirty-five." Obscenely late when you were over forty-five. "And by Maximum Overdrive, I mean killing fifty enemies while using Overdrive."

"'Overdrive'?"

"*Call of Duty*. And maybe one too many beers."

"Ah."

"Anyway, let me just grab a sweater and we'll get going. It's like September happened and summer is over. Bam. Might have been all that rain, I suppose. Hey, you want anything? Coffee?" He disappeared down the hall, the open door and his continuous chatter making an invitation. "There are some pretty good coffee stops in town. Have you had a chance to walk Main Street yet? You've probably done the historical stuff. Being an architect and all."

Smiling at the return of talkative Charlie, Simon followed him inside. "I had breakfast at Cachette last Sunday."

"Good food! Service isn't the greatest."

"They were a little slow."

Charlie reappeared with a sweater pulled halfway over his head. Simon mourned the loss of shoulders and pecs, while resisting the urge to smooth the disarray of brown curls as Charlie's head poked out of the neck hole. Charlie did the honors, sort of, running one hand front to back, and gestured toward the door.

The drive to town passed in a blur of short anecdotes and snippets of local history. It was obvious that Charlie not only knew Bethlehem inside and out, he loved it.

His commentary didn't feel insular or exclusive, though. He was excited by the rumor Johnny Depp might be buying property in Bethlehem. The revitalization of the old steel works pleased him—though he hoped the money from the casino would find its way to local schools.

As if relying on a satellite feed, his commentary cut off when they entered a parking structure. The sudden dimness of both light and sound felt strange until Charlie parked the car and glanced over. "I talked the whole way here, didn't I?"

"You paused for breath around Moravian College."

Chuckling, Charlie pushed open his door and stepped out of the car. Over the roof, he said, "If your ears start ringing, let me know."

The arts and crafts festival ran the length of Main Street from the brew pub at the top end, to Hotel Bethlehem at the bottom. Between, snaked a seething mass of humanity, flanked on either side by brightly colored awnings. The aroma of roasting corn and meat drifted through the air, and music played from a number of sources, one being the band stationed halfway down the street.

At the first stall, Simon stopped to "admire" a variety of misshapen lumps of glazed clay while trying to figure out what they were. The woman responsible for the pottery was engaged in conversation with someone who obviously saw more than clay. The pair gesticulated wildly over a tentacled green ball for a moment, and then the woman turned. She resembled her projects in form—being somewhat lumpy—but her face was all cheeky grandmother: gray hair tamed only from the front, left loose and wild at the back; lively eyes; and a smile so bright at the sight of Charlie, one might think they'd been separated for thirty years.

"Charlie!" She pulled him in close and noisily kissed both his cheeks.

Charlie's return hug was affectionate, if less noisy and kissy. "Cassie!" *Auntie Cassie?* "I want you to meet Simon, our new neighbor. Simon, this is Cassie Milstein, our friendly neighborhood auntie."

Cassie turned to Simon, hands upraised. "Oh, you are just gorgeous. Charlie, did you see his eyes!" She pressed her hands to her cheeks, fingers aflutter, before spreading them outward.

Simon allowed a smile, threat of incoming shoulder-squeezing and cheek-kissing aside, and offered his hand. "It's nice to meet you. Charlie's said you look after the neighborhood."

She took his hand in both of hers. As her grip tightened, Simon wondered if he'd ever see it again. "Yes! Did he give you my email? We have a loop. For neighborhood things."

"Cassie reports on all the stray cats," Charlie put in.

"Most of which are yours." Letting go of Simon's hand, Cassie reached up and patted his shoulder. "I cannot get over the color of your eyes, Simon. They are the most incredible shade of blue. They're not quite cerulean. Hmm. What color would you say they are, Charlie?"

Well, this wasn't embarrassing.

"Celestial," Charlie put in.

"Yes! Yes, that's it exactly!"

While Cassie waffled on about blue, and the meaning of a word Simon might never have attached to his eyes, Simon glanced over her head at Charlie, who had his lower lip between his teeth, and an odd expression on his face: uncertainty and perhaps surprise. Charlie quirked a quick, bashful smile before turning away, gripping the back of his neck.

"... glaze. It always turns out brighter than I expect."

Simon returned his attention to Cassie, and tried to remember what she'd been talking about. He gestured toward her display of lumps, the tentacled one in particular. "Do you have your own kiln?"

"Yes! At the house. You'll have to visit my studio. It's in the back garden." She picked up the little monster and turned it around. Up close, it looked less clumsy and more ...

"Are those eyes?" Simon took the piece and held it up for closer inspection. It wasn't something he could imagine displaying in his home, or office, or anywhere people might see it, but he could tell that Cassie had spent a lot of time on whatever it was.

"It's a beholder," she said. "A bit too large for tabletop use, of course, but quite collectable."

What? "It's very intricate."

"Thank you, dear. I spend a lot of time on each one. I think that makes them more personal."

"It's definitely very personal."

"Why don't you keep that one? A house-warming gift!"

"Oh, no, I—"

"She'll insist!" Charlie wore an ear-to-ear grin.

Best not to look at the thing in his hands—his expression might betray him. Instead, Simon tried for a grateful smile. "Thank you."

Cassie wrapped the "beholder" in tissue and put it in a bag stamped with *Cassie's Creations*. Charlie was kissed effusively again. Thankfully, Cassie constrained herself to arm squeezing when it came to bidding Simon goodbye. "Stop by anytime. I'll show you my studio. Oh, Charlie, you should bring him to yoga."

"Maybe," Charlie tossed over his shoulder as they moved away.

Simon resumed breathing two stalls later. "Yoga?"

"Don't worry. I wouldn't even subject Manson Trump to one of Cassie's yoga classes."

He'd fallen into another dimension, where people were named after the idiotic and insane and used lumps of clay with eyestalks to dispense condiments. New Jersey was not this weird. "Do I want to know who Manson Trump is?"

"The Boy." Charlie's eyebrows drew down, and the somewhat subdued look returned. "Liv's boyfriend. His name is Justin."

Ah, parenthood.

Charlie's expression brightened—the reason obvious as they came upon a stall staffed by teenagers. Olivia was there, engaged in conversation with a stunning girl. High cheekbones, flawless brown skin, dark eyes, a nose that could only be described as *regal*, and perfectly cast lips. Simon rarely felt a stir toward women, and never young women, but she was exceptionally attractive.

Olivia hugged her father with unabashed affection. When she stepped back, she glanced at Charlie's legs, eyes rounding. "Are you wearing new jeans?"

Charlie shrugged. "Phil and I stopped by Target last night."

Simon cast a critical eye over Charlie's butt—certainly worth attention, especially when enhanced rather than hidden. No way he'd bought those jeans at Target.

"Lookin' good, Charlie!" the other girl said.

And in this century, apparently, teenagers were on a first-name basis with adults. Lord, when had he gotten so old?

"Thank you, Rosalie." Charlie was gripping the back of his neck again.

Simon carefully diverted his attention from his neighbor's ass. He was too likely to get distracted.

Olivia's cheeks dimpled, and her eyes twinkled. "Can we have a funeral for the old pair?"

"What? No. The old ones are fine." Scowl lines marched across Charlie's forehead. "Or fine enough for yard work. Whatever."

Rosalie was laughing.

Olivia's smile narrowed as she lifted her chin in Simon's direction. "Hey."

"'Hello, Simon,'" Charlie said. "He's not a horse. Simon, you remember my daughter, Olivia? And this is Rosalie, her friend since birth."

"Hey," Simon returned with a half smile.

Olivia lifted an eyebrow.

"Hi, Simon!" Rosalie's bright and happy greeting closed that gap of a century, making him feel a bit younger. "How do you know Charlie?"

"I just moved into the house next door."

"You poor, poor man."

Charlie snorted. "Okay, let's see what the art club has for us this year."

Suddenly all business—their attitudes an odd combination between honor student and shy teenager—Olivia and Rosalie took them on a quick tour of the art displayed around their double-wide pavilion. The range of styles was impressive; manga-inspired character art, sketchy scenes, watercolor landscapes with a traditional feel, mixed media, collage, and an oil painting that, while extraordinarily beautiful and detailed, could quite possibly induce nightmares if hung anywhere near a bed. Or couch.

"It's the apocalypse," Charlie murmured somewhere close to his ear.

Resisting the urge to lean in and catch Charlie's lips against his neck, Simon applied this information to the painting. Okay, so those ghostly figures were actually ghosts. Screaming ghosts.

"What happened?" Simon asked.

"The land died." Olivia now wore a serious expression which, oddly, made her look more like her father. She glanced over at Simon. "It's a long story. You're probably not interested."

"Liv," Charlie warned.

Had Olivia spied him checking out Charlie's ass?

Folding her arms in front of her, Olivia began talking about fracking and earthquakes and terrorism, pollution, and disease. It was sad to hear such a tale of doom and gloom from a teenager, especially when it seemed edged with a belief that her painting represented the future. Did all kids think they were living in the end of times?

Simon struggled for a pleasant response. Optimistic, even. Difficult with Olivia burning a hole in the side of his head with a studiously unaffected gaze. He decided to be truthful. He had little enough experience with teenagers and had a feeling Olivia might have already decided to dislike him.

"It looks like a nightmare."

Charlie's eyes widened, but Olivia actually smiled. "Yeah." She nodded. "Yeah, that's exactly what it is."

Rosalie's drawings were an odd combination of mechanical and pastoral, as though Escher had decided to visit the countryside. Her line work was meticulous. Simon liked it a lot. Charlie encouraged the pair to show him a project they were working on for a competition, but they demurred, saying it wasn't finished yet.

Simon and Charlie left the stall and the next hour passed in a haze of names and faces spread across Simon's temporal lobe like a game of Memory. One he was doomed to fail. With time, he'd make a few matches. He looked forward to the day when Bethlehem felt less like a trip to the other side of the world and more like home. Somewhere he belonged. He'd never have Charlie's ease—the guy knew *everyone*—but quite liked the idea of eventually slotting into the community.

They ended their tour of the festival outside the Moravian Book Shop.

"Want to get some coffee, or something stronger?" Charlie asked.

Simon tipped his head toward the display in the shop's front window. "Is your book in there?"

Charlie gripped the back of his neck in what had become a familiar and somewhat endearing gesture. "Books. Yeah. They've got the whole series."

He had a series? "Let's go look."

Charlie hesitated only a second before recovering his sunny aspect and pulling open the door. "We'll turn left when we get inside. That's where the sci-fi is."

To the left, a wall of bright and vivid covers vied for attention: Dragons and swords and spaceships and moons. An anxious knot formed in Simon's gut. This was not his world. Art, he understood, and music was his passion. His love of architecture and sculpture went without saying. This imagining of other worlds was something else.

Though, he had to admit some of the covers spoke to him. There was art here.

He scanned the shelves until he caught sight of a book called *Ride the Wind* by C.R. King. A vortex-like thing twisted across the cover, in shades of blue and purple, with the silhouette of a small ship plunging through the middle. Four other books were shelved next to it, their spines all black with similar lettering and the same name, C.R. King.

Vaguely wondering about the *R*, Simon picked up *Ride the Wind* and turned it over to read the cover copy. Kaze Rider, wormhole travel, lost worlds, and an ancient evil.

Okay.

"What does the *R* stand for?" he asked.

Next to him, Charlie stopped fidgeting. "Not what I thought you were going to say."

"Is it a rude question?"

"No, not at all. I get asked that in interviews all the time. It's for Rothesay, which is my actual middle name. My mother had a crush on Prince Charles."

"Oh my God."

"I know."

"You don't have his ears."

"And if that's all I have to be thankful for in this life, I'll take it."

Simon chuckled. "So what did you expect me to say?"

"I figured you'd ask what the book was about."

"I read the back. Wormholes, secret planets, and something evil. It sounds—"

"Weird."

"Different." And now he'd have to buy the book and read it—not that he'd planned to do otherwise. He could do weird. Hell, he was the proud owner of a beholder.

"So, you've seen the book. Time for coffee?" Charlie asked. "There's a café next door."

"Sure, let me just pay for this."

"Oh, you don't have—"

"Are there beholders in it? Like, is this book going to tell me what I have in this bag?"

Charlie froze in place for a second, and then he laughed. Hard. Almost-doubling-over, hiccupping type of laughter. The entire store turned to look at them. Charlie slapped his thigh, drawing attention again to one of his long, lean legs, and straightened, hands pressed to his gut. "Oh God."

Simon responded with a feeble smile.

"You're . . ." Charlie patted him on the arm, grinning, chuckling. "That is the absolute best. Yep. I think I'm gonna keep you."

Simon fought the blush for as long as he could by concentrating on the clench in his gut. It was hunger. Or a need for coffee. Not a reaction to Charlie's open face, wide smile, and warm hand on his arm.

"I've embarrassed you. God, I'm so sorry." Charlie kept patting his arm, still chuckling.

Simon tried smiling more naturally. "No, not really."

"I have. Sorry. C'mon, let's get that coffee and I'll tell you all about Dungeons & Dragons."

Charlie could have told him there was a dragon living beneath the bookshop. All Simon heard was: *"I'm gonna keep you."*

His gut flipped again.

If only...

CHAPTER 9

Jory was back and sparks were flying between him and Kaze. Eight chapters later, they'd arrived at a scene where things could happen.

Sexy things.

This wasn't the book where Charlie would be opening the door on what his characters did in the bedroom, but now that he'd written his guys to the point where bedrooms loomed in their future—or a cozy piece of floor in an auxiliary cargo bay aboard the flagship of the Perseun Imperial Fleet—Charlie couldn't help wondering what might happen if no one interrupted them.

His outline wasn't particularly inspiring: *Perseun drones find Kaze and Jory hands on in a dark corner.*

Hands on.

They'd be touching each other's dick, right? Kissing was for teenagers. Multiple life-and-death situations later, these guys would be going for the good stuff. And they had to be quick. Would their pants be undone? Could a hand fit inside pants that weren't undone? Would there be enough friction if they stayed buttoned up? A patrol of drones were about to step through the door, exposing their hiding place.

Outside, a bird flew past the window, startling Charlie out of a somewhat disturbing daydream where Kaze was on his knees in front of Jory. And Jory's pants were definitely undone.

Wow. When had he moved from hands to mouths?

Could he put something like that in the book?

I don't even know how to write a blowjob.

Did guys like sucking cock?

Skin prickling, Charlie pushed away from the desk and stood. He'd go for a run until this weird feeling of expectation left him. Until he'd overcome the urge to write actual sex into a book that didn't need it. His feet weren't backing him toward the door, though. Instead, he approached the window and gazed out.

Looked next door.

He hadn't seen much of Simon over the past few weeks. An exchange of mail delivered to the wrong box, the occasional wave from their respective driveways, and Cassie's excuse for a neighborhood-watch meeting—hockey pucks disguised as cookies, served in her pottery shed slash yoga studio. Simon hadn't been able to stay for long.

Charlie studied the house next door.

Was Simon gay?

"Living alone at thirty- or forty-something doesn't make a man homosexual."

Having not been addressed directly, Simon's house made no answer.

Simon could be divorced. Or widowed. Though, he'd probably have mentioned that when Charlie dropped his little land mine. Simon never mentioned kids, and his only visitor drove a sleek black BMW Z3. Not that Charlie was keeping watch on his driveway or anything. He was just home most of the day. He saw stuff.

Why was he thinking about Simon right now?

The question was stupid and required no answer. Ever since the art festival, an increasing portion of Charlie's day had become devoted to thinking about Simon. The color of his eyes featured heavily in these small interludes. The shape of his face. His height and the breadth of his shoulders. The confident way he carried himself—like a man comfortable with his lot in life. The charmingly lost expression he got when confronted with something that didn't fit. Simon didn't do nerd stuff. Not games or science fiction or fantasy.

Of course, he had little idea what Simon did do for fun, because every time they saw each other, Charlie acted as though he were trying for an entry in the *Guinness Book of World Records* for words spoken per minute.

"So I like to talk." Even to himself, and he had a tendency to ramble when anxious.

But though he didn't know whether guys put their hands down each other's pants when trying to get off, Charlie did know what attention felt like. Possible interest. Simon's wasn't overt, but sometimes when he looked at Charlie, or touched him—a casual hand on the arm—there was something focused about his attention. As though he wanted Charlie to know this gesture was just for him.

It was like being flirted with in Morse code, and by the time Charlie translated each message, Simon had moved on.

Chewing pensively on his lower lip, Charlie sat down and leaned back in his chair. He'd accepted the fact he was attracted to Simon, and what that attraction meant. He could be honest about that. He'd always been curious. Never done anything about it, but he'd wondered.

Scrolling up, he read over the last line of the previous chapter. The odd feeling crept across his gut again. Maybe giving Kaze a same-sex love interest right now was a mistake. Increasingly, he'd become aware of the process of wish fulfillment that happened as he transcribed Kaze's adventures from his imagination to fictional reality. Who didn't want to be free to ride the wind from one adventure to another?

This wasn't sweeping a perfect crescent kick through two foes, knocking them off the edge of a cliff, though—not that he'd ever wanted to do that to some of Liv's teachers. Nope. This also wasn't discovering a vaccine for cancer.

Charlie grabbed his mouse and clicked a few times, opening a new window and navigating to Tumblr, which he generally avoided because . . . Tumblr. He had a page that he used to post cover art, the occasional giveaway, teasers, and contributions from fans. He'd surfed a few tags. Once.

People were weird and angry and strange.

He navigated to the search tab and typed: *gay sex*. He didn't hit Enter. Instead, he sat rigidly upright, as if lashed to a stake, awaiting the cleansing burn of fire. The back of his neck itched and his ears warmed. His breath fluttered oddly in his throat.

He hit Enter.

Holy shit.

What was air and how did lungs work?

As the results page populated with gifs of men bending over and kneeling in front of other men, kissing men, gripping cocks and balls, and squeezing nipples, Charlie figured now would be when his heart decided it had a condition, and his body would be found in front of a montage of his curiosity, stiff with rigor mortis and desire.

Jesus fucking Christ.

With a shaking hand, he clicked the small x in the top right-hand corner and closed the window. Then he breathed. The itch at the back of his neck had morphed into a burn that crept up over his scalp. He felt as though he were being watched. Skin prickling, he fought the urge to turn around. And to touch himself. His new jeans fit closer over his crotch than his old jeans had, and his cock was caught in a fold of denim. It hurt. Sort of. More, he ached for the friction of a warm hand, which was, sadly, the only attention he'd had since the last convention—and never in front of gay porn.

Charlie reached for his fly. He'd just loosen the zip. Give Little Charlie some room. Every contact between fingers and denim sent a shock through his groin. His erection swelled, jerking in anticipation of satisfaction. Belt undone, zip lowered, Charlie rearranged the cotton of his undershorts—half focused on making things more comfortable, half focused on the blissful torture of each casual brush of fingers.

Of course he ended up with his cock in his hand. Sweeping his thumb across the tip, he pressed down on his slit, catching a lazy bead of moisture. The sharp scent of pre-come tickled his senses. His balls tightened. Another swipe of his thumb had his dick jerking up—or maybe he'd tugged. *So good.* Scooting forward in his seat, he loosened his jeans, giving access to his sac. One hand down there, one hand up here...

Charlie scanned his desk for something to help him along, and spied a tube of hand cream. Even while he remonstrated himself for taking time out in the middle of the day to jack off, he slicked his palm with creamy white lotion. He gasped at the shock of the cool and wet. Then his fingers were following an age-old rhythm, flowing over terrain he knew better than the back of his hand: the familiar contours of his own penis.

He barely needed a visual aid. The glide of his fingers was enough. Closing his eyes, he summoned an image anyway: dark hair, a square jaw, and blue, blue, very blue eyes.

The first chime of his cell phone blended with the charge building at the base of his spine. The second didn't sync with the tempo of his strokes. The third nudged through his fantasy, ripping him back to reality.

Opening his eyes, Charlie reached for his phone—and watched, dumbfounded, as it popped out of his greasy fingers, shot across the desk, and clattered to the floor. Getting out of his chair with his jeans around his knees proved awkward. As did kneeling with his aching dick poking out in front like a compass needle. *There, the cell phone is over there. Thank you, compass-dick.* Charlie looked for something to wipe his hands on and hastily grabbed at his shorts. Every little motion set his hard rod bouncing around painfully.

He swiped his thumb over the green Call icon, leaving a smear across the screen, and raised the phone to his ear. "Charlie here."

Static answered him. At least, that was all he could hear over the wild thumping of his heart and the roar of his blood. This would be worse. Having a heart attack right here, kneeling beside his desk with his dick hanging out. One glance at his browser history would show what had set him off.

Just as he thought to check the caller ID, his cell phone chimed again. He swiped. "Hello? Hello?"

"Mr. King?"

"Yes." Breathlessness extended his *yes* into something almost depraved, but the voice on the other end didn't seem to notice.

"I'm calling from Liberty High School. Your daughter—"

Another rush of blood blackened Charlie's vision as all the possibilities hit at once. There'd been an accident. A shooter, an explosion, a kidnapping.

"—sex is not allowed on school property, Mr. King."

"What!"

"It might be best if you came down to the school. Are you free now?"

Nothing deflated an erection more quickly than the thought of his daughter having sex. On school property. With Manson Trump.

By the time Charlie found a parking space in the school lot, anger and fear had consumed him in equal measure, putting him in the worst possible mood for a conference with the school principal.

He announced himself to the desk staff, and was met with a sympathetic look that dialed his anger a single, impossible notch higher. The sight of Olivia sitting outside the principal's office nudged the dial back the other way. She was pale, her face pinched. Fear swayed him to the left. Anger swayed him back to the right.

"Liv."

"Dad..."

Before he could sort his feelings into words and questions, the door behind them opened and a tidy woman beckoned them inside. Introductions and curt handshakes were exchanged with Marleen Johnson, principal of Liberty High School.

"Where's Mans—Justin?" Charlie asked.

"I've already met with Mrs. Becker," Principle Johnson said.

Charlie turned on his daughter. "What did he do to you?"

"It wasn't like that! We weren't even doing anything."

"They said you were having sex!"

"What?" Olivia's eyes widened so far, the whites were visible all the way around.

"Who told you they were having sex?" Ms. Johnson asked.

"Whoever called."

"That's not what happened," Olivia said. "Oh my God."

"Then what did happen?"

"I—"

"Perhaps we could all sit down," the principal interrupted, gesturing toward the chairs in front of her desk, "and start at the beginning. Olivia, can you please tell your father what occurred after lunch period this afternoon?"

"I had study hall and . . ." Sudden color burned in precise spots on Olivia's cheeks, leaving the rest of her face pale. "I'm sorry, okay. I didn't think skipping study hall would be such a big deal. I usually get a pass to use the library or the art room anyway."

Charlie was used to the way children explained things. They always began with *it wasn't my fault* and ended with a story that had nothing to do with the actual infraction. Diversion, deceit. Hell, he'd been an expert at age ten. By seventeen, his parents had no idea what he did with his time. Or that he'd left school grounds so often that he lost his parking space in the lot. This lot. At this school. And, junior year, it had always been with Merry. They'd gone to the creek, skulked behind the new hospital and the old steel mill. The rotunda at the park. There had been a dozen places they could go, and they'd been fearless. They hadn't always opted for a pants-down encounter. Sometimes they used their hands. But they were getting off, having—

"We weren't having sex," Olivia said.

"What?" He'd missed it, again.

"We were kissing."

Blinking, refocusing, Charlie turned toward Principal Johnson. "You called me down here because my daughter was caught kissing?"

His panic started to recede, leaving blank spots here and there. Numb places. His brain felt like a fragmented disk. He had to stay out of his head and in the conversation. Stop imagining his daughter in that damned rotunda and figure out what was actually going on. He breathed. In and out. "Start at the beginning. Please."

Olivia started again. Apparently she had bumped into Justin on her way to the art room, and they'd veered off to the sports locker behind the gym instead. Intending to study, of course. But they'd fallen into a make-out session, and apparently clothes had been rumpled by the time Coach Ferris found them. Not undone, or hastily done up. Just loosened.

Charlie couldn't decide what surprised him more: that his daughter had skipped a class or been caught kissing—no, making out with a boy on school property. But before he could convince himself she'd been body snatched, the ghostly shape of the rotunda at the park drifted across his mind. God, he'd been there. Right there. No, he'd been worse. She must really, really like this boy.

Because this was a first offense, and she was a good student, Olivia was let off with a warning. A second offense would carry a mandatory suspension. A third would jeopardize her school career.

Charlie's ears began to ring again as he walked toward his car, Olivia lagging three steps behind him, her face crumpled like a wet tissue. He was the one who felt like crying. Every time his imagination tried to serve up what she must be doing with Justin outside of school property, however, his brain shut down and the ringing got louder.

Halfway home, Olivia broke the silence of the bells. "I know you're disappointed."

That was his best line. *I'm not mad, I'm disappointed.* "'Disappointed' doesn't even begin to cover this, Liv."

"We were just kissing."

"You're supposed to be learning. Studying. You're at school to do school things. Not kiss some boy."

"He's not 'some boy'!"

I know, Duck. I know. And that was a matter he'd have to deal with another time. Right now, he had more pressing business. "I don't want you in the house alone while I'm at Philcon."

"That's so unfair! It's not like I was caught in the locker room with the whole football team," she said hotly. "I was found kissing my boyfriend. The only boyfriend I've ever had, the only guy I've ever kissed. You're acting like I'm the school slut."

Stomach rolling, Charlie shook his head—not sure if he was dislodging the sound of her words from his ears or the very idea from his brain. "God, Liv, that's not what I think. Not at all. I'm concerned—"

"About me getting pregnant and having to get married at eighteen. News flash, Dad. I have more condoms in my bedroom than should be allowed for any teenager. I've promised I will use them a hundred times."

Rather than *a hundred promises*, Charlie heard *a hundred times* and shuddered. Maybe he should stop buying her condoms. Also, they were talking in circles again. And, again, he had lost the thread of the argument.

"I can't do this in the car," he said.

"I could have driven myself home!"

"You're not going to see the inside of your car until you're twenty." Which was grossly unfair, and he'd have to somehow get back to the school to pick her car up.

It was only a handful of miles from school to home. When he stopped the car in the driveway, Olivia got out with a dramatic sweep and door slam, demonstrating that sometimes she was seventeen going on seven. Did she think getting to the house first would give her time to hide?

Charlie had grown up in this house. There was no corner he did not know.

He squeezed his eyes shut, blocking out another flood of images. The corners he and Merry had found together. *I can't do this, Merry. I can't watch her get hurt.*

He knew the odds, and they were astronomically against Liv dying the same way her mother had. He had to find a way to let go of his fears. Easier said than done, though. This obsession of his was too closely related to the guilt he carried regarding Merry's death. It didn't help that he wasn't the only person who blamed him. His mother-in-law never let him forget the consequences of his youthful passion.

What would she think about the fact Liv had a boyfriend?

Now was so not the time to let his thoughts go there.

Charlie got out of the car, and it took a moment for him to register the lack of manic barking from the side of the house. Then he saw the hole in the hedge between his house and Simon's.

Of course it would happen today.

CHAPTER 10

Frank's voice fuzzed and popped as Simon drove through one of the many pockets of Bethlehem where cell phones clung to a single bar of life. Out of habit, he glanced down to check if the connection had dropped, returning his attention to the road when the static resolved into: "We still on for this weekend?"

"Are you sure you want to check out the casino?" Simon asked. "It's not like we're young enough to be dazzled."

"Hardly the point. Those who are young enough to be dazzled will be there, ready for a more worldly guide."

Simon mused on that a moment. He didn't really want to go out and pick up some young, starry-eyed college guy. But watching Frank make his moves was always amusing. He could play wingman, and checking out the scene around Bethlehem wouldn't be such a bad idea—though he was fairly sure the Sands didn't feature prominently.

He turned into his driveway and frowned at the sight of a figure crouched in one of his flower beds, arm rising and falling as they stabbed the ground. Wilted green stalks littered the driveway, and the earth seemed to have been thoroughly churned. The trespasser glanced up, and Simon recognized Charlie, whose face paled as he turned to toss something onto the pile of tangled shrubbery behind him.

"You still there?" Frank's voice blared through the speakers, jolting Simon back to the call.

"I gotta go. My neighbor is here and . . . I think he's digging up my flowers."

"Book guy?"

"Yeah, Charlie."

"And he's digging up your flowers. Huh. Pity."

"What?"

"The way you talk about him, I figured he might suddenly get an invite on Friday night." He'd talked to Frank about Charlie? "But if the guy is nuts—"

"I'll call you later, okay?"

Simon ended the call and stopped the car. He'd told Frank about Charlie's books. The surprisingly good books. Science fiction might never be Simon's thing, but Charlie told a great story. Reading his books was like watching an action movie, and it didn't hurt that the hero, Kaze Rider, often reminded Simon of the author.

Where would Frank get the idea he might invite Charlie out? What had he let slip?

And what was Charlie doing digging around in his garden?

Simon met Charlie near the destroyed flower bed. Charlie stood half in front of it, as though trying to hide the view. Guilt and something else played his features, his mouth twisting one way, his eyebrows drawn together. His chin pointed down.

"I'm so sorry," he said.

Simon opened his mouth and found he had no idea what to say. Life's manual hadn't prepared him for this particular situation.

"Herbert got off his chain and found a hole in the hedge." Charlie pushed a hand through his hair, leaving a brown streak across his forehead. "I was hoping I could repair the damage before you got home."

"Oh." Okay, that made sense. Sort of. Simon surveyed the damage. "Are you sure he came through the hedge and wasn't digging an escape tunnel?"

Making a vague sound, Charlie looked down and around before dropping to his knees to resume his digging. Or stabbing. He chopped at the earth, grunting with the effort. Dirt sprayed over his bent knees as he twisted a gnarled root free and tossed it toward the pile behind him. "I'm going to fix both beds so they're the same."

"No need to do that. I appreciate the thought, but they're just flowers." And bushes. "I was thinking of planting some mums, anyway. The garden could use an update. More color, I think."

Without looking up, Charlie kept digging and pulling stuff free. There was something focused about his attitude, as though he fought an unseen foe.

Simon tapped him on the shoulder. "Charlie?"

Charlie didn't respond for a moment. He dug, wrestled, and dug. Then, exhaling sharply, he glanced up.

"Are you okay?" Simon asked.

Charlie answered with a quick jerk of the chin.

"You really don't have to—"

"It's been a shitty day, okay? This is just the next thing. Once I'm done with this, my new roof is probably going to fall in. So I'd rather get on with it if you don't mind."

Simon stepped back, dropping his hand from Charlie's shoulder as he did so. He'd been nudged back, none too gently, by the barely constrained fury in Charlie's tone. He thought about going inside and ignoring the man stabbing holes in his dirt. But in the handful of weeks he'd known Charlie, he'd never seen a glimmer of temper or moodiness. Sure, he didn't know the guy well, but this didn't feel like Charlie.

"Want to talk about it?"

"No." Stab, stab. Then something cracked, and Charlie yelled and yanked his hand free. Blood spilled from between his fingers, trailing down his mud-caked hand. "Shit! Fucking piece of goddamned shit."

Simon grabbed Charlie by the wrist and hauled him upright. "Careful, we need to rinse your hand off. Put pressure there. Hold on." Charlie resisted before allowing Simon to tug him toward the front door. Simon fumbled for his keys, kicked the door open, and led Charlie straight to the kitchen. He opened the faucet and thrust their bloodied hands under the stream of water.

Charlie's yell was quieter than before. Less full of curses. In fact, the sound he made was mostly wordless. Bloody water sluiced down their hands, staining Simon's shirt cuffs and dripping into the sink where a muddy puddle formed and pushed back from the constant stream. When the water began to run clear, Simon pulled Charlie's hand out from under the faucet and pushed a wad of paper towels over the ripped flesh at the base of his thumb.

"Hold it there while I get my first aid kit."

Hopefully the cut wouldn't need stitches. The sight of blood—on his sleeves, under his nails—was starting to seep into Simon's consciousness. His vision blurred slightly at the edges. He grabbed the counter to steady himself. Now was not the time to wuss out. The remembered echo of Charlie's yells helped him stay on his feet. At least his neighbor wasn't the strong, silent type.

Charlie was peeking under the paper towel when Simon returned from the bathroom with his first aid supplies.

"How does it look?" he asked.

"Stupid." Charlie's expression was sullen and resentful. Then, eyes closing, he swallowed and breathed in. When he opened his eyes, he appeared more composed. "Sorry. I . . . I'm sorry. I didn't mean—"

Simon waved off further apology. "Don't worry about it." He turned his attention to the slice across Charlie's palm. It was ragged and angry, but not too deep. Blood oozed from beneath one flap of skin and dirt clung to the end of the cut. "This might hurt." Simon took the paper towel and dabbed at it.

Charlie drew in a breath and held it as Simon alternated between wetting down the towel and wiping the rest of the dirt away. Then he applied antibiotic ointment and a gauze bandage.

"When was your last tetanus shot?"

Charlie shrugged wearily.

"Want me to take you to urgent care?"

"No. I'm sure it'll be fine. Thanks for patching me up. I'll have to finish your garden—"

Simon cut him off again, this time by gripping Charlie's shoulder and giving a tiny shake as he urged him to pay attention. "Don't worry about the garden. It's not a big deal. Really."

Charlie's eyebrows crooked together. Emotion glimmered in his warm brown eyes for a second. Then his expression simply fell. Bleakness claimed him. It was as though all his vitality had swirled down the drain with the blood and mud. He lurched sideways, catching himself against the kitchen counter.

"Here." Simon guided him toward one of the stools around the front of the counter and pushed him down. "Sit."

Charlie sat and stared at nothing while Simon fussed with the coffee maker. He remained quiet while they waited for the hissing and burping to stop.

His eyes focused when Simon put a steaming mug in front of him. "What's this?"

"Coffee," Simon said. "With sugar and cream. You look like you could use it."

"Thanks."

"Want to tell me what's going on now?"

"If I start, I won't stop."

"That'd be okay." It would. Simon wanted to know what had so seriously derailed this normally vibrant and sunny man.

"I think my daughter is having sex with her boyfriend."

Okay, then. Simon waited a beat, in case Charlie wanted to keep going as promised, or possibly threatened. But it seemed that one statement had kind of done it for him. Also it looked like he might cry. Simon had never wanted to hug anyone quite so badly.

Instead, he pulled up the stool next to Charlie, sat down, and tried to imagine having a daughter. "Jesus."

"Right?" Charlie shook his head. "It's my greatest fear, you know? I was her age when Merry got pregnant. Well, a year and a half older, but I could have been her age. Merry and I were doing everything, every-fucking-where at seventeen. I was the horniest damn kid in Bethlehem.

"I'll never forget the day she told me she was pregnant. I thought I was going to throw up. Then I figured I wouldn't live to see sunset because her father was going to kill me. Then my father was going to dig me up and kill me again, to make sure I learned my lesson. *Then* it would be Merry's mom's turn."

Stunned by the depth of Charlie's confession, Simon reached for his own coffee. Taking a sip, he burned his lips and cursed softly.

Ignoring his cup, Charlie rolled on. "I got a call from the school. Liv and her boyfriend were in the sports locker. Kissing, she says, but their clothes were all messed up." He glanced up. "'Only kissing,' she said. 'Just kissing.' Something like that. Which means *this time*, right? That this time they were only kissing, but maybe some other time they got carried away enough to . . ."

Charlie swallowed. Paled. Swallowed again. "We've had the talk. All the talks. I stash condoms all over the house so she can't help but find them, but how do I know if she's using them? She doesn't talk to me like she used to. So, anyway, then we get home and the dog is gone." He swung his head from side to side. "Of all the days for him to break his chain."

"Charlie." Simon touched his arm. Held it steady. "Breathe."

"You're not supposed to raise a kid alone." Charlie's tone lent a mournful whine to his words. "It's not supposed to be like this."

Simon understood then that Charlie had loved his wife. He might have been surprised into marrying her, but he'd clearly not regretted doing so, and for the past eighteen years, he must have looked ahead. His wife had died and he'd kept forging ahead. Because he'd had to—he was a father. He'd had no other choice. And he didn't resent it. Charlie was a happy guy.

But this...

As he'd so succinctly put it, this was his greatest fear.

"Is there someone I can call?" Simon asked. He'd like to offer his support but, as a single and childless man, felt he couldn't do more than listen. Was that enough?

Charlie shook his head again. "I should take Herbert for a run. Clear my head."

"How's your hand?"

Charlie lifted his bandaged palm and peered at it. "Okay. Hurts." He flexed the hand. "I can still move it." He scooted forward, dropping his feet to the ground, and stood. "I'm going to head back next door. Thanks for . . ." He wound his injured hand through the air once, wincing as he did so.

You haven't had your coffee.

Pressing his lips together, Simon stood next to him and nodded. "Sure. Anytime you want to poke a hole in your hand, I'm here."

A half smile plucked at Charlie's mouth. He snorted. "Right." He glanced at the coffee and picked the cup up. Took a careful sip. His eyebrows rose. "This is good."

"You can take it with you if you want."

A slightly wider smile. "Nothing says welcome to the neighborhood like a mad man digging up your bushes. And now my blood is in your sink and your coffee mug is going to be forever lost somewhere in my kitchen."

Simon's return smile felt disproportionately wide. It wasn't because of the bandaging and coffee, it was Charlie trusting him with something so personal and precious. Simon hadn't even been able to offer any advice, but Charlie already seemed lighter. And, Lord, it had felt good to listen to someone else's troubles for a change. Made his own seem less.

"Should I take a cup in return, like a hostage?" he asked.

Charlie smiled. "It always starts small. Just a coffee cup at first. Then it's a ladder and power tools. Eventually, we won't know whose stuff is whose."

Why did that sound so nice?

"Thanks again." Charlie clapped his undamaged hand to Simon's upper arm. Twice, his hand staying put the second time.

An awkward moment swelled between them, where nothing was said, but thoughts clamored and the air crystalized, ringing with intent.

Would they step in and hug?

Step away and nod?

Move together and . . .

Simon glanced up from staring at Charlie's mouth. Shit. His chest tightened, locking all of his breath inside his lungs. Charlie's forehead wrinkled briefly. His fingers tightened on Simon's arm.

Then Charlie let go and stepped back. Producing a wavering half smile, he raised the coffee cup in salute, and left.

CHAPTER 11

"We have time for maybe two more questions."

A sleek gray arm shot up, followed by a guy wearing a skintight, reflective body suit. Really tight and really reflective. Charlie could see his biceps, pecs, abs...

Do not look at his crotch. Just don't.

Dumbly, Charlie pointed toward the silvery figure and swallowed. Hard. Costumes were the norm at any spec-fic convention. Schedule one in autumn and you were seriously out of place in jeans and a T-shirt. This, though... this wasn't fair.

"Is Kaze Rider gay?"

Charlie stroked his index finger over the small pink scar at the base of his thumb, where Simon had bandaged his hand. He'd formed a habit of stroking it when he was anxious. Not that he should be—he'd been expecting this question. Shelly had prepped him for it when they'd chosen an excerpt for the convention program. An extended teaser had gone up on his website this morning—and it was the scene from chapter twelve. The one where things could have happened in the auxiliary cargo bay.

"He's bisexual," Charlie answered.

"You don't think him getting back together with Jory in the final book means there was something he didn't want to admit to himself all along?"

Charlie tilted his head. "No. The—" He couldn't say *thrust*. Not here, not now. "Kaze's sexuality isn't a major theme in the series. It's a facet of his personality. Same as the fact his eyes are green. He's always enjoyed the company of women as much as that of men. He flirted with a Geroth bartender in the fourth book, and their gender isn't ever specified."

"So he's pansexual, then," someone else chimed in.

"He's just a guy," Charlie murmured.

"Do you believe gay heroes are important?" the silver guy asked.

"Yeah, I do." Kind of a no-brainer there.

"To you, personally?"

The panel moderator stood. "I think we're getting a little off topic. Does anyone else have a question relating to our previous discussion? We were talking about wrapping a series."

Another hand shot up and Princess Someone-or-Other asked about spin-off novels, her question directed at another panel member. Charlie took a moment to catch his breath.

A few minutes later, the moderator was thanking the audience for their attendance and participation, and the variously costumed crowd mostly left the small theater. A couple lingered near the door, waiting for pictures and autographs.

"Who was that guy?" Charlie asked Veronica Kirkwood, the author next to him.

"I think he was Iceman. He recently came out."

"Iceman from the X-Men?"

"Yeah." Veronica smiled. "Don't let the personal questions get to you."

"I don't, not usually."

"Did you do the panel on LGBT representation?"

Charlie shook his head. "No. It conflicted with my signing. And it's . . ." He shrugged.

"I get it."

"What?"

"You want your books to be about Kaze as a person, and his story. Not his sexuality or skin color or religious beliefs."

"Not really? Representation is important. I . . ." He needed something to occupy his hands. He tucked them into his pockets. "I just wasn't prepared for all the questions."

Smiling again, Veronica patted his arm and went to mingle with her fans.

After signing a couple of autographs and posing for a picture, Charlie escaped the conference room and nearly ran up the back of Iceman.

"Sorry if I got a little personal in there. It's just an important issue to me." Iceman offered his hand.

Charlie accepted the shake. "Sure, no problem."

"I'm a huge fan, by the way. I've already preordered the last book."

Smiling, Charlie pulled a card from his back pocket. "Drop me a line with your mailing address, and I'll send you all the bookmarks and bookplates and stuff. I think I even have some posters from a couple of years ago, the ones from book three." Kaze and Jory, back to back, weapons cocked.

"Hey, that'd be great!"

Feeling like a wilted rag, Charlie skirted the grand ballroom where the main convention was in full swing, walked an approximate mile of carpeted hallway toward the front of the hotel, and ducked into the bar. The panel had gone well, his quick reading getting a good reception. He needed a quiet moment, though. Time away from the crowds.

Charlie pulled the lanyard from his neck and tucked it into his shirt pocket, signaling he was "closed for business," and slipped onto a stool. He ordered a beer, wrapped his fingers around the cool glass of the bottle, and sighed. Even before he tipped it to his lips, he could feel the chill bubbles on his throat. Cons made for thirsty work.

A shadow fluttered to his left. Swallowing, Charlie put his beer back on the bar. A skinny guy of indeterminate age had claimed the stool next to him. At first glance, he seemed younger than he probably was. It was his inward posture—the roundness of his shoulders and dipped chin. But if living with a teenager had taught Charlie anything, it was that people under thirty did not wear cargo shorts and geek T-shirts.

Not those with friends, anyway.

The guy ordered a beer. When it arrived, he savored the first sip in much the same way Charlie had. No question he'd been at the con, T-shirt and lanyard notwithstanding. Obviously feeling the weight of Charlie's attention, he turned. While his expression moved from *You look familiar* to *Are you famous?* to *Weren't you on the panel I just attended?* Charlie gave his features a brief study. Wavy brown hair, startling blue eyes, pale but flushed skin. His nose was long and a little pointed. His mouth small, lips red. Chin narrow. The sprinkle of freckles across his nose wrestled with the evidence of laugh lines around his mouth and eyes. An old-young face. A guy close to his own age, by Charlie's reckoning.

"Were you just at the con?" the guy asked, gaze flicking to the center of Charlie's chest, where his badge would be if he were still wearing it.

An affirmative answer could mean he'd spend the evening debating Star Trek vs. Star Wars.

Then again, he had nothing better to do.

"I just escaped," Charlie answered with a grin. He lifted his bottle in salute. "To sore feet and ringing ears."

His companion lifted his beer and drank. The *clank* of his bottle back against the bar top startled them both. "Wait, I *do* know who you are. You're C.R. King!"

Here we go. Reaching for a humble smile, Charlie dipped his chin in acknowledgment. "Guilty as charged."

"Oh man, I love your books! Kaze is such a great hero. I love that he makes so many wrong choices, you know? Not that he's an idiot." *Gee, thanks.* "But he makes mistakes. Sometimes things work out, sometimes they don't. When they do, though, it shows how human he is."

"Uh, um, thanks. That's . . ." Pretty insightful. "That's kind of how he is, you know? Or how I wanted him to come across."

"Awesome." Guy was nodding. Then he stuck out his hand. "I'm Aaron, by the way. I attended the panel you did this morning with Gerry Stack and Liza Curlew."

Nodding, Charlie shook his hand. "That was a fun one."

Aaron looked as though he'd been given the secret to the universe. On the one hand, it was cute. On the other, his open adoration made Charlie feel weird. And guilty as hell. He was used to that, sort of. The feeling he didn't deserve so much admiration from fans.

Then something even stranger happened. Aaron didn't let go. The handshake had long ceased shaking but their fingers still clung together. The spark of recognition between them was that of author and fan, right? Aaron wasn't searching his gaze for something else?

Licking his lips, Charlie made his beer an excuse to let go, and wrapped his fingers around cool glass again. A moment later, he remembered to take a mouthful.

"So what made you decide to bring Jory Ondel back for book six?"

Charlie coughed, swallowed, and coughed again. The morning panel had been about recurring characters. The teaser for book six had been in that handout too. Being on a panel with a multiple *New York Times*–bestselling author (Stack) and the author of a twenty-nine-book (at last count) paranormal romance series (Curlew) meant that Charlie hadn't had to field any specific queries about his series.

He considered Aaron's question. "This is the last book for Kaze. I . . . wanted to give him something to live for."

"Someone, you mean."

A half smile pulled at the side of his mouth. "Sure."

"So you're not going to look into the repercussions of him not destroying the Norma Device?"

Oh, thank god. A nonsexual question. "I kind of like leaving that one open-ended. I mean, putting the device in the hands of the Carina Fleet should mean it's protected. That it'll never be used. But we don't know that for sure, right? I could probably write a whole new series from within the fleet. Make Admiral Nefain my new hero." Not a bad idea, actually. "It's not an immediate, world-breaking thing, though. It's a what-if, and life is full of what-ifs."

Aaron was nodding. "Why Jory and not Karleen? Don't get me wrong. I admire your choice, man. Book three was a surprise." He paused. "A good surprise. I think it's really brave of you to write a bisexual hero. Representation is important."

So Charlie kept telling himself.

"Honestly, I didn't know if my agent would go for it," he said. "Or my publisher. If I'd wanted them to get married and have babies, it might have been different."

"Yeah? Is that where you picture them at the end of book six?"

If he'd had beer in his throat, Charlie might have spluttered. As it was, he had to move some spit around to avoid choking. "Uh, um, I don't know. I haven't thought much about what Kaze will do after I retire him."

Liar!

Feeling the back of his neck prickle and itch, Charlie rubbed at the warm skin. "I just wanted to give the series a satisfying end."

Aaron was watching him intently, his eyes seemingly bluer by the minute. Lord, he'd only had one beer. What was it with him and blue eyes all of a sudden, anyway?

Aaron's expression softened slightly, forehead smoothing, and he leaned back and smiled. "You know the fan fiction sites will have them making babies within a week of publication. Hell, it's probably already been written."

"Fan fiction?"

"For Kaze Rider. You've never read any?"

Charlie opened and closed his mouth. He vaguely remembered a conversation with Shelly about something like this. "No. I, ah, don't think I'm supposed to."

"Good idea." Aaron chuckled.

Was it Charlie's imagination, or was Aaron becoming more attractive the longer they talked? No, he'd been attractive at the start, what with those eyes and his red lips. His geek uniform and easygoing manner. Long, slender fingers.

"So what do you do for fun?" Aaron asked.

This would be where Charlie mentioned his daughter—and perhaps a fictitious wife. Well, one that hadn't sadly departed five years ago. The bio in the back of his books was brief. His abbreviated name—C.R. King—and a bit about the awards he'd won for previous books in the series. That was it. No location, no family. If it'd been up to him, he'd have used a picture of Herbert, and a paragraph about how his master had taught him to use the computer so he could tell the story of his people.

Charlie didn't always mention his daughter and fictitious wife. Sometimes he flirted. Sometimes he went upstairs with the person he flirted with and got six months of sexual frustration out of his system.

Never with a guy, though, and he couldn't figure out if *Why not?* or *Why now?* was the more important question. The answer to the first was easy enough. Fear of the unknown, or maybe even a sort of complacency. He knew he clicked with women. Men he wasn't as sure about. As for why now? Heh. That answer was easy too. Simon. Meeting Simon had changed something within him. What he wanted and who he wanted it with.

But he was supposed to be thinking about what he did for fun. Two images immediately popped up. Phil's face was one, *Call of Duty* frozen on the TV behind him. Simon's face was the other. Simon in quiet moments, tending the cut under Charlie's thumb, or poring over the collection of plans for the house.

Charlie cleared his throat. "Ah, *Call of Duty*?" Why had his voice risen at the end? Fun shouldn't be a question. "We're still playing *Advanced Warfare*. We played with *Infinite Warfare* for a while and I know everyone's raving about *World War II*, but the campaign in AW is so fu—freaking amazing." Aaand now he was geeking out.

"I totally agree! So many cool mission objectives too. How did you find the WASP drone?"

"Frustrating as hell. And the highway mission. Jumping from truck to truck?"

"God, yeah."

"Phil and I spent hours on that one." Mostly because one kept jostling the other right when they were supposed to jump.

"Is Phil your partner?"

"Huh?" No beer, spit, or choking. Just plain old confusion.

Aaron's eyebrows crooked together. "Sorry, you kept saying 'we' and the whole thing with Jory, I made a leap."

"Phil's a friend. Um, my best friend." And brother-in-law. "We started kindergarten together. I'm . . . I'm single."

"Oh." Aaron's body language changed, the shift both subtle and obvious. He leaned forward, sliding the arm he had resting along the bar toward Charlie until their fingertips almost touched. "You know, we could borrow an Xbox from the hotel. They got a bunch in for the con—a couple too many."

"You want to play *Call of Duty*?" Even as he asked, Charlie knew the question was stupid—because of course Aaron wanted to play *Call of Duty*. For five minutes.

What do I do? What do I do!

Swallowing, Charlie pulled his hand back along the bar, the small pink scar at the base of his thumb tingling. "I, um . . ." He glanced up at Aaron, trying to read his expression.

Why *hadn't* he hooked up with a guy at one of these cons? He'd looked. He could remember thinking and wondering. Exchanging handshakes with men like Aaron, knowing on some level that he could ask them back to his room. It would have been the perfect situation in which to check his fear. Instead, he'd gone for the girl. Every time.

In the protracted silence, he studied Aaron's features. Blue eyes, pale skin, red lips. Simon's face, but not. He remembered again what Simon had looked like the day he'd bandaged Charlie's hand, and the long moment when they'd stood there, touching, gazing at each other. When Charlie had nearly leaned in and kissed him.

Something inside clicked, and barely formed thoughts tripped from the end of his tongue. "Um, there is sort of someone. We're not, ah, he..."

Okay, words weren't working for him right now.

Also, he'd given his interest a *pronoun*.

He'd given *voice* to his interest.

This time his blush didn't confine itself to the back of his neck. Was it possible to die of embarrassment with a side of confusion?

Aaron huffed out a soft laugh. "Oh, yeah, there's someone." He grinned. "How about if we stick to *Call of Duty*, then?"

Charlie relaxed. Breathed as though he'd forgotten what air tasted like. "Yes. Yeah, thanks. I'd like that."

Aaron pushed back from the bar. "Just so you know, you're still making all my dreams come true."

Charlie blinked.

"I'm playing Xbox with C.R. King!"

Charlie laughed. "I could be really, really bad at *Call of Duty*. You could spend your whole evening teaching me how to actually play."

"Even better. I can brag that I showed you how to get Maximum Overdrive."

"Wait, you've gotten Maximum Overdrive? What are we standing around here for?"

CHAPTER 12

Resisting the urge to rub his palms over his thighs, Simon plucked a proposal from the top of the neat pile and flipped through the pages. It was all there, as he had known it would be: mission statement, precis, plans, elevations, costs. Promises. It was a good packet. A great proposal. Larger versions of the plans, elevations, and renderings were arranged on easels around the room. An old-fashioned touch considering the technology available, but the Beckwith and Lynley pitch hinged on the distinction that everything old was new again.

Voices outside the conference room announced the arrival of Sierra Mason and her team. Arthur ushered them in and introductions were made. Ms. Mason had brought along her lawyer and her business partner, who was also her . . . wife. Huh. Simon glanced at Arthur. Would he have a problem with this? The older man seemed to be cataloging the differences between Sierra and her spouse, Penelope Mason. Where Sierra had dark-brown skin, dark hair, and dark eyes, Penelope looked like she'd stepped out of a Scandinavian travel brochure. Blond, blue-eyed, and fresh-faced—even the freckles across her nose were endearing.

Arthur extended a hand to Penelope. "A pleasure to meet you."

Smiling, Simon offered the same greeting.

"My project manager couldn't be with us today, but if we like what we see, he'll be at our next meeting," Ms. Mason said.

After exchanging a glance with Arthur, Simon indicated the seats and started the presentation. "Both Arthur and I have an affinity for the history of Bethlehem."

Chins dipped respectfully and gazes flicked across the plans arrayed behind him. Simon quickly moved to the overview of Burnside Province as he and Arthur envisioned it and began.

The neighborhood, as they had designed it, would be modeled after the historic farm it was named for. Every house would have a name denoting its location at the original farm—Summer House, Granary, Wheelhouse—and the land surrounding each would be of irregular shape and size, making some lots larger, others smaller.

"Someone always wants the largest lot in the neighborhood," Simon explained. "The retired professor will want the house at the end of a long driveway, and the young family will want the entry-level house. The one they can afford."

Heads were bobbing, expressions still engaged.

The next part was Simon's favorite. The actual house designs. There were twelve to choose from, many modeled after registered buildings. There were authentic farmhouses—one of which looked a lot like Charlie's place—and more formal residences. Outside, they all resembled scrubbed and polished versions of their 1700s counterparts. Inside, the homes featured modern, light-filled open spaces.

"All of these plans can be adjusted to accommodate larger and smaller room sizes. Within reason, the bathrooms can be moved and expanded."

Arthur took them through the financials and timelines next. Then the Q&A began. Simon had anticipated all the client questions except the last.

"Do you really think people want to live in farmhouses?" Sierra asked. Her voice carried a subtle undertone. She wanted to know why he loved these designs so much. She'd clearly picked up on his enthusiasm for the project and wanted to know where it came from.

"There are pretend colonials and Tudors and revivals of everything all over the Northeast. The people who buy them often wish they were living in the real thing—but they're either not up for a restoration, or would rather not deal with century-old plumbing. These houses are a compromise that won't feel like a compromise. The price point guarantees that. These are not cheap knock-offs. They'll appeal to people who appreciate that distinction. And for those who don't, the price will be just right." Expensive enough, and with a good address.

Sierra glanced at her wife, and Simon felt a pang as they exchanged a look only a long-standing partner could read. It was a small thing, but he missed that connection with another person. Knowing what someone else was thinking; knowing they could read your thoughts in return.

After exchanging another wordless look with her legal guy, Sierra turned back to the table with a warm smile. "Thank you for seeing us today. We still have one other presentation to view. Regardless of what we decide for this neighborhood, I hope we can seek further proposals from Beckwith and Lynley. I very much enjoyed meeting you both." She stood and offered her hand.

It wasn't a no, but neither was it a yes. It was more a *we like what we see, but aren't sure you're right for this project*.

Setting his smile to "professional," Simon stood and shook everyone's hand again. He managed to remain polite and courteous until everyone had left and he and Arthur were picking up discarded packets.

Had they even taken one to look at?

"I think that went rather well, don't you?" Arthur said.

"No? I don't know? Maybe? Did they take a packet?" Simon lifted the stack he'd gathered from the table.

"Of course they did." Arthur smiled. "And we can mail them another with a follow-up note thanking them for seeing us."

Right. Yes. Perfect.

Simon started breathing again, but the oxygen didn't feel fresh or refreshing. "Do you really think it went well?"

"I think they loved the houses, but didn't want to effuse in the first meeting. It'll come down to price. You'll see."

God, he wished he had Arthur's confidence. This wasn't his partner's next best chance, though. His remaking. His attempt to run away from home and find his future.

How could his life remain so uncertain when it was already half done?

When he arrived home, Simon's mood dipped a little farther as he contemplated the bland exterior of his rental house before glancing at the gate in the hedge. Would Charlie like to see the plans for Burnside Province? Given his knowledge of the area and local history, he could offer valuable insight, and having lived in the sort of house Simon wanted to build, he'd certainly have some advice regarding room size and aspects. Charlie could tell him if his designs worked, from a consumer point of view; what didn't work; and what he could improve.

Also, it'd be nice to commiserate with someone. Frank was currently on the West Coast interviewing someone famous, important, or both. Calling him in the middle of his afternoon would be needy.

Simon collected one of the presentation packets and approached the hedge. He couldn't see much of the house from here. The view was actually better from the top of the driveway, near the mailbox, where the hedge meandered down to bush level, exposing Charlie's front garden.

Not that Simon spent a lot of time checking for mail...

Oh, who was he kidding? He couldn't even say it was Charlie's house that fascinated him anymore. Not entirely. On occasion, he still gazed at the tall fieldstone chimney with something like lust. It was Charlie himself who continually drew his attention next door, though. The man whose gaze he caught more often than he should. The widowed father who wrote science fiction adventures. Who'd given his hero a male partner in book three.

Ever since that moment in the kitchen, when Charlie had looked at him with something like want, Simon hadn't been able to think of much else.

There was music coming from Charlie's house. Wondering if Charlie had company, Simon sidled toward the hedge. He stopped a foot short of the defiant spread of deep green.

A Peeping Tom would push his face into the hedge and spy.

When leaves started poking him in the face, Simon stepped back with something between a cough and a laugh. Apparently his Peeping Tom skills included quiet, unaware creeping too.

He didn't hear the dog running toward the hedge until after the crash—Herbert against the foliage, Simon down to the ground. Lying there gasping for air, he belatedly recalled the sound of accelerating paws.

"Herbert!"

Though the hedge stubbornly clung to its leaves year round, it had thinned substantially since the summer. Simon had a clear view of Olivia on the other side trying to extract her dog from the complicated tangle of branches.

Don't look up. Please don't look—

"Oh my God, are you okay?" Olivia moved a few branches aside, then let them go to run to the gate. She burst through, hauling Herbert alongside. The dog danced next to her, pulling at the grip on his collar.

"I'm fine," Simon wheezed. "Just . . ." Wishing the ground would open up and swallow him.

"Hold on, I'm going to put Herbert inside."

"Really, I'm fine." Simon rolled to his side, aware he was flopping around like a hooked fish.

Thankfully, Olivia had disappeared. Over the ringing in his ears, Simon heard voices on the other side of the hedge. He doubled his efforts to stand, not wanting Charlie to find him sprawled across the grass. A young man poked his head through the gate before running to Simon's side and helping him up.

"You're not Charlie," Simon observed, dusting himself off.

Not-Charlie smiled dazzlingly at him. "Mr. King is in Philadelphia."

"Justin." Olivia's voice had a warning tone to it.

Justin glanced over his shoulder. "What?"

Olivia danced from foot to foot a moment, chewing on her lip. It took Simon's oxygen-deprived brain a couple of seconds to connect the gesture to her father. When she was anxious, she looked just like him.

Composing herself, she said, "Are you okay? Should we call someone?"

"I'm fine, I just fell. Herbert surprised me and I . . . fell." Wow.

Olivia's and Justin's expressions echoed his silent thought—with the fancied addition of *I hope I never get so old I fall down for absolutely no reason whatsoever.*

"So. Charlie's away?"

"Yeah, he's at a con this weekend."

"Con?"

"Philcon. It's actually in New Jersey. It's like thousands of science fiction nerds crammed into a single hotel. Guys with bushy beards wearing kilts. They talk about aliens and sex for three days."

"Sounds like fun."

Justin snorted and Simon shared a grin with . . . Oh, this was The Boy! Did Charlie know Olivia was home alone with The Boy? A ghostly finger poked Simon in the back. Should he say something?

"Do you need anything while your dad is away? Are you set for . . . food?" Teenagers ate, didn't they? When they weren't having sex with their boyfriends. God, Charlie was going to freak. Simon couldn't imagine any other reaction to finding out Olivia had spent a weekend alone with her boyfriend.

"Oh, I'm not staying here." Olivia's expression soured. "Dad was worried either an asteroid would hit the house—just this house—or that a biblical flood would separate our neighborhood from the rest of Bethlehem, trapping me alone on an island, which would then get struck by an asteroid."

Justin gaped. "Seriously?"

Olivia gave her boyfriend one of those looks that combined eye rolling and lip curling. It was kind of endearing. "You have no idea."

"I thought he didn't want us sleeping over."

"That too."

Simon cleared his throat. "So . . ."

"Oh," Olivia said. "We're just here to feed and walk Herbert." And play music. Right.

"No sleeping over, then," Simon said, glancing from one to the other.

Behind his immature dusting of stubble, Justin blushed, and that was endearing too. Simon couldn't remember being that young.

Olivia was chewing her lip again.

Oh Lord.

Simon found himself in a position he wasn't quite prepared for. He could do the adult thing. In fact, he'd been accused of doing the adult thing so well, he might as well have skipped childhood. These weren't his kids, though, and that wasn't his house—chimney and fieldstone envy aside. But he considered Charlie a friend.

"Listen—"

"I'm staying with Rosalie. Really." Olivia pulled out her phone, showing him a blank screen. "You can call if you like. Verify I've been there since Thursday night."

Simon shook his head. "Not my job. But, hey, if your dad goes away again, I'd be happy to walk Herbert. Or look after the cats."

Olivia seemed caught between reactions. Her eyes flashed, her lips twisted, her shoulders lined up all square. She glanced at Justin, who sensibly remained quiet. She returned her attention to Simon. "That's nice of you. I'll let him know."

"Yoo hoo!"

Olivia's eyes widened. Justin spun around. From inside the house, Herbert started barking. Then Cassie popped through the hedge.

She took in the small party, smiling brightly before greeting them with, "Well there you all are," as if they'd gotten lost on the way to the bathroom. Cassie gathered Olivia into a quick hug, kissing the side of her head. "I heard music. Having a party without dear old dad?"

"We were hanging out some while we took care of Herbert," Olivia said.

"Aren't you a good girl?" Cassie looked up at Justin and smiled her kindly old aunt smile. "And you must be Justin. I've heard all about you."

Justin's blush deepened.

Cassie turned back to Simon, taking in the grass still clinging to his pants. "What happened to you?"

Simon tucked the Burnside packet behind his back. "Gardening."

Cassie made a sweeping gesture, encompassing all. "Well, I've made lemonade and these odd little cookies. Come on, before they get cold."

"Justin—" Olivia began.

"You don't want your dad to think Simon and I left you and your boyfriend alone in that house, do you?" Cassie said.

Olivia looked down at her feet.

Justin tried for a smile. "That's kind of you, ma'am."

Aww, wasn't he sweet?

Before Simon could back up a step, Cassie hooked her arm through his. "I've been wanting to talk to you about my studio, anyway. I was thinking of putting in a skylight." She jerked her chin toward the shuffling teenagers. "Come on, I'm sure the cookies will be better warm."

Really, he had no choice but to follow.

Really, he didn't mind.

In no way could he ever have imagined befriending someone like Cassie. The woman made inscrutable pottery and kept trying to break his back (yoga) and teeth (cookies). For the first time in his life, however, Simon felt as though he were part of a neighborhood. He had friends outside his circle of mostly gay and often lonely men.

Then there was the fact Cassie had lived next door to Charlie since he was twelve years old. She knew a lot of stories.

Smiling to himself, Simon began preparing a list of leading questions.

CHAPTER 13

As always, Charlie spent a few days after the con lying low. He'd avoided the crud, but was thankful he'd scheduled no freelance work over the next month—he had a book to finish, after all. He did write some, then spent an inordinate number of hours sprawled on the musty old couch behind his desk convincing himself that Tumblr was the eleventh circle of hell—and that once he stepped through the gate, he'd never find his way back.

Twice he approached the gate between his property and Simon's. Twice he forgot the excuse he'd manufactured for visiting and turned back. Once, he waved enthusiastically at Simon's car as it rolled down the street past his house. He'd been thinking about the gate again. Or visiting Simon. After the taillights disappeared around the corner, he stood on his front path, cursing himself for being the most idiotic human being in existence, until Cassie came out to ask if he wanted to do yoga with her.

He'd spent the rest of the day on his couch, nursing what felt like a broken spine.

Friday evening found him pacing his hallway, waiting for Phil. When he heard a truck pull into the driveway, he ran for the door, slowing to a walk as he pushed through to *amble* down the front steps all casual-like, and absolutely not having to clamp his mouth shut over the pronouncement that he was unquestionably bisexual and had a thing for the guy next door.

"Hey!" Phil said, all but tossing him a pizza box. "How was the geek fest?"

"Geeky." Charlie flipped open the lid and smiled. "Hmm, my favorite."

"Olives and anchovies, just for you."

"C'mon, the beer and Xbox are ready." Discussing his sexuality would have to wait a bit. Pizza, beer, and *Call of Duty* were serious business.

They were on the family room couch washing away the grease with healthy swigs of Stella, wiping fingers with imperfect squares of paper towel, when Phil said, "Damien thinks he's pansexual."

Charlie glanced up from trying to slide a corner of towel under his thumbnail. Oily fingers and Xbox controllers were a huge NO. Especially when they had achievements to achieve. "Huh?"

"Pan. Sexual. Ever heard such a thing? I'm pretty sure it's got nothing to do with kitchenware, by the way."

"No, it's like, ah . . ." Charlie frowned. "I think it's like bisexual." *Which, hey, what a coincidence, basically describes what I am.* Charlie took a slow and careful sip of his beer. "What do you think about it?"

"Fuck, I don't know. I mean, I'm not going to go all caveman on him. He's my son. He'll always be my son. He can love who he loves and I'll stand proud at his big gay wedding. What I don't get is the word. What happened to being gay or lesbian or something?"

"People can still be gay or lesbian."

"Have you figured out if those women on the corner are, you know . . ." Phil's eyebrows did a little dance.

"If you're asking if I've mustered up the courage to ask if their close and personal relationship includes sex, no. I just kind of assumed. They're obviously not related and they never talk about the men in their lives."

"Huh."

Charlie leaned over the arm of the couch to snag his laptop from the end table. He flipped it open and typed *pansexual* into Google. "Okay, 'pansexual' means 'not limited in sexual choice with regard to biological sex, gender, or gender identity.'" He glanced up at Phil. "So . . . ?"

Phil's eyebrows were doing the thinking thing, twitching together in the middle of his forehead, skin all creased over the top. "Biological sex?"

"Whether you have a dick or not."

"So, he doesn't care what, ah . . ." Phil waved up and down, indicating his chest and groin. "Parts someone has?"

"Yeah."

"Okay, so what does 'asexual' mean?" Phil asked.

"Why?"

"Because that's what Penny wants to be."

"Penny is eight."

"When I tried to point that out, Bethany read me the riot act. I'm not allowed to tell her sister, or any of my kids, that they'll change their mind when they get older."

"What did Jen have to say?"

"She held it together until we got to bed and then sobbed into my shoulder because Damien might not make any beautiful babies."

"He might. He might just have to jerk off into a cup first."

"Dude."

"Or adopt. There're enough babies out there needing good homes."

Charlie's finger hovered over the Tumblr icon. What did pansexual sex look like? *Like sex, you idiot.* He glanced over at Phil, who sat hunched in his corner of the couch, picking at his thumb. Charlie drew in a quick and not at all electrifying breath. "Did you ever used to look at Billy McHugh in high school?"

Phil glanced up. "Huh?"

"Never mind."

"Billy McHugh as in captain of the football team?"

"Yeah."

"He's gay. Did you know that?"

Charlie nearly dropped the laptop. "No way! How did you find out?"

"I heard something from one of my cousins who heard something from a friend of his in Philly who does plumbing." Phil's network of useful cousins extended far and wide.

"I used to have a crush on him," Charlie said.

"If you're going to say, 'see and I turned out okay,' save it. This is a bit different."

"I think if I hadn't gotten Merry pregnant, that we would have taken a break when we got to college." Phil's gaze narrowed.

Oh, Charlie had his attention now. "Because I wanted to experiment." He waited a beat before adding, "With guys."

To his credit, Phil didn't crawl backward over the arm of the couch to put three feet of leather-clad upholstery between them. Nor did he proclaim that the whole world had gone gay.

"Sorry," Charlie said. "I don't mean to put aside this thing with Damien. We can talk about that if you want. I just . . . I've wanted to talk to you for a couple of weeks now and this seemed like a good time."

"A couple of weeks? What happened? Did you hit your head and suddenly remember fantasizing over Billy McHugh? Oh God, did you used to jer—"

"Not going to discuss private time with you. Jeez. Already this conversation borders on the weirdly personal, even taking into account the fact we're basically related."

"Speaking of, how did Liv do while you were away? Cassie report any suspicious lights over here?"

"No, but she did find Olivia and The Boy here one afternoon"—Charlie made air quotes—"'hanging with the dog.' Sounds like my other neighbor already had the situation in hand, though."

Damn his itchy, prickling fucking neck. Charlie rubbed his nape.

"So are you telling me you're this pansexual thing too?" Phil asked.

"I'm bisexual." Now that he'd found his way to bisexuality, he wanted to hang on to it. Explore its truth with Simon, maybe.

"You were really good with Merry, man. I thought you two were for life."

Swallowing a sudden lump, Charlie dipped his chin. "We would have been. Just because I've been looking at guys doesn't mean I ever . . ." He made a circular motion with his hand. "I loved her with everything I had."

"I'm sorry."

"No, it's cool. I know what you're thinking, but it's not like that. Not for me, anyway."

"Is there . . .? Are you telling me this because you met someone? Was it at the con?"

"A guy did try to pick me up at the con, actually."

"Have you done dudes before, at these cons?"

"No!" Charlie took a breath. "No. I did hook up with a couple of women. After, you know..."

"Of course it was after. You'd never..."

An uncomfortable quiet bloomed between them. Charlie didn't measure his days so much by *before Merry* and *after Merry* anymore, but tonight her ghost felt close. What would she have thought of his confession? She'd probably have been heartbroken at the idea he'd have gone off to college without her. But if they were meant to be, he'd have come back to her, right?

Oh, Charlie, it was so long ago.

Charlie cleared his throat. "It's my neighbor, Simon."

"The architect guy?" Phil looked thoughtful. "Are you sure you want to do this? Here? Now?"

"It's not that small a town, and we've got two colleges here. There are people of other orientations among us." Charlie's smile felt small. "Besides, there are only a couple of opinions that really matter. Yours, Liv's."

"What did she say?"

"I haven't told her yet."

"You gonna tell your parents?" Phil asked, still missing or ignoring the broad hint.

"I don't know. Maybe after I ask Simon out on a date and see if I crash and burn or not."

"You're going to ask him out?"

"I'm thinking about it."

"Should you maybe ask if he"—Phil gestured vaguely—"likes guys first?"

"Good idea."

Phil studied him a moment, all serious and intent. "I don't have to tell you I'm good with this, right? You know you could start wearing sandals with socks, and you'd still be my brother from another mother."

Another lump tried to interfere with the swallowing process. Charlie forced it down. "Thanks."

Phil grinned. "I don't ever want to know if you've thought about me naked, though."

Charlie's laugh sounded so much like a bark that Herbert put his head up and licked his chops, whining softly. "Dude, no. Don't even . . ." Charlie waved his hands. "Put that out of your mind, completely."

Phil was laughing too. "What? I'm a man in my prime."

"I thought you didn't *want* me to think about you."

"Well I didn't until you made such a big deal about not wanting to. What's wrong with me?"

"Brother from another mother?"

Chuckling, Phil reached for his beer. "C'mon, it's time to play. We've only got a couple hours until we have to wait on the porch for Olivia to miss her curfew."

Charlie groaned. "Don't remind me. You want to talk about Damien some more?"

"Nah. Not tonight. I need to think about this biological sex thing some more."

"Damien would probably be happy to tell you about it."

Phil nodded slowly. "Yeah. Okay, let's kill stuff."

A curious sense of peace and determination mingling in his chest, Charlie picked up his controller. "Bring it on."

CHAPTER 14

Sitting behind the abandoned secretary's desk at the offices of Beckwith and Lynley, Simon absently watched the world pass by the front window and thought about his neighbor. They hadn't exchanged more than a wave from driveway to driveway since Charlie had returned from his convention. Simon had been busy with plans for a client who wanted an entirely new kitchen—unfortunately not farmhouse style—and he assumed Charlie had other things to do besides walk his dog and plot galactic domination.

If not to examine Charlie's kitchen, even under false pretenses, what excuse could he come up with for visiting?

His rumination was interrupted by a phone call from Arthur. "Ms. Mason and her team will be at the office in an hour," he said.

"They've reached a decision?"

"Hopefully a favorable one," Arthur replied. "They wouldn't drive up from Philadelphia unless they wanted to discuss terms, though."

"Right. I'll tidy up the conference room and get something from the café next door."

"See you soon."

The conference room needed no "tidying," but he straightened all the chairs anyway. Wiped down the table. Set out coffee and pastries. Put the Burnside plans on the easels, took them down, put them up again, and then stacked the entire project in presentation order on a single easel.

He was just stowing the extras in the closet when Arthur arrived, Sierra Mason's team at his heels. Sierra, her wife, their lawyer, and—

Sun glinted from a blond head as Brian Kenway followed the party inside, ducking instinctively as he guided his tall frame through the doorway. Simon blinked a couple of times, willing the familiar features to blur, for Sierra's project manager to become someone else. Someone he'd never worked with before—never slept with, lived with, been in love with, been betrayed by, had left his home and state for.

For this to not be happening.

Brian looked up, and their gazes met. Briefly, his expression brightened, as if he'd spied an old friend, and then the lines of his face settled into a smile Simon knew all too well. Brian had known Simon would be here. He had connected the Lynley part of Beckwith and Lynley with him. Brian's morning had started with the expectation that Simon would be present for this meeting, and he was prepared to be professional about it, as though the twelve years they'd spent together had been little more than a business arrangement.

Sierra Mason was in front of Simon, offering her hand and a warm smile. She'd said something. Simon had an impression of her voice, but not the words. He clasped her hand in a firm shake. "Good to see you, Ms. Mason."

"Sierra, please."

He found a smile, plastered it across his mouth like a mask, and let it set. Greeted the rest of Sierra's team, knowing Brian was waiting to be last in line. Would a black hole form between their fingers as they tried to shake hands, swallowing up Bethlehem, then the world?

You've been reading too much science fiction.

Brian stuck out a hand. "Simon. You're looking well."

Simon returned the briefest handshake he could get away with, pulling his fingers from Brian's grasp before the world could end. Sierra was eyeing them curiously from the other side of the table as he gestured toward the chair next to him—the last one, damn it—indicating Brian should take a seat.

Sierra got the ball rolling. "As you've no doubt guessed, we've come to discuss your proposal with the hope that we can reach an agreement to work together." She nodded toward her lawyer. "We've only a couple of points to go over, all of which I'm sure will be no obstacle. Mostly matters of branding and scheduling."

Paperwork shuffled across the table, a packet that included their proposal, suggestions and changes highlighted and interleaved, and the meeting began. Simon tried to concentrate. He'd been excited about this project, but Brian's presence beside him functioned like a sinkhole, dragging at him mentally and physically.

How had he not known Brian was a part of Sierra's group?

Because Arthur had done the financials. He'd researched the names, the previous projects, the solvency of Mason & Mason.

Someone was speaking to him again. Simon glanced up from the paperwork into expectant silence. "Sierra wanted to know if you had any additional thoughts regarding the project boundaries," Arthur said.

Simon inspected the page in front of him again, not even certain it was the right one. Every word seemed to say *Brian*, and he wasn't sure the voice in his head was his own.

It's not supposed to be this way. This is my fresh start. My future. Mine!

And if he didn't pull himself together, he'd lose it.

He glanced at the page and saw it was the right one. He read the first line of every paragraph, and began forming his reply. Calm seeped in from the edges, seeking the excitement he had for this project. The steel that had seen him through the breakup of his life reasserted itself. Straightening in his chair, he took the meeting by the reins and rode it.

Afterward, when hands were being shaken all around, pastries served, and coffee dispensed, Simon edged toward the door. He needed a minute. Just a little one. One second in a space not occupied by Brian Kenway.

Brian followed him into the hallway. "Simon."

Without looking at him, Simon shook his head. "You'll be dealing with my partner, Arthur Beckwith. He's the project manager. I'm only the architect on this one."

Brian put a hand on his arm. Despite his misgivings, Simon looked up.

"It's good to see you," Brian said. Damn if he didn't seem as though he meant it. As though he'd actually missed Simon. Missed *them*.

"Don't." Simon tugged at his arm.

"I gave them your name. Your firm. Beckwith and Lynley."

"What?"

"I wanted you to have this project. I knew it would be perfect for you."

Coffee soured in Simon's stomach. "How dare you."

"I didn't do it to be kind. I did it because you're the best choice, and you proved me right. They barely even considered the other proposals. Yours was the best by far."

That didn't make him feel any better. "Why are you here?"

"Same reason as you."

"This isn't your deal, Brian. You like to make McMansions in Jersey. One plan, two variations. It's easy. You don't have to think."

Brian rocked back a little. "Ouch." Then he tilted his head. "Did you ever think that I might have been bored and frustrated too?"

Was he talking about their work, or their personal life? Simon shook his head.

"I thought enough time had passed that we could do this." Brian's tone was soft, almost intimate. "I want us to be friends. I know you don't. I know I hurt you too badly for that. But maybe working on this project together can bring us back to some place of mutual respect. How it used to be, when we liked each other."

Simon didn't want to remember having liked Brian, but couldn't help it. This man had been his partner in every sense. Now, all Simon wanted to do was ask the question he'd never had a satisfactory answer to. Why? Why had Brian taken everything they'd built together and thrown it away?

The projects, Simon understood. Though soul sucking, the money they'd made had meant they could move on to something better. The cheating, though. Finding the man whose faults you overlooked because of that charming damned smile, among other things, in bed with someone else—not once, not twice...

God, he'd been a fool.

Simon cleared his throat. "I'll work with you. There's no choice there. I'm invested in this project." He stabbed a finger toward the conference room. "Those houses are the best I've ever designed."

"They're beautiful, Simon. They really are."

"I don't care if you think they're ugly. I want to build them, so I'll work with you. But you can forget about the respect part. You can't have that back." It would be too high school to tell Brian he didn't want to like him, either. So Simon simply nodded to punctuate his statement, his thoughts, and turned to stalk away, seeking a properly uninterrupted minute. A true breath of fresh air.

After Sierra and her team had left, Arthur approached him with a worried expression. "Is everything all right?"

Simon nodded, shook his head, then nodded again. "I have a personal history with Brian Kenway. I'll try not to let it intrude. He's..." He pushed out a sigh. "He's a damned good project manager. Not terribly imaginative, in my experience, but hard-nosed enough to keep the contractors on schedule."

Arthur studied him a moment. "My concern is you, not the project. When Kenway walked in, you looked as if you'd seen a ghost."

Grunting softly, Simon turned away to collect the used coffee cups. "Like I said, personal history."

Arthur waited another beat before speaking. "My generation was never much for personal things. History, yes, or stories we can tell that are more entertaining than our own sordid lives. But our personal lives were supposed to remain our own. To this day, I can't decide if it was better that way."

Simon gave him a questioning glance.

"I'm aware most of Bethlehem believes my associates are ghosts," Arthur continued. "There was only one, though. Jeremy Klein. He was my partner in all things until he passed." He wore the expression of a man reminiscing over deep loss and old grief. "It's difficult to move forward from that. Especially in a small community. So I honored his memory—each facet of it—by making Jeremy into a host of associates. My partner, my friend." A quiet breath. "My lover."

Gaping wasn't polite, but how else to react?

"I hope I have not misjudged you," Arthur went on. "That my... personal history isn't something you—"

"No. You haven't. I appreciate the confidence."

"It's considered rude to imagine one knows another without question, and this world is so obsessed with labels. But I recognized you when you first came to visit me, Simon. That's not why I was eager for the partnership, you understand. But I felt nonetheless that we could make beautiful things together. That in you, I had found someone to pass my associates on to."

Moved beyond measure, Simon took Arthur's hand. They exchanged something like a handshake, a secret message between men of a certain persuasion. A somber smile, a sharing of trust.

"Thank you," Simon said, for the gift Arthur had just given him. Not the sharing of his personal history, though Simon appreciated that more than he could express, but the understanding, and the belief that this, too, would pass. That life went on, and that beautiful things could be built from the ruins of anything—of memories good and bad.

If only he could absorb Arthur's decades of patience along with his words and advice.

Tomorrow is another day.

CHAPTER 15

Hearing the faint hum of music, Charlie hesitated outside Simon's door. Maybe he had company? On a Monday night? Charlie glanced down at the six-pack dangling from his hand and shuffled his fingers a bit, easing the line where the cardboard handle had cut into his skin. Then he put the beer down beside the step, tucking it into a shadow. Monday wasn't really a beer night. He put the book under his arm on top of the beer. If Simon had company, Charlie didn't want to be the guy who showed up with book two of his series like some reverse-stalker.

Ditto the Cheez-Its. He put them on top of the book.

Maybe the puzzle was too much as well. Charlie peered into the bag, the porch light not really bright enough to do more than throw a dim, plastic shadow across the front of the box. Charlie pushed the noisy plastic bag down by the step as well, hiding it next to all his other stupid ideas.

Officially out of excuses to visit, except for the real one, he prodded the doorbell and waited while the music inside swelled in volume. Sounded sorta like movie music. Maybe Simon was watching something?

Should he push the bell again? Knock?

The music ended, and Charlie's finger jabbed forward, making the decision for him. By the time footsteps approached the door, the back of his shirt felt damp. Charlie half turned, readying his retreat. If he could get to the hedge by the time Simon—

The door opened. Simon stood there, silhouette untouched by the porch light. He looked at Charlie, then glanced at the apparently not-well-hidden pile of stuff by the step. "What's up?"

"I brought you some things." Worst pickup line *ever*.

He couldn't see Simon's face, but had the impression of a furrowed brow and pursed lips. He'd shown up on the doorstep on a Monday night with a random pile of shit. How else would Simon look?

"Want to come in?" Simon asked.

"Sure." Charlie stooped and gathered his stuff.

Leaving the door open for him, Simon retreated down the hall. Charlie tugged it closed, then wondered if he should have left it open. Simon might mean for him to leave as soon as he'd dropped off his crap.

Why was everything so weird all of a sudden? Was it just him, or did Simon seem a little off as well?

The short hall ended in light—a bright, open-plan space Charlie vaguely remembered from when he'd cut his hand on the garden trowel. He gazed about and got an immediate impression of his reluctant host: Clean lines; broad and quiet spaces. Tidiness. Order. In contrast, Charlie felt loud, crunchy plastic bag crushed against his chest notwithstanding.

Simon paused by the island counter separating the kitchen from the living area. The same counter where he'd doctored Charlie's hand. He leaned one hip against it and took a sip from the glass in his hand—an amber liquid with the viscosity of old whiskey or brandy—and directed a questioning expression at Charlie.

"Maybe this isn't a good time," Charlie said.

Simon's gaze landed on the book tucked under Charlie's arm. His mouth twitched. Was that the hint of a smile?

"I'm up to book four," he said.

"Oh?" Neck prickling, Charlie glanced around, as though searching for evidence. Wait, that meant Simon had read book three. That should make this easier, right?

Noticing the piano in the far corner of the large space, he asked, "Was that you? Playing?"

Simon made an affirmative sound.

Charlie looked back just in time to catch Simon's expression shifting through an interesting pattern. Sorrow, anger, guilt, fatigue, and . . . grief? "Are you okay?"

"Not really."

"Would you like me to go?"

Simon seemed to consider his request before lifting one shoulder. "It's just work. You're fine."

"The proposal for that farm place?"

"I told you about that?"

"Yeah, you mentioned it when I showed you the plans for my house."

"Oh, right. We got the project."

"That's awesome! Congratulations." So why did he look as though he'd had that project, and every one he might consider for the next ten years, rejected?

Simon offered another half shrug in response.

Okay, something wasn't quite right here. "Listen, I know we don't know each other very well, but you seem, um, upset." Charlie started lining up his excuses on the counter. The beer, the book, the box of crackers, and the puzzle. He fiddled with the corner of the puzzle. "I can listen, if you want. Be righteously angry about whatever it is on your behalf. And not just because I owe you for when I tried to cut my hand off."

Something in Simon's expression softened at that. His mouth moved again. Slightly. Another amused twitch. He nodded toward the puzzle. "What's this?"

"Oh, I found it at the art store. It's like this 3-D puzzle made out of paper. It's a castle in Europe."

"Neuschwanstein."

"Bless you."

Simon's laugh was rusty, but his face brightened with it for a moment. He took the box and turned it around. "This is really neat."

"You haven't seen them before?

"Not this one, no." He glanced up. "Why . . . ?" He gestured at the rest of the stuff with the box.

Charlie bit his lower lip, hard. "I wanted an excuse to visit and this is what I came up with."

Simon returned a blank expression.

"I'm not that imaginative, okay?"

Simon was shaking his head now.

In desperation, Charlie waved toward the piano. "So, you play?" *He already answered that one.* "I mean, how long have you been playing?"

When Simon didn't answer, Charlie turned to look at him and met a gaze of quiet but intense blue. Damn, he was gorgeous. Just... so well put together. If Charlie tried hard enough, he might pick out some imperfection. One eye slightly bigger than the other, or maybe the line of Simon's nose wasn't quite straight. Should a man's lips be that red? His chin had a slight cleft. Was that a good thing or not?

Aware he was staring, Charlie dropped his gaze to the unbuttoned collar of Simon's shirt and the V of crisp white undershirt. Did he have hair on his chest? Were his nipples as red as his mouth, or would they color up when he was turned on?

Oh, sweet Jesus. Heartbeat thrumming in his throat, Charlie took a step forward.

"Do you actually want to know how long I've been playing?" Simon asked.

Charlie shook his head. "Well, yes, I do. But not right now." He took another step.

Simon seemed to lean in, closing the distance between them. Then he took a deliberate backward step. Not a sway, not a stumble.

Charlie swallowed as the back of his neck caught fire.

"Sorry," he mumbled toward their shoes. "I . . ." He flicked his fingers in the direction of all the stuff on the counter. "I don't know how to do this. I don't have a lot of practice, and I've never tried with a guy before, and I forgot to ask if you would mind, but that seemed like the wrong question. I'm not sure what the right question is. We're not in a bar, damn it." His breath was coming faster, now, still flickering oddly in his throat. "If I've made a mistake, I'm really sorry. I didn't mean to offend you. And if you have no idea what I'm talking about, then, um, maybe we should just forget this. I'll take the book. You can have the Cheez-Its and beer. We'll say it's—"

"Charlie." Simon grabbed his arm, his hand warm through the cotton of his long-sleeve T-shirt.

Charlie had been backing away, mostly looking down. The heat across the back of his neck hurt. He was definitely having a "the floor can split open and swallow me at *any* time" moment. He glanced up, found Simon standing in front of him, that amazing mouth right there. Forgetting about everything else, Charlie leaned in and kissed him.

It didn't feel as strange as he'd thought it might. Simon's lips were softer than he'd expected. Sweeter. But his return kiss wasn't some tentative, fumbling caress. Not the uncertain connection between two people who didn't know each other—who wouldn't know each other any better in half an hour's time, despite having gotten naked and sweaty. Simon kissed him with focused intensity. Kissed him as one might kiss a lover.

With a groan, Charlie leaned in farther, opening his mouth. Simon responded immediately, his tongue sweeping through once. Wanting more—a deeper connection—Charlie reached for Simon's face. Touched his hair. Curled fingers around the back of his neck. His dark hair was soft and clean, the skin of his neck warm. So warm. In fact, the whole of Charlie's front was hot from the press of Simon's body—an impression of firm musculature, strong legs.

Suddenly there was an unaccountable space between them. Simon had put down his glass, and was holding both Charlie's arms, fingers still warm over the shirt, but he was pushing Charlie away, even though the expression on his face showed nothing but want. His eyes practically glowed with it. His mouth was even redder than before.

"I can't do this," Simon said, dropping his hands and taking another step back. "I'm sorry, but I can't."

"Why?" There were other questions, but this seemed the most important.

Simon shook his head. "It's not the right time."

"It felt right to me." It had been a good kiss. Oddly personal and fucking hot. Just thinking about the feel of Simon's lips against his would be enough to give him a hard-on. *Don't think about it now.*

Being rejected while sporting an erection would be really, really sad.

"Charlie." His name was a sigh. A sad one. "I'm not in a good place right now. I came here to sort myself out, and I'm not done yet." Pain furrowed Simon's brow, the hint of grief darkening his eyes. "Particularly not today."

"What happened?"

"I don't want to talk about it."

"You can't just kiss me like that and not talk about it."

"You kissed me, Charlie."

"You kissed back!"

"I know and I'm sorry. Please . . . don't make this more difficult than it already is."

Why does it have to be difficult?

Dipping his chin, Charlie backed off. Halting the southward roar of his blood required too much concentration for him to deal with the *why* right at this moment. What he did know was that he needed to leave. Before he did something he'd regret. Before Simon bruised his ego beyond repair.

Still, he turned before he reached the hallway. Glanced back. The fact that Simon remained right where he'd left him seemed strange. Charlie had half expected him to disappear. To leave an empty space like the one Charlie felt in front of him—to match his sense of loss. But Simon just stood there, looking like he'd lost something much more valuable.

Catching his breath, Charlie did the only thing that made sense. He left.

CHAPTER 16

Simon watched, unable to move, as Charlie turned away a second time. The quiet *click* of the front door closing behind him seemed entirely unsuited to the moment—as though the sound crew had picked the wrong tape. The wrong effect. Surely someone had forgotten the dialogue cues. The quiet was too loud, too discordant.

There was no music.

Reaching for his scotch, Simon let his weight drop onto the closest stool, half expecting it to slide out from under him. He would welcome a fall to the floor. The smack against the back of his head, his hip. The splash of whiskey across his hand and sleeve. Even sitting, it seemed the world tilted slightly, tempting, taunting.

"Jesus Christ." He tipped the glass and drained the last of the liquid, savoring the burn as he swallowed. The bubble of heat moving down his esophagus and into his chest did little to warm him, though. Instead, it pulled at his heart and lungs with a weight heavier than the grief he'd brought home from the office.

He'd just killed something so wonderfully light and bright. Squashed it dead.

"Damn it."

Asking why he'd done it would be an exercise in futility. It was Brian's fault. Brian fucking Kenway. Why today? Why had he had to step back into Simon's life today? Of course, if he'd kissed Charlie tonight, taken him to bed, would he have handled a visit from Brian any better tomorrow?

I don't fucking know.

Looking at the small pile of gifts made his heart hurt. Charlie was such a sweet guy. Nice in a way that seemed utterly guileless, but wasn't, really. He'd gathered this collection of stuff with an express purpose.

Except maybe the Cheez-Its. They made no sense whatsoever.

Neither did pushing Charlie away, not after weeks of circumspect wanting. Of trying not to flirt and constraining his touches to what felt natural and friendly. Stalking that damn hedge, contriving excuses to visit. Watching Charlie walk Herbert every night. Missing him when he hadn't got to the window in time.

Why had he pushed this funny, engaging, generous, kind, stupidly handsome guy away?

Clutching his empty glass, Simon breathed until the urge to throw it passed. From somewhere in the house, his cell phone played an obnoxious tone, the one he'd chosen to actually catch his attention—not that he felt like giving it right now. Would Charlie call him? No, he'd never given Charlie his number, despite the "fact sheet" he'd received the day he'd asked for information about the cable company.

Brian wouldn't dare call him, would he?

Maybe instead of trying to answer the call telepathically, he should hunt down the phone.

It was in the hall, in his coat pocket. The call was from Frank.

Simon hit Redial out of habit and failed to find the Cancel button before Frank answered. "There you are."

"Sorry, was busy trying not to break things in the kitchen."

"And you're normally such a good cook."

"I wasn't cooking."

"Have you been drinking?"

"Brian came by the office today." Simon's throat tightened over the last word.

"What! Why?"

"He's the project manager for Burnside Province."

"How did that happen?"

"The universe up and decided it hadn't finished fucking with me, and it didn't end there, either. Tonight, Charlie came over with this armload of stuff and kissed me."

"Wait. Hold on, I'm lost. Charlie?"

"My neighbor."

"Was he just really happy you're reading his books?"

Pushing out a sigh, Simon ventured back into his kitchen and eyed his empty whiskey glass. He could use another. He shouldn't have another. "I don't think this move is working out."

"Okay, let's rewind and start from the beginning. When did you find out Brian was working on this project?"

"This morning."

"Did he know you were the architect?"

"He recommended me for the job."

Frank's silence had a stunned feel to it.

"Right?" Simon pressed his free hand to his forehead.

"He didn't suggest—"

"No, and I'm not that stupid or desperate. I'm done with Brian."

"Can you work with him?"

"I kind of have to, or ditch this project."

"You can't do that."

"I could, but I'm not going to. Who knows, maybe this will be a good thing. Brian is a great project manager. If we can keep it professional, we could make this work. It's the sort of project we always dreamed about working on together." Simon stopped speaking as his voice wavered.

"I can't imagine how hard this must be for you."

"It shouldn't be, Frank. It's been close to a year. It shouldn't be this hard."

"You two were together for a long time."

"Yeah."

"What are you going to do about Charlie?"

"I—" Another sigh cut him off. Simon rubbed his head harder, as though he might rearrange his thoughts, have them make sense. "I think I basically killed that before it could start."

"Might be for the best. I mean, if you're this cut up over Brian—"

"Fuck Brian."

"That's what got you into this situation."

"Not laughing."

"Yeah, that wasn't really funny, but maybe a good fuck is what you need. Doing your neighbor might not be the best move if you plan to renew your lease, though. Could get awkward."

"Charlie isn't a one-night prospect. He's too . . ." *Don't say* sweet. "He doesn't strike me as a player." Didn't kiss like one, either. Simon's lips tingled with the memory. The bold sweep of Charlie's tongue, the groan he'd made. The way Charlie's fingers had sifted through the hair at his nape.

"If I come down there and take you out again, you're just going to brood in a corner like you did last time, aren't you?"

"I didn't brood. I was enjoying my drink." Simon picked up the empty whiskey tumbler and turned it so the etched glass caught the light.

"Mm-hmm. Why don't we do a weekend in the city?"

"I don't need to get laid."

"Yeah, you do. I'd offer up my own—"

"Frank, don't."

"I'm not pining for you, Simon."

"Okay, good."

"I'd still—"

"Jesus Christ."

On the other end of the line, Frank was laughing. "You're too easy. Have a drink and go to bed. Or play piano. Something thunderous or sad. Maybe you could use a good cry."

Simon gripped the glass. "You seriously think I'm going to sit and cry at my piano over Brian?" He'd been damn close when Charlie rang the bell.

"That's the spirit."

"Goodbye, Frank."

"Think about this weekend," Frank said before clicking off.

Simon put the phone and glass down on the kitchen island and picked up Charlie's book. He'd liked this one even better than the first. Book three, though, had been the one that had opened his eyes, had him hunting every line for a thread of Charlie's true thoughts. Had Jory been a plot device, or Charlie's feelings on the page? With that in mind, Simon had wanted to start again from the beginning, see how much more of his neighbor he could find within the text.

He flipped open the cover and saw writing on the title page. *Because we all need adventures.* He'd signed it *Charlie*. Not C.R. King, but Charlie.

"Goddamn it!"

Simon put the book down and stalked toward the piano. Thunderous. That was what he needed. Something so loud and so involved, he couldn't hear himself think for a while.

CHAPTER 17

One of the advantages of getting your girlfriend pregnant at eighteen, and subsequently marrying her, was a life devoid of rejection. Charlie had never been turned down for a date. Never rebuffed after a single kiss. He'd gotten a "let's just keep this friendly" vibe from a couple of women he'd tried to chat up at conventions, but that was it.

Well, except for the file of short stories no science fiction or fantasy magazine thought had value. But they were slices of another Charlie. Not the real Charlie who now sat dejected at his desk, staring at chapter something with no impulse to write.

If he pressed his face to the window and squashed his nose sideways, he could see the house next door. A greasy mark on the glass suggested that he'd tried sometime in the recent past, though Charlie blamed another slice of self for that one. Brooding was much more comfortable, until he thought over the four things he'd left in Simon's kitchen.

Five if he counted his pride.

Having not suffered personal rejection before, he also had no experience of the symptoms, or how the disease progressed. Tuesday hadn't been so bad. He'd drifted in a bubble of disbelief, as though Monday night were confined to a dream. Something that hadn't actually happened. Reality caught up with him Wednesday morning—about halfway through his run. He'd been leaning against a tree, stretching out his hamstrings, when Simon's face intruded on his thoughts. An unwelcome sweaty feeling followed.

Today, he just felt depressed. Thinking about his depression—and why he sat staring at nothing—only depressed him further. He was thirty-seven years old. He should be beyond three days of epic brood over being shut down and out.

Man, that kiss, though. What an amazing kiss.

His cell phone danced around the desk, inviting Charlie to accept an incoming call. His stomach swirled as he picked it up, expecting to see that it was Liv's school (not welcome), Phil (maybe welcome, as long as they didn't talk about Monday night), or Simon (calibrating response...).

It was Shelly.

"'Lo."

"Charlie! I was starting to worry."

Sometimes Charlie suspected Shelly had cameras hidden in his attic den. She always seemed to know when he wasn't writing. Though, the fact he hadn't answered her last three emails was probably a more reliable indicator of his nonproductive state.

"I'm still on target to meet my deadline." If he rationed sleep and brooding time over the next ten days.

"Good, good. I was hoping to talk about the ending. I love what you've sent me so far, but—"

"I haven't plotted the end yet. You know I never really think about how everything will shake out until I get there." Charlie shut his eyes, blotting out the sight of the keyboard he'd barely touched over the past few days. Every time he tried to concentrate, his thoughts wandered next door, toward Simon, the *man* he'd kissed.

"Have you figured out their escape from the fleet prison?" Shelly was asking. "Also, I wanted to talk to you about motivation."

In other words, she hadn't quite loved what he'd sent so far.

Olivia's car turned into the driveway. Charlie checked the time: three thirty. What time did school finish? With all the after-school activities and homework parties, he hadn't had a clear idea of when the school day ended for a number of years. He certainly hadn't seen his daughter much before five over the past few months.

Something was wrong.

"Shelly, I gotta go." He tossed the phone onto the desk, and ran for the stairs. Olivia stumbled into the kitchen when he opened the back door. Her distressed features crumpled as big, fat tears sprang from her eyes. "Dad..." She flung herself into his arms.

Remaining upright under the onslaught of sodden seventeen-year-old accomplished, Charlie hugged her close to his chest. "It's going to be okay, Duck." He had no idea what had happened, but it was his job to make sure whatever it was went away. His girl would be okay.

Olivia cried for about ten minutes, saturating the front of his shirt. He felt words land with the tears, but couldn't make sense of any of them. He rubbed her back and murmured nonsense, oddly content to wait until the storm passed. For the first time in weeks, he had a purpose—even if it could be described as *snotty hanky*.

Finally, sniffing between hiccups, Olivia stopped bawling. She still clung to his shirt, but it seemed safe to start guiding them toward the kitchen table. "C'mon, let's get you a glass of water."

He desperately wanted to ask what was wrong, but asking anything related to the tears would trigger a fresh batch. Best to hydrate and calm and wait for her to talk, which would probably require a dry shirt and a roll of paper towels.

Ten minutes later, the story began with "Justin and I broke up."

Anger seared a path across his heart. "What did he do?"

"No-th-ing." The hiccups were back. "I . . . We . . . Dad, why does it hurt so much?"

Charlie opened his mouth and closed it again. He'd been going to ask if Liv had talked to Rosalie. Surely her best friend would have better advice. But though it hurt to see his daughter so distressed, a part of him was glad she'd come home—even if it was because Rosie hadn't been available. Second choice was better than not being in the loop, and he only had another year and a bit to truly be here for his daughter.

Man, she looked wrecked, though. Why didn't the first aid kit have something in it for a broken heart? Charlie crouched by her chair and collected his daughter in another awkward hug. She sobbed into a fresh patch of shirt, her head butting into his ribs. When she was done, she was about as red and wrinkly as the day she'd been born. Charlie had to suck back the burn behind his eyes.

He patted her hair, smoothing the snarl of loose brown curls away from her hot, sticky forehead. "Want to tell me what happened?"

"No." Hiccup. "Maybe." Sniffle. "Do we have any ice cream?"

Charlie dropped to his heels and massaged his numbing thighs. If he stayed crouched much longer, he'd lose all feeling in his legs. Slowly, he stood, holding on to the back of her chair for support. "What flavor do you want?"

Liv lifted one shoulder in a quick shrug, the gesture oddly reminiscent of Simon's. He'd offered a lot of one-shouldered shrugs on Monday night.

Had he been in need of ice cream?

And I took him Cheez-Its.

Charlie pulled a random tub of ice cream from the freezer and scooped out two generous servings. Sitting opposite Liv, he dug into his bowl, savoring the cool burn against his tongue. Oh man, why wasn't he eating ice cream for lunch every day? This was like the best idea ever.

Olivia started crying again, quietly, tears tracking down her cheeks as she sucked ice cream off her swollen lips. His daughter was a messy crier. She got that from him. Merry—Merry had always wept serene tears, even after the doctors stopped delivering good news with the bad.

Charlie reached over and caught her free hand, squeezing her sweaty fingers into his palm. "It's okay. Finish your ice cream and then start at the beginning."

"I got scared. I— The thing is— I mean . . ." She let out a deep, shuddering breath. "Dad."

"I'm so sorry, Liv."

Liv shook her head. "I liked him so much, but everything was moving too fast, and I wasn't ready to get that attached."

"Umm . . ."

"Sometimes I feel so young and stupid and other times I feel like I'm rushing toward the end. I don't know what it is, I know I won't see it coming, but it's right there. Big and black and implacable."

He hadn't been The Boy's biggest fan, but surely Liv hadn't broken up with Justin because she believed the world was coming to an end? Shouldn't the end mean clinging to the ones you loved? Had she loved him? An odd sensation crawled through Charlie's chest, and he didn't know if it was guilt that he was glad to have her back or sadness on Liv's behalf.

And why, for the love of everything square and cheesy, did she think the world was going to end? What was behind this morbid fascination of hers? After Merry's death, they'd both gone to counseling for a while. Maybe it was time to revisit Dr. Cambria. "Liv?"

She looked up.

"Sweetheart, this world-ending thing." The burn was back behind his sinuses. "What does it mean?"

Instead of lifting her gaze heavenward and smacking gum, Olivia put her head down on the table, over their hands. Charlie stroked her hair for her, just as he'd done when she was a little girl. After a while she whispered, "I miss Mom."

Now he really did want to cry. "Have you talked to Rosalie?"

"She had the dentist this afternoon."

So that was why his shirt was ruined. "Want me to call Grandma?"

Her head rocked over his hand.

"Tell me what you need."

She was crying again. Charlie's heart ached for her. Seeing his little girl in so much pain was about the worst experience ever. A sharper hurt than Merry's death, because he'd known that was coming. At the end, he'd sighed more than cried. A deep exhalation of release. Now, he stroked Liv's hair until she lifted her head and started eating her melty ice cream soup. He should try to say something adult. Do the competent-parent thing.

"I know it feels like your world is ending right now." Was that what she meant by *big, black, and implacable*? "And you're probably not going to feel any better tomorrow, or maybe even the next day. But some day after that you'll wake up and your heart won't hurt so much. You'll be able to think past getting through the next five minutes. Then you'll see ten minutes or an hour. Half a day. Sometimes getting through a whole day will feel like a miracle, and other days you'll feel guilty about it, which is dumb. Because life goes on. Then days will pass, and you'll basically be living again and— What?"

Liv's mouth was hanging open, a soft whine on her hiccupped breath. Charlie shuffled off his chair and pulled her back into his arms. Jesus. He was the worst father ever.

"Is that how you felt after Mom died?" Liv finally asked, her voice dry as toast.

Oh. Oh, so . . . Shit. Charlie nodded. Olivia was buried in his chest. He rested his chin on the top of her head. "Yeah. I'm sorry, Liv. I didn't mean to say it like that. I'm sure you'll be okay soon."

"I had no idea you were so sad. You never said anything."

"Wasn't your job to listen." He'd had the stars for that. Sleepless nights on the roof of this old house with only the endless sky for company. "You needed me to keep going."

"Sometimes I thought you were glad she was gone, and I hated you for that."

"Never, Duck. Never. I won't lie and say I wasn't relieved in some way. Cancer is an awful way to die. I was glad she wasn't in pain anymore. And that you didn't have to watch her shrinking like she did. I was happy you could come home to a house that didn't smell like death." What an awful thing to say. "But I was never glad she was gone."

"Do you think you'll ever fall in love again?"

Charlie squeezed his eyes shut. He couldn't answer that question right now. Couldn't even think about his own heart, and the fresh little bruise on the right-hand side. He pulled out of the tangle of Liv's arms and crawled back into his own chair. Nodded toward her bowl of swirly chocolate milk. "Drink your ice cream."

Giggle-snuffling, Liv complied, picking up her bowl and drinking.

"So is it a done deal with Justin? Can't you tell him you panicked, or made a mistake?" *God, save me.*

One shoulder hitched upward. "Maybe. He was pretty upset. I've never seen a guy look like that. I think I really hurt his feelings. But I don't know if I'm ready to go back to what we had, though. I've got stuff to sort out." *Don't we all?* "But if I tell him I want to be friends, he'll take it as a final sentence, even though that's what I want most right now."

"Give him a few days." Charlie resisted the urge to close his eyes again. He'd been terrified by the idea of his daughter getting involved with this boy; now he was telling her how to patch things up. But this wasn't about him. Liv was hurting and likely Justin was too. Charlie couldn't always be a crap father. "His pride is probably hurt as well. It's not easy to take a no from someone you care about."

Olivia nodded.

In for a penny... "Then try to talk to him somewhere peaceful. No distractions. No one else around. So he can be himself when he talks to you, okay? And start with the good stuff. Always start with the good stuff."

Olivia continued bobbing her head up and down.

"Want to talk to Jen?" Phil's wife might have some better advice, what with having the whole female perspective and all. "Grandma will tell you how beautiful you are if you need to hear that. Or just listen."

She squeezed his hand, her grip firmer and less sweaty. "No, I think I'm good. Thanks, Dad."

Shortly afterward, Liv climbed the stairs to her room, the cadence of her unhurried footsteps familiar and soothing. The music started a minute later, something loud and mournful. Charlie sat and stared into his half-empty bowl of ice cream. With all the swirls, the surface looked like a faraway planet. He let his thoughts unhook and sent them in there—into his bowl of cold soup—and tried not to cry.

It'd been five years.

Five long years.

Five long years without the specter of a known end.

Five years of getting over it. Getting up and out.

He was doing okay on his own, wasn't he?

Unbidden, Charlie glanced at the kitchen door, through the glass panels of the top half to the gate in the hedge.

He was trying, damn it.

CHAPTER 18

The first gift had arrived three days after Charlie had kissed him: a Styrofoam 7-Eleven cooler on Simon's front step with a single, ice-packed tub of ice cream inside. No note. It had to be Charlie, though. Cassie would have left inscrutable pottery.

After staring at the tub for ten minutes, wondering if it would be stupid to eat a random gift of ice cream, Simon served himself a bowl and ate it. Curiously happy memories warred with the discomfort of knowing Charlie was thinking about him.

Two days later, a new puzzle sat on the step. Another miniature 3-D construction, this time the stone edifice of Hogwarts rendered in foil.

No note.

Simon didn't acknowledge either gift. He planned to, but his nights were filled with drawing and planning, interrupted by the occasional mournful sonata. He also read book five of the Kaze Rider series, and the teaser from book six posted on Charlie's website, which had—strangely enough—inspired him to use half a tube of lube in repeated demonstrations of his appreciation.

Who masturbated over science fiction?

You weren't jerking off over the story, Simon.

November turned cold, and the weekend passed without a gift. Simon spent the evenings talking himself out of lurking near the front door. His plan to catch Charlie in the act of dropping off ice cream or crackers or a puzzle felt self-defeating. What if it wasn't Charlie?

What if it was?

What if Charlie had given up on him?

Ten days after The Kiss, Simon sat at his desk thinking about the feel of Charlie's lips on his. He imagined he could still taste him. Still see the hurt and confusion on his face as Charlie turned to leave.

Brian intruded on his thoughts, sitting on the corner of the desk and tapping the plans for Burnside's front gate—which would be less a gate and more a frame, a gap in the historically accurate wall that would run to a hundred yards on each side of the neighborhood entrance before being replaced by split rail fencing.

"What are you doing here?" Simon asked.

"This signage is perfect," Brian said, ignoring him. "It says farm without the manure."

"An important distinction," Simon noted dryly. He looked at his watch. "I didn't know we had a meeting today."

"We don't. I just stopped by to check if we'd be ready to start putting up signage next week."

"You could have called."

"I could have." Brian stood. "Okay, then. I'll meet you on-site on Monday?"

"Sure."

Brian's expression became one of studied nonchalance. "Got weekend plans?"

A bottle of whiskey, my piano, some brooding about Charlie.

None of it was any of Brian's business, though Simon sensed Brian wanted it to be. He hadn't outright issued an invitation, but after twelve years, Simon knew how he operated.

"I'll see you Monday, Brian."

When Simon got home, a gift waited for him on the front steps. The tangled mess that had been his gut slowly unraveled as he took in the beautiful orchid. Deep-green leaves flanked a single, knotted stem. Bright-pink blooms clustered like tear drops. Simon picked up the pot and walked to the side gate.

Charlie was in his yard, as he often was—even in the fall, daylight fading rapidly around him—hammering together what might be a chicken hutch. Beside him, Herbert chewed on a plastic chair leg, making little grunting noises. There was a cat sprawled nearby, on its back, paws all curled. Hopefully not dead. It wasn't the same cat that often lurked on Simon's patio, sometimes leaving small, headless corpses.

Simon waited, holding his flower, until Charlie glanced up—probably to reach for more nails.

"Hey," Simon said, wondering if *hiya* or *hello* might have been better.

Eyeing the orchid, Charlie stood. His smile wasn't as bright as it used to be—a hesitancy underlined it. Hope or the anticipation of another rejection?

"I wanted to thank you for the flower. I'm, ah, assuming it was you."

Charlie's smile widened a fraction. "You need some color in your house. And something bent." His eyes widened briefly. "Curved, or not straight. Crap. This is why I shouldn't talk. I'm really bad at this talking thing."

One corner of Simon's mouth curled upward. "Are you trying to tell me I'm not gay enough?"

Charlie moved to cover his face with his hands, nearly braining himself with the hammer. Bracing his forearm across his forehead instead, he breathed into a pause, quietly, steadily. Then he dropped his arm, and leveled a direct look at Simon. "I'm sorry I barged into your space, and messed it up with my clumsy come-on. I didn't stop to ask if you were into guys, or take into account the fact you might have lost someone. Or might not even, you know, want to... whatever with me. I just got it into my head that I needed to know what it would be like to kiss you, to kiss any guy—not that you were the most handy one. It's your eyes. They're so damn blue, and I haven't thought about anyone on a daily basis in so long, and I had to know."

His face was red, and the quiet breathing had accelerated into a soft gasping, as though Charlie had just finished a run. Simon stepped in, closing the distance between them, and paused for long enough for Charlie to step back, dodge aside, or simply raise a hand. Say no. He stiffened a little, eyes widening, but otherwise remained still.

"Any guy?" Simon arched an eyebrow.

"You in particular."

"Why the ice cream?"

Charlie's eyelids fluttered, briefly. "Because there's no way anyone can eat ice cream and feel sad."

Oh God. Simon's next breath shook slightly. "The puzzle?"

"Because you needed time to think, and something to do with your hands."

"What *are* you trying to tell me?"

They were standing so close together that the straightening of Charlie's shoulders was a twitch at the periphery of Simon's vision. The *thunk* at their feet would be the hammer. Then Charlie was leaning in, a hand rising to curl behind Simon's neck. He paused there, for the space of a single breath, before pressing his lips to Simon's in a gentle kiss.

A whisper passed between them, a susurrus of words. Simon didn't bother figuring them out; he tucked his free hand behind Charlie's shoulder and pulled him closer, angled his head slightly, and deepened the sweet, tentative kiss.

Charlie's lips were the sort a man might dream about. Full and plump and utterly distracting. Simon kissed both before tending the top and bottom in turn, exploring the mouth he'd fantasized about. The tip of Charlie's tongue sent a tingling burn across his skin. He shivered. Goose bumps prickled his nape, his shoulders, his arms. The kiss deepened again, becoming less tentative, less question, more statement.

Simon stroked his hand down Charlie's arm. The sharp, clean scent of Charlie's sweat filled his senses. The taste of Charlie thrilled his tongue. Prickling skin gave way to keen-edged arousal. A southward rush of blood.

Head light, thoughts swimming, Simon pulled away. Just his lips. Charlie chased him, caught him in another kiss, and Simon got lost somewhere on the way to reason, answering the surer flick of Charlie's tongue, the sweetly satisfied exhalation of breath.

Charlie bumped into him, nudging him backward. Simon broke out of the kiss again, stepping away to lessen the chance of losing himself a second time. Third time. The sun could have set and the stars come out. A year might have passed by. As he stood there, panting, gaze locked with one of deep and velvety brown, only the weight of the small pot in one hand served as a reminder of why he'd come next door.

Surely it hadn't been for a kiss.

He'd have traveled much farther for this kiss.

The growl of Olivia's car turning into the drive broke the protracted silence. It stopped with a groan and pump of indecipherable music. Charlie glanced toward the front of the house, anxiety crawling across his face. The music cut off as Olivia opened her door.

"I have to..." Charlie nodded toward his daughter.

Simon swallowed and it hurt. Was this it? Had they hit a higher obstacle than Simon's lack of preparation for the emotional onslaught of Charlie's interest? Maybe Charlie wasn't out to his daughter. He'd been married to a woman and had obviously cared deeply for his late wife.

"I needed to know what it would be like to kiss you, to kiss any guy..."

"Can I come over later?" Charlie asked.

Surprised, Simon glanced toward the approaching teenager, sure she'd smell the attraction between him and her father. Were they standing far enough apart? Had too much of his blood rushed to his cock? He looked back at Charlie and saw a lazy smile. Half-lidded eyes. Satisfaction. Not the face of a man who never wanted to kiss him again. The face of someone who wanted more.

"Yeah. Sure." Simon breathed. "I'll leave the door open for you."

Lifting a hand in greeting to Olivia, he turned and fled. He needed a cold shower. And... another cold shower.

CHAPTER 19

A writer should be able to come up with a better excuse than: "I'm heading next door to help Simon figure out where to put his new plant."

Olivia barely twitched an eyebrow. She'd stopped talking about the big blackness at the end of the road. She didn't have time. She and Rosalie seemed to be completely absorbed by the mural project—were in fact going to work on it this evening. They'd won a section of wall, and had been spending every free night figuring out the dimensions of the larger version of their vision.

Of Justin, Charlie had heard nothing. So long as Olivia wasn't crying into a bowl of melted ice cream, he was okay with that.

Should he shower before heading next door? Would Olivia wonder why moving a plant around required a thorough scrub and clean clothes?

The front door opened and closed as Rosalie arrived. Female voices floated through the house, softening as they descended into the basement. A minute later, the thump of music moved through the floor.

Charlie peeled off his clothes and stepped into the shower.

Afterward, he wiped steam from the mirror and gave himself a pep talk. "Take it slow. Don't talk too much, and don't assume he wants you as much as you want him."

That kiss, though...

"Take it slow."

One of the cats followed him through the gate before sauntering off toward the back of Simon's house as Charlie approached the front door. He stepped inside and called out, "Hello!"

"In here."

Charlie started toward the kitchen just as Simon poked his head into the hall.

"Can I get you something to drink?" he asked before disappearing back around the corner. Bottles rattled as the fridge door opened. "I've got beer. Someone left a six-pack here last week."

Moving up behind him, Charlie wrapped his arms around Simon's middle and kissed the back of his neck. Cool air from the fridge competed with the temperature of Simon's skin, an ever-fluctuating breath of hot and cold. Simon turned, his arms coming around Charlie. Soap and aftershave mingled with the bland chill of refrigerated air. Thought became sound and scent. Heat. Smooth skin, lips.

God, his lips. When Simon *wanted* to be kissed... Wow.

Every part of Charlie fell into the void. Bottles clinked and the cool puffs of air disappeared as the fridge door closed. More important were Simon's hands and the way they transcribed Charlie's back, skimming up and down as though learning the topography of his spine, shoulder blades, and hips. They were pressed so close together, Charlie could feel the weight of Simon against him. The warmth of his skin—again. The hardness of his form. Chest, abs, thighs.

Simon tasted like whiskey and aftershave. Something smokier. Every stroke of his tongue sent sharp shocks through Charlie's torso. Every charge terminated at his groin. When had a kiss last tightened his balls? Hardened his cock? And he couldn't stop moving his hands. Echoing Simon's exploration—mapping his back, his shoulders, and the long, shallow indent of his spine. The curve of his ass.

Breathing, groaning, moaning, grunting, gasping. Charlie couldn't tell which sounds were his. A flush of embarrassment started and died, was replaced by the burn of desire. He leaned in, only to discover he had nowhere to go. Simon's body covered his, and the kitchen counter held them in place. He grabbed Simon's hips and pulled, desperate to get closer. A deep rumble echoed through his chest. Then Simon was sucking on his neck, tongue flicking back and forth. Charlie lifted his chin. His back arched, his hips thrust forward, and his harder-than-hard erection butted up against answering stiffness.

"Oh fuck."

He'd said that, right? Simon was busy feasting on his neck.

Charlie pulled their hips together again. Simon caught his hand and moved it away from his hip. Why? Then Simon was fumbling between them, the *clink* of Charlie's belt competing with their grumbling moans.

Something gave around Charlie's hips—his jeans loosening. A moment of panic gripped his chest. He stopped breathing, gathered air for a word. *Yes* or *no*? Simon wrapped warm fingers around Charlie's cock—still trapped inside his briefs—and stroked. Any notion he might say no, stop this glorious nonsense from happening, dissolved. Charlie thrust forward and reached down to tweak his underwear out of the way.

Simon was pressed so close to him, his constrained erection nudged the back of Charlie's hand. Charlie tugged at Simon's pants— grateful he'd foregone a belt. Button, zip, more cotton—something hard and hot behind. He looked down, ending Simon's apparent fascination with his neck. Their lips brushed together in a half kiss. Charlie tilted his head so their foreheads came together. This close, he couldn't see Simon's eyes, just a vague impression of celestial blue. He slipped his fingers inside Simon's briefs and wrapped his hand around another man's cock.

Time stopped. Breath ceased. His heart took a pause. A tremble passed through him, head to toe.

A whisper caressed his cheek. "You okay?"

The impression of blue retreated a little, became two distinct eyes as Simon waited for him.

Grabbing the back of Simon's neck, Charlie pulled him forward again so their foreheads touched. This was safer, closer, but somehow more anonymous. He couldn't see the questions in Simon's eyes when they were blurred. "I'm okay."

He began stroking Simon's cock. Simon reciprocated, their hands moving in sync for about ten seconds before Charlie stopped thinking about how to do this and just started doing it. He explored as he stroked, measuring length, girth, and weight. Seeking the prominent vein on the underside, noting Simon was cut and shaped not unlike him. Maybe a little longer. Thicker. He pressed his thumb into the divot at the top of Simon's cock, collecting moisture from his slit, and stroked downward. Again and again, knowing instinctively how hard to squeeze, how much glide to leave between his fingers and sensitive skin.

Simon leaned forward, initiating another kiss. Feeling he had enough of a handle on things—on hot, hard flesh—to lose himself again, Charlie met the kiss. Immediately deepened it. All too quickly, the kiss fell out of alignment as Charlie dropped his head and keened softly. Simon kept nudging his balls, and he'd discovered Charlie liked a quick twist at the end of his stroke. Somehow, Charlie kept his hand moving up and down, but he knew his efforts were feeble. Simon's hand felt too good. The breath across his cheek too erotic. He shuddered. Whined.

Gasped a single word: "Coming."

Simon stroked him through the climax, milking and squeezing until Charlie cried out for a second time. His knees wanted to buckle. He had a vague idea that the back of his hips might be bruised from the counter. None of it mattered more than the lick of cool air across his tingling and damp cock. Simon's fingers in a gentle caress.

Gulping air, Charlie tightened his grip on Simon's hard shaft. Then he let go for long enough to wrap Simon's fingers with his, collecting enough spunk to slick the slide. Simon opened his mouth, gasped, then lost whatever he might have said to a stream of soft curses. Charlie stroked and tugged, employed a twist, and repeated whatever made Simon hum. Soon, Simon was nudging him backward, the buck of his hips rocking them into the counter. Then he was gasping, trying to speak again. Coming in hot jets of semen that spilled over Charlie's fingers.

They leaned together for a while, panting against one another's neck. Charlie licked at the sweat on Simon's skin. Huffing out a chuckle, Simon kissed Charlie's jaw. He raised his head and dropped a sweet kiss to Charlie's lips, then pulled back far enough for his eyes to become distinct once more.

"I hope you closed the front door behind you."

Charlie shrugged. "I honestly can't remember if I did or didn't." And he didn't care. Drawing Simon closer, he kissed a mouth further reddened by his attention. Tasted lips that weren't sweet, but were. Reveled in the warmth of Simon's response, the soft kisses he returned.

He was floating in a bubble of calm, knowing that once they separated, tucked spent cocks away, and started washing their hands, the reality of what he'd just done would hit him.

Maybe now would be a good time for that beer.

"Hey." Simon's nose nudged his. "You doing all right?"

Having fallen out of the kiss, Charlie drew in a quiet and steady breath. "I started thinking. Preventative measures may be required."

"Oh, Charlie."

Was it too soon to love the way Simon said his name?

Simon moved away, leaving him cold and bereft. He opened a drawer, grabbed a cloth, and moved to the sink. "Let's get cleaned up."

Right. Just think about getting cleaned up.

Wiped, tucked, and zipped, Charlie followed Simon across the broad expanse of his living room toward the couch. The cold bottle of beer in his hand made his knuckles ache. His legs still felt unsteady. He sank gratefully into a square cushion, surprised by how soft and comfortable it was.

"I thought this couch would be harder."

"An uncomfortable couch is a waste of space," Simon said, sitting close, but not too close.

Charlie reassessed the living room, all the clean lines and bare spaces. While the room seemed bereft of softness, it wasn't cold. There was personality here, of a quieter and more ordered man. The orchid sat north of middle on the square coffee table. Taking a swig of his beer, Charlie swallowed meditatively as he scanned the rest of the place. The piano, the neat bookcase, the framed prints on two walls. The lack of curtains covering the floor-to-ceiling windows lining the entire back-facing wall.

Shit.

He nodded toward the windows. "And you were worried about the front door." He glanced over his shoulder at the kitchen area. "We just gave all of Bethlehem a show."

Simon smiled. "The only visitors to my backyard, so far as I know, are your cats. They leave me presents from time to time."

"They must like you."

"I've never been wooed with headless corpses before."

"It's an acquired taste."

"How's the thinking coming along?"

Charlie winced. "Stalled until you asked." He patted the cushion next to him. "You should move closer and distract me."

Rather than scoot across the couch, Simon leaned back, putting an arm over the top of the cushions. "I think we're at three-and-oh for action versus thought."

"Is this what it's always like? With guys. I don't think I've ever come so fast with so little effort before."

"Are you saying my handjob was half-assed?" Simon's eyebrows quirked upward.

"No. God, no. I meant me. You. This." Charlie gestured back and forth between them. "I'm not used to any of this. Usually I'll buy a woman a couple of drinks, talk with her some, then invite her upstairs to my room. At cons. I've only ever picked up women at cons and only after . . ." *After.* Fuck. "In the past couple of years." He shook thoughts of Merry free. "And I never sit with them afterward, drinking beer. This is different." He pressed a hand to his forehead and groaned. "And I promised myself I wouldn't talk too much."

"I'm okay with talking if you need to talk."

Charlie glanced over at Simon and marveled at how composed he was. Then again, he obviously wasn't reeling from his first gay experience. "Phil said I should ask if you were into guys before I made a move."

"Phil?"

"My friend. Oldest friend. We grew up together."

"You talked to him about me?" Simon's composure softened a little. Flexed as he seemed to take on board the fact Charlie had been thinking about him for longer than it had taken to launch himself through the front door, landing lips-first on his neighbor.

"Yeah. Right after I told him I thought I might be bisexual. Shit. 'Think' is the wrong word. I know I am. You're not the first guy I've looked at. Thought about. You're the first one I threw myself at, though."

Simon's smile was kind. "I'm flattered."

"You should be. Not everyone gets a ride on the good ship Charlie." *Holy fuck, where had that come from?*

Simon was laughing at him.

"Next time I come over here, I'm wearing a gag."

Sobering slightly, Simon gave him the quirked-eyebrow again. "Kinky."

Charlie smacked the cushion next to him. "Get over here and distract me. I'm digging a fast grave by myself."

Chuckling, Simon released his hold on the back of the couch and scooted closer, settling right next to Charlie. He put his arm around Charlie's shoulders and dropped a kiss to his forehead.

"That's better," Charlie said, snuggling against Simon's side.

CHAPTER 20

Simon stiffened as Charlie leaned in. He'd invited it, of course, by shifting over and circling Charlie's shoulders with his arm. The kiss to the forehead. Charlie inspired such tender damn feelings in him, though. And it was... strange. Different.

Simon was more used to being the one in need of tenderness.

"You're not much of cuddler, are you?" Charlie said.

"It's been a while."

Charlie drew back a little and picked at the label on his beer bottle. Simon watched. A gently expectant quiet bloomed between them. If not tended, questions would probably roll in soon, leaving unanswered echoes. They didn't yet know each other well enough to do comfortable silence.

After pulling a shred of paper from the bottle, Charlie looked up. "Why tonight, and not last week? It was the flower, wasn't it?" He was obviously trying for a grin, but his expression was too anxious to pull it off.

"In part. Why did you leave it for me?"

"I told you. You needed something curvy in here."

"Why do you care about what I need?"

"You haven't answered my question."

Tempted to reestablish some distance, Simon pondered a response that wouldn't involve spilling his life story—and oh, how Brian would enjoy knowing that he was such an integral part of that story.

"I've heard it's bad form to swap ex stories on a first date," Simon said instead.

Charlie frowned. "This is a date?"

"No. This is a hookup without the benefit of having visited a bar or Grindr first."

"I feel so much better about it now." Charlie leaned forward as if to push off the couch. "So, I should probably—"

"It was a bad breakup. About a year ago now, and I was pretty much over it, but he's project managing Burnside Province. The night you came over, I'd just found out. Had just seen him for the first time in eleven months."

"I'm sorry."

"Don't be."

"I figured it was something like that. That you'd lost someone. That's what the ice cream was for."

Did Charlie have any idea how sweet he was? How, as a widower, had he not had that sweetness burned away? If anyone knew loss, it must be him.

"Were you together a long time?" Charlie asked.

Figuring what Charlie really wanted to know was why they'd broken up, Simon said, "Too long, as it turns out. About twelve years too long. No, scratch that. I'm pretty sure he didn't cheat the first two years."

"Ouch."

Charlie took another sip of his beer. Simon amused himself watching him swallow, remembering the taste of his neck, the way his throat moved when he moaned. He'd known Charlie would be vocal. What would he be like in bed, naked, bared beneath Simon's hands?

"A woman looked at me like that once. It was about a year after Merry died. I ran. It was the scariest thing I'd ever seen."

Simon laughed. "I can imagine what she was thinking, right up until the point where you fled."

"Hah." Charlie put his half-empty beer bottle on the coffee table. "So, I feel like this is going to get weird soon. I should probably go before it does, or before I start talking nonstop again." He glanced up, then down at his knees. "Umm . . ."

Without permission, Simon's hand rose, moved to the other side of Charlie's downturned face and gently nudged his chin, encouraging Charlie to face him. Taking over, Simon stroked his thumb along Charlie's bristly jawline. The vulnerable expression Charlie turned on him nearly undid every resolve Simon had yet to make. It was that sweetness again, and the uncertainty. Simon leaned in to kiss him, measuring his movement so that Charlie would have time to pull away if he wanted to.

Charlie didn't pull away. He met the kiss with an openness that surprised him. There was no game here, no strategy. Just a . . . man. A man with a wide, kissable mouth. A man who didn't feel the need to thrust his tongue into the center of every situation. Simon enjoyed his restraint, the tentative brushes, the soft kisses. The quiet murmur in Charlie's throat.

The kisses were sweet. Just like Charlie.

Touching his forehead to Charlie's, Simon said, "It doesn't have to be weird."

It was, though, because he wasn't ready for this. For Charlie's newness and questions, for the fact that he was everything Simon could want in a partner. His noise and brightness. His color. His niceness.

Charlie dropped a last, light kiss to Simon's lips, and stood. Smoothed his hands over his thighs and patted his back pocket as though checking for his wallet. "Thanks for the beer." His forehead creased. "And, umm, you know."

Simon dipped his chin in acknowledgment.

"I'll . . ." Charlie gestured toward the front door. "See you soon?"

"Sure."

Simon didn't follow him to the door. He continued staring at the short front hall long after Charlie had left, though, his mind somewhat fallow. It was only when he turned to regard Charlie's beer bottle that the questions rolled back in, sewing themselves into every furrow of thought.

CHAPTER 21

Charlie turned into the paint aisle of the hardware store and stopped just short of knocking down a familiar stranger with the blunt javelin of the porch post that extended three feet beyond the end of his cart.

The back of his neck warmed. He almost imagined a rushed breath against his skin, heard the quiet growl of a climax. Simon's. He could still taste Simon on his tongue, smell him. Remembered the feel of every kiss from the night before.

"Simon."

His voice had been a bare whisper. He hadn't even meant to say Simon's name. Nevertheless, Simon heard him and turned, an automatic smile lifting the corners of his mouth. "Charlie."

Oh God, this was awkward. All the calm Charlie had gathered while selecting replacement rails, posts, and a couple of planks for the steps had evaporated. He cast about for something to say. "I'm shopping for the porch project."

He should be writing, but, well, this wasn't the only flashback he'd had to last night.

Simon sidestepped the post threatening his groin. "So I see." He indicated the display of paint swatches. "I, er, had a quiet afternoon at the office, and was thinking about paint for my place. Maybe in the kitchen to define the space. Or the wall behind the piano. Add some color to the room."

"I kinda like it the way it is. It feels like you."

A dark eyebrow arched over one extraordinary eye. Jesus, Simon's eyes. So goddamn blue.

"It's calm," Charlie explained. "And, this is going to sound weird, but the open space suits you. You have this expansiveness to you."

"I've always thought of myself as a fairly closed-off sort of person."

"Really? You don't come across that way. Well, you're quiet, but I like that. Gives me more space to talk."

Simon's smile shifted toward genuine. "I think this is the deepest conversation I've ever had in a hardware store."

"You obviously don't visit often enough. I got quite philosophical over my choice of planks for the new steps. I had to sort through two stacks until I found alternating waving lines. I'm pretty sure the assistant who helped me is still scratching her head in confusion. Seriously, who hasn't read Lao-Tzu?"

"You didn't ask her that, I hope."

"Not in those exact words."

"If you're planning to paint the steps, why does it matter what the wood looks like?" Simon asked.

"I'd always know what was underneath." It was stupid, Charlie knew that. But somehow the choice of wood had become important. The feet of the people he loved would touch these steps every time they entered his house. "Want to help me choose paint colors?"

"Seeing as I apparently don't need any for myself, sure."

Charlie was intensely aware of Simon's presence as he moved to stand next to him, in front of the paint swatches. He could feel the heat of Simon's skin, or remembered it. Either way, air got harder to draw as his lungs became somewhat less responsive.

"Are you planning to paint the rest of the house? Trim, shutters? Or do you want to match the existing colors?" Simon asked.

Charlie sucked his lower lip into his mouth for a thoughtful gnaw. "Hmm, that's a good question. Do you think the trim needs updating?"

Simon began talking about the fieldstone, the chimney, and the lines of the house. How the shutters matched one period, which most of the windows were from, and the back half of the house another one. How he liked the jumble, the awkward line of the kitchen addition and the rooms upstairs. As he spoke, he picked up paint swatches, using some to illustrate a point, others to punctuate.

Charlie had never heard Simon say so much before, or seen him so animated. He'd been excited when Charlie had shown him the plans, but not this passionate. And relaxed. That was the most amazing part.

Whereas Charlie's ramblings changed course, and usually had no point whatsoever, Simon's discourse on his house was like poetry.

Also, the way he gestured with his hands, thumb stroking across this and that square of color, was fucking sexy.

"You're looking at me like a slice of cake you found at the back of the refrigerator," Simon said, one side of his mouth lifting in amusement.

"I want to see you again." Charlie's cock was nearly hard, and the urge to thrust Simon up against the paint display all but irrepressible.

Eyebrows crooking together, Simon glanced over Charlie's shoulder, then refocused on Charlie. "Maybe we should—"

Charlie turned around, saw no one, and turned back again. He swallowed. Rubbed his palms against his jeans. Had he read the situation incorrectly?

"Sorry, I . . ." Damn it, now he could feel another blush coming on. He backed up a step, putting much-needed space between them, and spoke to his shoes. "Um, thanks for the advice. I'm going to think about the paint for a bit." He grabbed the cart handle.

"Charlie."

Charlie navigated his way out of the aisle, careful not to knock paint brushes and scrapers from the shelves with his porch post. The back of his neck itched and burned. He had no idea what he was doing, and the muddle inside his head made his stomach flip. Was he falling for a guy, or was this just a sex thing? What actually defined the boundaries of bisexuality? Was it sleeping with guys, or actually being in a relationship with one?

Was he really prepared to explore this side of himself at thirty-seven?

Would Simon even let him get that far?

"Charlie." Simon caught his hand, pulling him to a stop. Charlie looked up. "I didn't mean to put you off." Simon's tone was low and urgent. He removed his hand, leaving Charlie's stinging with neglect. "I just wasn't sure how comfortable you'd be flirting in a public place."

"Oh." *Oh*. He hadn't even considered that aspect.

"Can I follow you home?" Simon asked. "Talk with you when we get there?"

Breathing out, Charlie nodded. "Sure."

The drive back to his house seemed endless and too fast all at once. Charlie kept checking his rearview mirror for Simon's car. Staring too long at the vague shadow behind the windshield. Simon turned into his own driveway, and appeared a couple of minutes later, using the gate in the hedge. In silence, he helped Charlie unpack the back of his SUV, stacking the wood and railings on one side of the porch. Then he grabbed Charlie by the elbow and pulled him around to the back of the house, by the kitchen door. Pressed him up against the fieldstone wall and kissed him.

CHAPTER 22

Simon had lost track of the number of times they'd kissed, but had a vague idea it wasn't supposed to get more exciting. Once they'd learned one another's mouth, taken the edge off, kissing was merely a means to an end... wasn't it?

Obviously not to Charlie. He kissed with curiosity and inflection, as if he was using his lips to get to know the rest of Simon. God, what would it feel like to be naked with him?

Framing Charlie's face with his hands, Simon softened the kiss, pulled back, gifted two more gentle touches to Charlie's lips and inclined his forehead so their faces hovered close together. This seemed to be their thing, how they took a pause.

"Does that answer your question?" Simon asked.

"What question?"

"Can we go inside?"

"God, yes."

Charlie took his hand, the slide of fingers across Simon's palm at once sweet and exciting. Brian had rarely held his hand. Charlie tugged Simon through the kitchen door.

"You left the door unlocked?" Simon glanced over his shoulder at the door now standing slightly ajar, and pulled Charlie backward so they could close it properly.

"I've gone away for the weekend and left the front door open."

"How—"

Charlie stole the rest of his question, backing Simon into the fridge with the force of his kiss. Simon indulged him for half a minute—maybe longer—before putting his free hand to Charlie's chest and backing him off.

"Wait."

"What?" Grinning, Charlie leaned in against his hand.

"Should we maybe go upstairs? Or to my place. I have doors that lock."

Charlie's eyes took a moment to focus. "It's barely afternoon. Liv won't be home for a couple of hours." Taking possession of Simon's hands, Charlie stepped back, easing Simon away from the fridge. "Upstairs is a good idea, though."

A shudder moved through Simon—a pinch of fingers at the back of his neck, a ghostly trace down his spine. The feeling grabbed at his balls. His cock hardened. Left on his own with only Charlie to stare at—the man holding his hands, mouth quirked in a sexy half grin, eyes as bright and warm as an autumn day—Simon could come in his pants. Just from looking. From being desired. Had anyone *ever* looked at him like that?

Charlie gave his hands a quick tug. Their lips joined together again, magnets seeking attraction. Feet moved, shoulders hit doorways. Breath and footsteps, gasps and moans followed them down the hall and up the stairs. They left their shoes on three different steps. Shirts on another. By the time Charlie pulled him into a room off the upstairs hallway, belts were undone, and Simon's pants barely clung to his hips. Charlie's jeans were around his thighs.

Simon hadn't noticed if the front door stood open.

Charlie disengaged long enough to kick the door closed behind them, giving Simon a chance to check out the room. It was a bedroom. Charlie's, presumably, though the absolute lack of feminine touches was a quiet surprise. Charlie had been married for a long time. The house had a definite family feel to it, but this room was bare. Large and under furnished. The only clues that someone actually inhabited the space were the unmade bed—a mattress and base with no frame—an overflowing laundry hamper, and a nightstand crowded with books.

Charlie stood in front of the bed, kicking off his jeans. "Sorry about the mess. I didn't know I was going to have sex today."

A million responses jammed Simon's vocal chords. Pushing his pants from his hips, he selected one. "So, that time you left the front door open. They emptied the house, right? And this is the room you're still furnishing."

Charlie's laugh was short and sharp. "No. This was my parents' room, and they took the bedroom set when they packed off to Florida. Living room and dining room too. That couch downstairs is from the basement, and I keep meaning to replace it. Way too many inappropriate teenage memories attached to that couch." Looking away, Charlie surveyed the room, pausing when he reached the bed. "Sheets are clean." He glanced up, and for a moment, standing there in his underwear, he seemed unsure. Vulnerable.

And utterly fuckable.

Charlie's skin was lightly tanned all over, a shade darker on his arms and around his neck, showing he spent a lot of time outdoors. He had a sturdy build. Not thickly muscled, but strong. Steady. Long legs, his thighs and calves defined. His shoulders and chest were cut, but not sharp. He didn't lift weights, he lived life—as evidenced by the slight curve of belly, beneath which might lurk some abs.

A smattering of red-brown hair stretched across his chest, slightly thicker between his pecs and trailing off to nothing until his navel. Beneath striped boxer briefs, his cock had taken an impressive stance.

Simon glanced up to find Charlie giving him the same long, lingering once-over. Stepping out of the puddle his pants made on the floor, Simon approached on socked feet. He took Charlie's arms, smoothing his palms up from the elbow, his thumb tracing the definite curve of biceps on up to deltoid.

"I don't care if the sheets are clean." He did . . . and he didn't. He dropped a light kiss to Charlie's lips. "I'm here for you, not your sheets."

He backed Charlie toward the bed, pausing while Charlie sat and scooted backward. Simon pulled his underwear down over his erection, kicking the warm and rumpled cotton aside as he climbed onto the bed after Charlie. The scent of arousal rose up from his skin, making his heart pound. Charlie lost his briefs somewhere in the jumble of sheets and reached for him. Simon fell into his arms, breath puffing out as they collided and rolled to the side, lips already seeking lips again.

Between kisses, Charlie gasped, "I wanted . . . to look at you . . . longer. Maybe after I touch . . . and kiss you . . . all over."

"Good plan." Any plan involving Charlie being more than an inch distant, his skin not flush and warm against Simon's, was to be discarded immediately.

Nudging a leg between Charlie's thighs, Simon brought their cocks together, gasping as one hot charge met another. He pressed a kiss to Charlie's shoulder. Charlie lifted his chin, and Simon nuzzled his neck. When fingers wrapped around his cock, Simon glanced down to find Charlie had him in hand. He thrust into the firm grip. Charlie swiped his thumb across the crown and down. Sighing through another pinching shudder, Simon bucked his hips.

He reached between them to claim Charlie, grasping his shaft. Charlie arched his back. His hips jerked forward, thrusting his cock through Simon's hand.

"God, yes." Charlie still had a hand on Simon. He squeezed. Grabbed Simon's hip and pulled him in. "Closer."

Simon leaned down to kiss Charlie's shoulder, drawn again by the strong curve. He loved the apparent strength in Charlie's frame. The solidness of him. If he weren't so turned on, he'd have given in to the urge to fit himself into the pattern, lock himself against Charlie's body. Cuddle—even though cuddling was not his thing. He wanted to be held by this man. Feel broad arms around his back. Bask in the warmth of him.

Kissing a trail from shoulder to pec, Simon took his first taste of nipple, flicking the hard point with the tip of his tongue before giving it a soft suckle. Charlie arched forward, thrusting through Simon's fingers. He let go of Simon's hip to rub his palm over Simon's abs. Simon swallowed a chuckle. He'd forgotten how ticklish he got when aroused.

"You feel so good," Charlie said.

"You too." He added another stroke down below. "Got any lube?"

Charlie stiffened slightly, eyes widening. "No."

Simon stroked his cock. "Handjobs feel better with lube."

"Oh." Returning to his warm and pliant self, Charlie grinned. "For a minute there, I thought we were going to have a discussion I'm not ready for."

"Not today." For as much as Simon wanted to be inside Charlie, being next to him was enough. Holding him, stroking him, watching him fly.

"I've got hand lotion." Charlie rolled toward the nightstand and yanked open a drawer.

"I'm not even going to get started on how you have any skin left on your cock."

"It's got keratin and shit in it. I usually jerk off in the shower, anyway." There was an image. Charlie rolled back with a big bottle of store-brand lotion. "Here."

Nothing for it. Simon pumped out a decent-sized glob and grinned. "This will only hurt for a second." He seized Charlie's cock with his cold and slippery palm.

"Holy Christ! Jesus. That's . . ." A moan swallowed the rest of Charlie's words as he thrust into Simon's rapidly warming hand. "Fuck, yeah."

Another dollop, another cold squeeze—Simon grunting this time—and they were minutes from heaven. Or maybe already there, pumping and stroking in a syncopated rhythm that, while not ideal, was getting them off. Simon sought out Charlie's mouth, kissed him breathlessly as they rocked together. Then he nudged Charlie back a little, moving half over him. Charlie went willingly, and when he was settled, Simon collected both cocks and stroked.

"Oh fuck. Do that again."

"With pleasure." Simon thrust down and forward—gently—as he stroked them together. Charlie arched up, swearing softly. They moved with each other, at a new and slower pace, and this truly felt like sex. Both of them working toward a common goal, both of them feeling so fucking good.

Then Charlie's hand was between them, and he urged Simon backward. "I want to try."

Simon rolled onto his back and smiled as Charlie climbed on top, braced a forearm on the bed and grabbed their important bits, squeezing their hard-ons.

One stroke, one thrust, and Charlie's eyes fell shut. "Oh my fucking god. This is it. This is what we're doing." Charlie hips were pumping forward, punctuating his sentences. "This is— I don't—" His words began to break up as he rocked faster.

Beneath him, Simon did his part by arching into Charlie's thrusts. He lent his fingers to the hot and messy press of turgid flesh between them, caressing his own cock as much as Charlie's. It all felt good. The best part, though, was Charlie moving over him, in time with him, face flushed with pleasure.

Well, that and the pressure and friction. The low, tight rumble in his balls. The sweet pain of impending orgasm.

Charlie opened his eyes and straightened his arm. He mouthed something—silently for a change—and jerked into a climax, hot fluid rushing between their fingers to land on Simon in a rush of sizzling droplets. Another thrust, another jet. The scent of sex rose between them, tugging Simon's own climax loose. He came with a growl, still driving up and forward into their joined hands. Charlie shuddered, moaning. Maybe whining. Simon pulled him down into another kiss, their lips brushing together in breathless passes as the motion of their bodies steadied and calmed. Charlie melted into him, tongue taking a lazy tour of Simon's mouth. Then he rolled off to the side and lay there shuddering, breathing heavily, occasionally letting go a muttered "fuck."

Buzzing and content, englobed by the warmth and lassitude of a stellar climax, Simon let his eyes drift closed. He floated in space next to Charlie and tried not to let his thoughts range too far. He didn't want to think about what a mistake this might have been, even if it felt far from accidental or wrong or thoughtless. Being with Charlie was amazing.

It felt right.

This was the first time Charlie had been to bed with a man, though. The handjob in Simon's kitchen could be put aside if need be. They'd been standing and still dressed. This . . . this had been accomplished with intent. They'd undressed each other, tumbled down onto the bed together, moved in sync. Regardless of where they went next, they were lovers—if only for a single, blissful moment.

How would Charlie take that?

How would he, Simon, react in turn?

Downstairs, a door opened and shut. Then a voice called out, muffled by distance and the closed bedroom door. "Dad?"

CHAPTER 23

Charlie thought he might be having a heart attack. That was what a stabbing pain in the chest and desperate need for breath was, right? His left arm wasn't tingling, but that might only be because it was trapped under Simon—*the naked man in his bed.*

"Fuck." Tugging his arm free, Charlie sat straight up and swung his legs toward the edge of the mattress. "Shit, shit, shit." This was not how he wanted to explain his sexual change of address to Olivia. He glanced over his shoulder at Simon, who was doing a good impression of a landed fish.

"Should I climb out the window or something?" Simon whispered.

"Not yet. Let me see what she wants." Talking while his heart beat in his throat was a disconcerting experience. At least it hadn't stuttered to a halt yet. Charlie looked around for his shirt and then remembered he'd left it on the stairs somewhere. Along with Simon's button-down and undershirt. He had a vague impression of them moving through the shadows, tossing clothing aside, rubbing hands over skin and kissing. "Fuck."

He lurched to his feet and hit up the laundry hamper for another shirt.

"Dad?" Liv's voice was closer. She was in the front hall. Maybe on the stairs. "Why are your shoes and shirts all over the stairs?" Definitely on the stairs. "Dad! Are you up there?"

"I'm here! Hold on, coming down."

"What are you doing?"

"Getting dressed."

"Okay."

After a year of scaring each other senseless when Liv was eleven, they were both pretty good about not barging into each other's room without knocking. Charlie dragged the first shirt he grabbed across his belly, plucking at the cotton with his fingers to wipe away sweat and semen and . . . God, his fingers were so sticky. He tossed the shirt aside and picked up another one.

Simon remained frozen on the bed, eyes wide.

"Just looking for a shirt," Charlie called through the door.

"I've got a handful out here. Is this one new?"

"Huh?"

"This dark-blue one with the buttons. I haven't seen it before."

"Phil and I went to Target again last week."

Simon started convulsing on the bed. Charlie shot him a glare, pressing one finger to his lips. Clapping a hand across his mouth, Simon obviously worked to restrain his laughter. Charlie tossed a shirt at him, hissing, "Clean up."

"Huh?" Olivia asked.

"Nothing."

Charlie flung the sheets around, searching for his underwear. He found them, tugged them on, and hunted down his jeans. Simon had finished swiping the shirt across his stomach and chest, every pass leaving the hair pushed in one direction or another. They both really needed a shower. Waving his hands like a traffic-control officer, Charlie directed him from the bed to a corner. Simon picked up his pants and underwear along the way.

"I'll try to get your shirt, otherwise"—Charlie waved toward the laundry hamper—"sorry, it's laundry day."

Wiping his hands on his jeans, he approached the door and opened it. Liv stood blinking in the hallway. "Is someone in there with you?"

"No." May he burn in hell forever without a single box of Cheez-Its.

"I thought I heard you talking to someone." Liv was leaning away, hesitantly. Obviously curious, but also . . . well, hesitant.

Who wanted to catch their father having sex? And she had to smell it. The funk clung to his fingers and nostrils and probably all of his clothes. "Let's go downstairs."

Frowning, Liv turned and led the way back to the staircase. "I just wanted to tell you I'm going to Rosalie's tonight. I want to stay the weekend with her."

"We're supposed to be having brunch with Cassie on Sunday."

"I could meet you there?"

"I guess that would work." Charlie stepped over one of Simon's shoes, a black lace-up with the laces still tied. He kicked one of his boots aside and stepped over the other one before turning to push all the shoes to the side.

"What's with all the shoes and stuff on the stairs?" Liv asked when they reached the bottom.

"I was getting ready to do laundry."

"You're acting weird." Liv handed him the dark-blue shirt and a whiff of Simon rose up from the material. Swooning wasn't something Charlie had ever considered doing, but that puff of scent... Wow.

He steadied himself against the wall. "Sorry, thinking about the book. So, why did you need to tell me about Rosalie's? You could have just texted me."

"You're always like, 'Why didn't you come home first? We're a family. I want to see you for more than five minutes a week.'"

She even had his voice sorta right.

With a rueful smile, Charlie reached out to ruffle her hair. Thankfully, Liv ducked. There would be no way to explain why their next-door neighbor's semen was stuck to her curls.

"Sooo..." Liv folded her arms and tilted her head.

"Sooo?" Charlie folded his arms, tucking Simon's shirt in against his chest.

"Do you have a girlfriend?"

His heart made one last attack, slamming against his breastbone hard enough to leave a bruise. "Huh?"

"Upstairs. I heard you talking to someone. And the trail of clothes." Her eyebrows pinched together. "Oh my God, are you—"

"This isn't a movie. Jesus. Real people don't get undressed on the stairs."

Liv gave him the *Santa isn't real* look.

"I don't think I'm ready to have this conversation right now," Charlie said.

Liv gave him the other *Santa isn't real* look. The one reserved for ten-year-olds and punctuated with a question mark.

"Isn't it kind of early for you to be home?" Charlie checked a nonexistent watch before gesturing toward the kitchen. "I need to wash my hands."

Unfolding her arms, Liv flounced toward the kitchen, huffing and puffing. Were boys this dramatic? If he'd had a son, he could have screwed who he liked, right? So long as meals arrived on a reasonable schedule and clean underwear showed up from time to time.

Charlie shoved his hands under the tap, scrubbing at his palms. He reached for a towel, and the pipes in the wall started knocking, the sound as familiar as breath to anyone who lived in this house. Someone was in the upstairs bathroom. Both he and Liv glanced up at the ceiling. They looked down at the same time, gazes colliding.

Liv arched a single eyebrow, and in that moment so resembled her mother that Charlie's chest constricted. His poor heart.

"Okay, I have someone over. I'm . . ." He braced his hands against the side of the sink. "I'm sort of seeing someone."

Liv brightened instantly. "You are? That's great!"

"It is?"

"Well, yeah. Rosalie and I talk about hooking you up with people all the time. You're not *that* old." *Thanks.* "You shouldn't be alone."

"I really, really don't like the idea of you and Rosalie talking about hooking me up. That's just wrong."

Liv did the left-up-and-down-eye-rolling thing. "It's not like we're sleazy about it. There's this teacher at school, she's so nice. She's read all your books!"

Jesus Christ.

Charlie inhaled. Time contracted and expanded concurrently. Out there in the universe, stars were born, cooled, and died in a flash of light that carried the history of civilizations. And it all happened between one breath and the next as he tried to work out what to say to his daughter.

"Liv, this person I'm seeing—" Were he and Simon "seeing" one another, or just fucking? He probably shouldn't make that distinction to Liv. "It's . . ." He swallowed and winced. Someone had filled his throat with razor blades.

"It's...?"

"It's a guy. I'm seeing a guy."

"Like... a friend?" The question could be her way of giving them both a thinking pause, but her eyes told the real story. Wide, but not too wide. The lovely brown shining with curiosity and something else. Something— "You have a *boy*friend?"

"I don't know if I'd call him that. We only just started, umm, getting together."

"Wow. So not what I expected." She hadn't dialed 911 yet, nor had she called either of her grandmothers. "So, umm, you and Mom. Was that an accident?"

Oh God. Charlie shook his head hard enough to scramble his brains. "No."

"But—"

"If I had a woman upstairs, would you be asking if your mom and I were an accident?"

Liv's brow creased gently. Then she shook her head. "No. I guess not, it's just—"

"I loved her, Liv. She was everything to me."

"But what about me?"

Did he need to tell Liv that his days began and ended with her, that sometimes it felt like she was his reason for existing? He reached across the counter to squeeze her hand. "I wouldn't change any of it, Duck. Not for all the world."

A creak announced that someone had reached the bottom stair. Liv's gaze shifted in the direction of the front door. Charlie turned around. From where he stood, he couldn't see into the hall. He wasn't sure Liv could either, or that there would be enough light for her to identify the man standing there.

Charlie picked up the dark-blue shirt. "I'm just going to give him this. Wait a minute, okay? We'll talk more."

Liv got off the stool. "Can I meet him?"

"You want to do this now?"

Simon could probably hear every word they said. As if understanding this, Liv lowered her voice. "Do you want me to meet him? Like, is he going to be around for a while?"

I don't know.

Maybe?

I sorta hope so because I really like him.

Do I really have to answer this question this minute?

Charlie compromised, giving Liv a truncated nod. "Just give me a sec, okay?"

He turned into the hall and stopped. Simon was right there. He held a hand out for his shirt, then gestured toward the kitchen with his handful of blue material. Swallowing again—more easily this time—Charlie turned around again. Liv was standing behind him.

Another rip in space-time swallowed the moment. Another endless bubble of nothing and everything closing around the space in the hall as Simon and Liv took one another's measure.

Then Liv smiled. "I should have known it'd be the hot neighbor."

CHAPTER 24

Olivia's absence left a curious vacuum in the house. Simon listened to her car backing down the driveway and wondered if Charlie felt this way every time his daughter went out. The man in question was staring toward the front door, thoughts obviously tripping through stardust.

He turned around, offering Simon a shaky smile. "So, that went well."

"Your seventeen-year-old daughter called me 'the hot neighbor.' I'm not sure if I should be flattered or horrified."

"That's nothing." Rubbing at his chest, Charlie started pacing the kitchen. "I think my heart nearly stopped sixteen times in the last hour."

Conversation had pretty much ground to a halt after Simon had come downstairs. Hiding on the second floor had felt craven, though. He didn't want to be Charlie's dirty little secret, and had been gratified to hear Charlie telling Liv the truth. It had been a brave move and one that answered a lot of the questions Simon had had before the bang of the front door had pierced his happy after-sex bubble.

Now fear slithered in around his comfortable buzz. Was he ready for this? For Charlie? Ready to *be around for a while*? He hadn't heard Charlie's response to Olivia's question, but had to assume it had been somewhat affirmative. Otherwise things would be more awkward.

Charlie was still pacing the kitchen.

Simon caught him at the end of the track. "Hey. Listen, I really need a shower." Every movement tugged at his chest hair and pubes. "I'm going to head next door and give you some space."

"I—"

"You usually hang out with a friend on Friday night, right? Unless you want to explain how you spent your afternoon, you should probably get a shower in too."

Charlie's grin was of the slow and seductive variety. "My shower's big enough for two."

"Christ, don't tempt me."

Simon leaned in for a kiss. Charlie met him in the middle, his lips warm and sweet. His kiss was thoughtful, just shy of distracted. Simon touched his cheek. Pulled away to gently bump their noses together. "I'll talk to you soon, okay?"

"Okay."

Once home, Simon roamed around the kitchen and living area, aimless. He might as well have taken Charlie's distraction and brought it next door with him. He wanted a shower, but also had the curious sensation of having abandoned a task before it was done.

Should he have left Charlie alone?

Why had he left Charlie alone?

His phone interrupted his third circuit. Simon tugged it from his pocket and checked the screen. Frank. "Hey," he answered. "I was just about to jump in the shower. Can I call you back in a few?"

He didn't want to talk to Frank while he still smelled like Charlie.

He didn't really want to not smell like Charlie, either.

Showered and dressed in clean clothes, Simon poured out a healthy measure of scotch, picked up his phone, and parked himself in the corner of the couch.

Frank answered on the first ring. "Done washing away your sins?"

"Are you spying on me?"

"Why? Should I be?"

"I slept with him."

"I think we're having two different conversations."

"Not sure we're having any kind of conversation yet."

"Then let's start at the beginning. Who did you sleep with?"

"Charlie."

"The book guy?"

"Why do you always call him that?" Simon had no idea why it bothered him. Maybe because he got the impression Frank wanted

Charlie compartmentalized, or labeled. One of several items rather than a central feature.

"Aren't we testy? Was he a disappointment?"

"Now you're being catty." Simon said.

"Have we met?"

"I . . ." Simon stopped short of saying *I like him*. "He wasn't a disappointment. Far from it."

"He had a wife, didn't he?"

"I know what you're going to say next, and I'm pretty sure I'm not his big gay experiment."

Silence rolled over the line.

Huffing out a sigh, Simon filled it. "Can you just be a friend and listen? Maybe offer some advice?"

Frank sighed. "Sure. Tell Frankie all about it."

"I can't keep my hands off him, Frank. Every time I see him, it's like static happens between my ears. It's the way he looks at me. All this want, and his mouth—Jesus Christ, his mouth."

"You were about due a fling."

"I don't think it's a fling. Since when have I ever done flings, anyway? Is that even a word people use anymore?"

"Beside the point. What's going to happen when you get him out of your system? Or when he decides to taste the rainbow?"

"What do you have against monogamy?"

"Well, the one stellar example I have of it was a complete and utter farce."

Cheeks heating, Simon swore at the phone. "What's up with you? Why are you being such an ass?"

"I'm worried about you, okay? For nearly ten years, I listened to your insecurities about Brian. Your company, your relationship. And that's fine. That's what friends are for. I know you'd do the same for me. Have done. But what always got me was the fact that you couldn't see when Brian was being an ass. You always figured his faults were yours. It got exhausting. This past year . . . I've liked seeing you be you, Simon. Seeing you make things happen for yourself."

"Then why doesn't this make you happy? Charlie could be just what I need."

"Or he could break your heart. You know the rule. Don't date someone who's only recently decided they're gay."

"He's not gay."

"I rest my case."

Simon exhaled sharply. "He's bisexual and pretty open about it." To himself, Simon, his daughter, and at least one friend.

"Great, so he's got twice the field to play."

"Seriously, Frank?"

Frank grunted. "How long has he been single?"

"I know what you're thinking, but that's not Charlie. He's had twice the field all his life and has had, as far as I know, exactly one relationship."

"Okay, I take it back. This is probably a discussion you need to be having with Book Guy, anyway."

Simon growled.

"Fine. *Charlie.*" Frank sighed. "You know I don't have a specific bias against bisexuality, I just . . . Be careful, okay? I love you, Simon. I don't want to see you hurt again. I really don't. It'd break my heart."

"I appreciate your concern."

After ending the call with less controversial chatter, Simon tucked his phone away and stared sightlessly at the tall windows. He understood Frank's concerns; they were his own. But it was his risk to take. Surely the way Charlie made him feel was worth it?

He hadn't touched his whiskey. Picking up the glass, he studied the amber swirl of liquid for half a minute, the decision to drink it inextricably linked to what he planned to do next. Then he swallowed it, wincing at the burn. As warmth raced down his throat and across his shoulders, he picked up his phone and dialed.

Charlie answered a couple of heartbeats later. "Hey."

"I hope I'm not interrupting anything."

"Waiting for Phil to get here with pizza."

"Right. Listen, I wondered if you'd like to try a date."

"A date?"

"Dinner. Out."

"Or I could cook for you."

They wouldn't get to the meal then, and that was kind of the point. "Maybe another time? I . . . I thought if we went out somewhere, we could get to know each other a bit better without falling into bed within three seconds of breathing the same air."

Charlie's laughter bubbled through the phone. "Understood. When do you want to do this and where did you have in mind?"

"How about tomorrow night? Do you want to choose where? You know the area better than I do." And would more accurately pick a place where he'd be comfortable, where he'd be okay showing up for dinner with another man. Because with the way Charlie looked at him, it'd be obvious they were more than friends.

After a quick pause, Charlie said, "Okay. I think I know just the place. Pick you up around seven?"

Simon smiled widely at his phone. "I'll pick you up. I did the asking, after all."

CHAPTER 25

Charlie was determined not to be a cliché. Regardless, his limited wardrobe was spread across his bed. He'd made the bed first. Fresh sheets and all. Dates usually led to sex, and he was still living down the embarrassment of Simon having witnessed "Charlie, Day-to-Day."

Maybe they'd go back to Simon's after. Simon probably made his bed every morning. Slid out of barely disturbed sheets and twitched them into place.

Did he sleep naked?

Focus, Charlie. Focus.

His point of focus sucked, though. His wardrobe was limited to two pairs of jeans—one tragically old and one probably too young—a collection of convention T-shirts and sweatshirts, a handful of flannel, and the suit he pressed into service when confronted with a dress code.

He selected a white button-down with a faint blue stripe, wondering if his father had left it behind when he moved to Florida. He laid it against the newer pair of jeans and nodded. Not exactly Fifth Avenue, but not "I just left the geekiest convention ever" either.

The shower presented him with a fresh set of inquiry. How thoroughly should he wash? Would there be a conversation before Simon wanted to check out his ass, or would they go right there, high on after-dinner drinks and lust?

More importantly, did he want to go there? Maybe Simon would offer to go first—though Charlie got the distinct impression Simon was more a top than a bottom. No single reason why, just a feeling. Maybe it was that despite his quietness, he had a way of directing every encounter they had.

How did guys figure out who did what?

Rather than waste the rest of his prep time daydreaming, Charlie showered. Thoroughly. Then he dressed, forsaking his usual boots for an old pair of black lace-ups he found in the back of his closet. They looked pretty spiffy *and* they matched his belt. That seemed important.

Pity he had to cover everything up with a scuffed old leather jacket. He and Simon really should have started dating in August.

Finally, he took to prowling the front door while massaging his wrist. He'd had a watch once, but stopped wearing it after Merry died. It had reminded him too much of how slow a minute could be when someone he loved was in pain.

Lights flashed through the evening gloom, and Charlie stepped outside to meet his date. He climbed into the passenger side of Simon's car, and spent two seconds wondering whether they should kiss, before Simon leaned over and pecked him on the lips. The clean scent of Simon's skin wrapped around him like a crisp autumn morning, spicy and invigorating, and when Simon pulled away, Charlie caught him behind the neck and drew him in for another kiss.

"You sure about this dinner thing?" he murmured between tastes of perfect lips and Simon's deft tongue.

Simon inched forward so their foreheads rested together. "Yes. You look nice, by the way."

Charlie disengaged so he could cast a depreciating glance over his outfit. "I think I'm wearing my dad's shirt."

Simon laughed. He was dressed impeccably, of course. Dark pants and a clean white shirt that showed his physique to advantage. A jacket that didn't go with a suit. Sports coat? Not professor-ish, just . . . nice. With Simon's dark hair curling just behind his ears, his amazing eyes, and beautifully reddened lips, he was perfect. Charlie hummed appreciatively. "You're like a *GQ* model or something."

Simon brushed his thumb along Charlie's jaw. "And you're gorgeous."

The back of Charlie's neck prickled. Clasping it, he nodded toward the end of the driveway. "We should go, before I drag you upstairs to my completely made-up-with-fresh-sheets bed."

Simon laughed again. While he was stunning at rest—like someone from a billboard—when he laughed, Charlie saw the Simon he liked best. His posture always changed when he was amused. He relaxed. His eyes lightened—probably as the result of his eyebrows lifting. And his laughter was truly joyous—as though he were rediscovering humor after too long away.

Charlie sought Simon's free hand for a quick squeeze before letting go so that Simon could drive.

Simon turned a quick smile in his direction. "Okay, where are we going?"

Charlie directed him to town, to the same parking lot they'd used for the art festival. It was different being there again at night, but the same sense of excitement and expectation clutched at his gut. He was in the company of someone who fascinated him, and figured they'd have a good time. Hoped they'd have a good time.

When they reached the intersection of Broad and Main, Charlie pointed out the brew pub on the corner. "It's like a bar and grill. They make their own beer and the burgers come from their own cows." Was it too casual a choice? "It's not, umm, super intimate, but it's friendly and lively inside. The staff is nice. And they don't mind if you hang on to a table for a while."

Simon smiled. "Sounds good." His tone suggested it wasn't perfect, though.

"Do you want to try somewhere quieter? Or fanc—dressier? There's a great Italian place down Main a bit." Dark corners and candles in old wine bottles. Maybe that was more Simon's scene. "Or—"

Simon took his hand, surprising him into silence. "I'm sorry," he said.

"For what?"

"The restaurant is perfect, Charlie. You could have suggested McDonald's and I'd have gone along with it. I'm just . . ." He licked his lips. "I'm a little nervous. It's been a long time since I did this."

"Oh."

Simon glanced down at their hands. Charlie was aware of other people passing them and wondered if they were looking at their hands too, speculating. Simon traced his thumb across the back of Charlie's hand, and gave him an inward smile. "That's part of the reason why I wanted to go out tonight."

"Okay." Charlie bumped his shoulder to Simon's. "We'll save the romantic Italian place for our first-month anniversary."

Simon's mouth dropped open.

"What, the kids all celebrate by the week. I figured I was giving us some breathing room." Simon's features were slowly shifting toward the laughter Charlie really enjoyed. "C'mon."

Simon lifted his hand, as if to remind Charlie they were still joined at the fingers. "You ready for this?"

Refolding his sweaty fingers around Simon's palm, Charlie nodded. "Yep."

He lost his nerve right outside the restaurant, sliding his fingers from Simon's in a badly disguised movement. He didn't need two hands to open the door. It was kinda heavy, though. He waved Simon through, and they did the reservation-yes-table-ready-follow-me thing.

Charlie had chosen the restaurant for his stated reasons, but it wasn't until he spotted the couples and families that he realized he'd been hoping for the camouflage of the Friday after-work crowd. It wouldn't have been unusual to see colleagues, all male, eating together. Tonight? Not quite the norm. He wasn't embarrassed, or didn't want to be. He was . . . anxious. Hoping he didn't see anyone he knew—because introducing Simon as a friend would feel like a lie and he wasn't ready to get into the exact nature of their relationship.

When their server asked what they wanted to drink, Simon studied the menu and looked up with an expression of pleased surprise. "They have scotch." Score one for Charlie. "I'll have the Dalwhinnie neat."

The dalwhatnow?

"You, sir?"

"Valley Golden. A pint."

The server left, and Charlie let an outward breath deflate him enough to render him limp and properly folded into his side of the booth.

"Doing okay over there?" Simon asked.

"Yes." The answer was automatic, and in need of reprisal after Simon quirked one eyebrow. "Would it be totally inappropriate for me to say I feel like everyone's staring and wondering which one of us . . ." Charlie fluttered his fingers.

Thankfully, Simon smiled. "How many times have you seen another couple in a restaurant, or anywhere, and wondered what they do in bed? If she's a screamer, or if he likes to be spanked while he's wearing frilly panties."

"I don't own any frilly panties. Just so you know."

Simon grinned. "Unless one of us ducks under the table, no one is going to give us a second look."

"I'm sorry. I planned to be much cooler than this. I was until we got inside the restaurant."

Their drinks arrived, and the conversation took another break while they ordered burgers. Then the server left again, and Charlie swallowed a stupidly large and painful volume of beer while Simon sipped his whiskey.

Charlie cleared his throat of bubbles and residual ache. "So, now that we're actually on a date, should we talk about our exes some more?"

Simon's left eyebrow arched up again. It was a sexy look. "Have you ever been on a date before?"

"I watch a lot of Netflix."

Simon put the back of his hand to his mouth. Above the line of his fingers, his eyes brightened, the corners crinkling. His shoulders shook. He was laughing. Charlie thought about getting all offended and indignant for about a second before joining in.

"Your candor is refreshing," Simon said, still smiling.

"Great. Now I feel cute."

Simon chuckled again. "You are, Charlie. Ridiculously, adorably, but not quite insufferably."

Charlie rubbed the back of his neck. His fingers were as warm as his skin.

"Can I ask you something?" Simon said.

Charlie nodded.

"Why *haven't* you dated?"

The question had a tentative quality, careful footsteps across an attic full of memories. Charlie had the idea he could evade or offer up a flippant response, and Simon would back off.

"After Merry died . . ." A heavy sigh pulled his shoulders down. Charlie dragged a finger through the puddle of condensation forming around the base of his beer glass. "For a long time I figured that was it. That she had been my one chance. The love of my life. It didn't make sense to move on, you know?"

Simon's expression indicated he did know. That he'd been there.

"Sorry," Charlie muttered. "Was that too much of a downer?"

"No. We're not sparkly new adults waiting for our first-week anniversary. We've lived and loved. Our scars are supposed to make us interesting."

"What about you?"

"I don't have an urn to cry over, just more than a decade of confusing memories. Some good, some not so good. And, wow, I'm sorry. It's not the same."

It was odd seeing Simon flounder. He didn't ramble the way Charlie did, and when he delivered more than a handful of words, he tended toward prosaic elegance. He said what he meant. Nicely.

"Twelve years is a long time," Charlie offered. It felt like a completely inept response, but Simon looked so down. And self-conscious.

"But he's still here."

Charlie cut through the air with his hands. "You don't need to do that. My story is sad, but that doesn't invalidate yours. We don't need to compare scars, just acknowledge we both have them. Right?"

A small smile edged at Simon's lips. "Exactly right."

"And we have good memories too. For me, it wasn't all Merry being sick. I had the joy of Liv, of watching this amazing person grow up. And even when Merry couldn't get out of bed, she would try to be happy, and though it broke my fucking heart, all the time, she'd make me happy too. Because she was . . . light."

Simon's expression had turned inward again.

Wincing, Charlie said, "Okay, my turn to say sorry." He reached across the table and beckoned. Simon slid his hand over the smooth wood until they met in the middle. Charlie gripped his fingers. "Better here than in bed, covered in you know what."

Simon's laughter was sudden and shocking. He pulled his hand away and turned his head, knuckles pressed to his lips. Heads turned, but the conversational buzz of the restaurant quickly swelled back around them.

"You're regretting asking me out on a date, aren't you?"

Simon shook his head. "No. I'm more thinking that this was the best idea I've had all year."

Their burgers arrived, and Charlie clapped his hands together in delight. Even Simon looked impressed.

Before they could tuck in, Charlie held up a hand. "Before we eat, let's cap this portion of the date. Finish it." He took a deep breath. "I knew I was bisexual before I married Merry, but right now, I wouldn't change a thing. Except maybe for her illness. But I've done my time, and I'd like to think you moved next door right when I was ready to figure out what I wanted to do next. Not to make you sound like a project, or something I'm doing on the way to something else. I just don't want to scare you by saying 'what I want to do for the rest of my life.'"

Simon was shaking his head again, slowly, his mouth quirked into a soft smile.

"Your turn," Charlie murmured.

Simon took a deep but quiet breath. "I spent twelve years of my life living and working with a man I believed was The One. The most pathetic part of my story is that I probably knew he wasn't about ten years ago. But he was as close as I figured I'd get, and I was okay with that. Sad, I know. Stupid, yes. Apparently my self-worth needs work. But I can honestly say that while him leaving me was about the most devastating thing that has ever happened—making me look the fool because he was the one who cheated while I decided I didn't deserve better—I can also say that it was the most generous thing he ever did for me. Letting me go. He broke my heart, but without that wound, I'd never have had the chance to heal."

Charlie's eyes stung. He ducked his head to blink.

Pull yourself together.

Yes, his wife had died, but this raw confession of Simon's was so real. They weren't reenacting something from a movie. They were sharing the most profoundly painful experiences of their lives. Over burgers and beer.

"Simon..."

"Yes?"

"I think we've skipped about three dates."

"That might have happened yesterday when your daughter caught us in bed together."

"Are we doing this all wrong?"

Simon wrapped his fingers around Charlie's hand and squeezed. "No. I think we're doing it just right."

CHAPTER 26

"What a beautiful day." Simon leaned back inside the doorway of the office, quite unable to wipe the smile from his face.

"Did you win the lottery or something?" Arthur asked.

"No." But Simon felt like the rare November sunshine slashing across Main Street. Saturday night had been amazing. It had been the best date Simon could remember. They'd cut the strings on several weights before eating their burgers, setting the balloons of their hearts and minds to bob freely in a bright-blue sky. The rest of dinner had passed in a blur of light conversation and laughter.

By the time they'd returned to Charlie's place, the evening had felt curiously complete, even though they hadn't gotten to the thanks-for-dinner sex part. They almost hadn't needed to. Simon had already been stripped bare, fucked apart with words, and pulled back together by warm affection. But Charlie's kisses had propelled them inside and up the stairs to Charlie's *"made-up-with-fresh-sheets"* bed, where Simon had introduced his new lover to an old favorite: the blowjob. Charlie had proved a most eager and talented student.

A great date. Great after-date sex. Then a lazy Sunday morning in bed with a man whose smiles rivaled every sunny day.

"Good." Arthur's quiet voice brought Simon back to the present. "Can't have you taking a world tour when we're about to break ground."

"Is that what you'd do with a lottery win?"

"Oh, yes. I've always wanted to travel."

"Why didn't you?"

Arthur had been running a successful firm for years. Surely he had the funds.

"I always meant to, and then with one thing and another"—old grief and a flash of wistfulness passed across Arthur's face—"I never got around to it. I've seen quite a bit of our beautiful country, of course."

Simon smiled. "Maybe next year, hmm?"

"Next year?"

"When you retire."

"Oh, right. Yes. Perhaps then."

Last week, Arthur's waffling regarding his retirement date might have concerned him. Today, Arthur would retire when he retired, and he and Charlie would—

"Good morning." Brian's appearance was a rude interruption.

"What are you doing here?" *And why did I leave the door open so you could just wander in, like a ... like a ...*

"I came to see if you wanted to ride over to the site with me."

"Why would I want to do that?"

"I don't know, Simon. Maybe because we're going to be working together for the next umpteen months and it would be nice if we could sit in the same car and drink coffee and discuss the project like functional adults."

Arthur chose that moment to clear his throat.

Simon drew absolutely no satisfaction from the flush creeping across Brian's cheeks. Well, not much. Turning to Arthur, Simon asked, "Do you want to drive or will I?"

"Actually, I planned to take my own car. I've an appointment later this morning."

Brian directed a pleased damn smile at Simon. "I'll come with you, then."

Brian waited until the car was moving before talking, perhaps convinced Simon would be less likely to toss him out once they were on their way. "I would like to stop for coffee if it's not a problem," he said.

"Not worried I'll drop you somewhere and leave?"

"You're not that childish."

Simon turned into the parking lot of Dunkin' Donuts. The drive-thru window was closed.

Brian snickered softly. "Maybe you are that childish." He opened his door. "Want anything?"

Simon's "No" sounded just shy of petulant, but he would rather drink drain water than Dunkin' coffee. He was actually surprised Brian had gone inside. He returned a few minutes later with four cups wedged into a cardboard tray and a bulging bag.

"Brian—"

"For the rest of the team."

"Right."

"I did get you a donut, though. Boston Kreme."

Damn him.

They drove in silence for a while longer, Brian fussing with the lid on one of the cups, sugar packets, stirrers, and the donut bag before turning to Simon. "You know, I always liked your infuriated look, but I really would like to not do this in front of Sierra and Penelope." His next comment was infinitely more embarrassing, mostly because it was true: "You're the professional one. That was part of our charm as a team. I was the color. You were the businessman. The one our clients trusted."

"Are you still the color?"

"Of course."

"Do you—" Simon ground his teeth together.

"Do I what?"

"Do you miss it? Our business."

Brian didn't answer for a moment. He fiddled with the coffee cups again, stirred one needlessly. Then, quietly: "Yes." He glanced over, meeting Simon's gaze for a second before Simon had to turn away. Remember he was driving. "I know that from your perspective I tossed away twelve good years," Brian said.

"No, you didn't."

"I quit on something we'd built together."

"I didn't see it that way. The market went south, and we were sick of building Cracker Jack toys."

"And when our business was faltering, I packed myself up and left you."

Unsure how to judge Brian's tone, Simon glanced over again. Looking back at the road, he said, "If you're going to tell me you did me a favor—"

"I miss you, Simon."

"Don't do this."

"I know I fucked up. Multiple times. And I know I have no right to ask. But maybe we could try to be friends. Because that's what I miss the most. Just... being with you."

"Because you spent so much time just being with me. Honestly, I don't know how you fit me into your schedule of massages and weekend wine tours and what-the-fuck-ever else you were doing with all the men who weren't me."

"You know what I kept wondering?"

"Oh, please tell me."

"Why you put up with it."

Wincing, Simon gripped the wheel so hard his knuckles burned. "I can't do this now."

"I'm sorry."

"For making this the most unpleasant morning of my life since November twenty-third?" What kind of fool was he, treasuring the date Brian had packed up and left?

"I'm sorry for all of it. I know the words don't mean much. That a donut won't buy your forgiveness. And I'm not asking for all we had. I know that ship has sailed, but I want to salvage something."

"So you can stop feeling like a heel?"

"Because I miss my best friend."

Simon sucked in a breath that might as well have been acid. Thankfully, they were one turn away from the site. Relying on autopilot—and the fact that diesel trucks rarely ventured this far off the highway—Simon got them around the corner and parked neatly against the grassy embankment that would soon feature his fucking architecturally appropriate entrance gate. Blood whistled in his ears, and sweat trickled down his ribs. Without looking at Brian, he exited the car and walked away from the group clustered near the backhoe. Fists clenched, he climbed the embankment, breath coming in short, sharp rasps.

Why today? Did Brian know where he'd spent his weekend? And with whom? Was Brian jealous? Did that matter? God, why now? Why, when he'd finally connected with someone in a way that mocked everything he'd thought he'd had, did Brian have to shoehorn in and say, *"I miss you?"*

Why was it that every time Simon took a step forward with Charlie, Brian was there to drag him two steps back?

Simon stopped at the top of the rise, locking his knees against the urge to run down the other side and across the fields waiting to be plowed under by progress—by his houses, his beautiful farmhouses. As he took in the view, the whistle in his ears began to fade, replaced by the quiet rush of a crisp breeze.

His phone buzzed in his pocket. Simon pulled it out and woke the screen. It was a text from Charlie.

Just saying hi in case I forget to for the next however many days. Book. Deadline. Need to write. Will you be my reward for getting it done?

Simon exhaled, his breath misting in the cold air, and smiled. He lifted his chin, eyes closed against the glare of autumn sunshine; let the vague warmth bathe his face; and thought back to Saturday night—about the tenderness he felt inside every time Charlie looked at him, smiled at him, kissed him.

"Will you be my reward" . . .

He answered the text: *Absolutely.*

The following day, Brian showed up at the site with coffee from Starbucks. Simon left his cup untouched.

Two days after that, a donut bag appeared on his desk. Simon contemplated the bag for five whole minutes, his mind revisiting the small gifts Charlie had taken to leaving on his doorstep a few weeks before. What was it about him that inspired men to woo him with *things*? Surely words were more effective.

Perhaps he was difficult to talk to.

Was he difficult to talk to?

A few more minutes passed as Simon pondered that one before eventually arriving at the conclusion he should be working rather than looking for the secrets of the universe in a donut bag.

The following day, Brian was next to the untouched bag, one hip resting against Simon's desk.

Letting go a sigh that Frank would call *wonderfully dramatic*, Simon picked up his keys. "I need to go to the site."

"I'll come with you."

The drive passed in silence.

It wasn't necessary for Simon to be on-site so much at the beginning of a project. But he always was. As the bulldozers cut away portions of the hill to allow for the muddy track that would one day become a winding road, the shape of the land changed in subtle ways. The ideal locations for some of the houses shifted, as did their aspect. He shuffled plans and consulted. Redrew.

At the site, Simon parked out on the road and made the trek to the highest point. Brian followed him up the slope of the track, muttering about the mud sticking to his new shoes, and turned with Simon to survey the neighborhood. For a moment, having Brian next to him was irritatingly familiar. This was what they did—had done: work the plans together. Brian wasn't an architect. He was the bigger-picture guy. He'd take Simon's pieces and slot them into the puzzle.

"Would you rather have this view at the front or back of your house?" Brian made a sweeping gesture that encompassed the downward slope, the glimmer of water running in a thin line around the bottom of the hill, and the forest beyond. From there, it was just trees. A field of dark trunks and mostly skeletal limbs obscured by the gloom of a November afternoon. On a clear summer's day, the fringes of Allentown might be visible, but as no more than a speck of civilization here and there before swathes of green.

"It's a pity there are no real hills down here," Simon mused. "A view of something like Budd Lake, or the west side of the Kittatinny Mountain."

"Put that view here and you'd be pricing out most of your prospective clients."

Simon glanced over. "Do people really care about the house? Or is it all about the view?"

"You ask me that every time."

"I do?"

Brian's smile was a touch wistful. "Yeah. And I always tell you it's the house. They think it's the view. They buy the land for the view, but they live in the house."

"Which they learn to live with the same way some folks have to learn to live with their mother-in-law."

"See, this is why we made such a good team. And why you should stick to designing houses and not selling them."

Simon laughed.

Brian joined him, seeming more amused by Simon's laughter than his joke. Then, sobering slightly, he ruined the moment. "Want to go get some coffee?"

Simon turned back toward the view. "I had coffee this morning."

"We could discuss the changes in the lots. I'd like your advice on which house styles would look best where."

"You know someone is going to want the Craftsman on the front lot, right next to my split-rail fence." Simon glanced over in time to see Brian grimace, and spoke again. "I'm seeing someone, Brian."

Brian's expression went through an odd metamorphosis. Then he took a turn at gazing across the valley. It shouldn't be like this. Brian had no right to any feelings regarding Simon's life, or his relationships. Now, over the past year, or . . . hell, for the entirety of his life.

Before Simon could muster up the anger he was oddly weary of, however, Brian turned to him with a small smile. "I figured you had something going on. You're not as sulky as you were a couple of weeks ago."

"I was not sulky."

"Yeah, you were. Monday, though . . . Monday, you were seeing angels and rainbows dancing across the street."

"What? When?"

"When I showed up at your office. You were looking out the door, but not seeing anything real."

Simon snorted.

"I'm sorry if you feel like I backed you into a corner," Brian continued. "I was jealous."

"Mm-hmm."

Brian sighed. "Is he local?"

Simon held up a hand. "I don't want to talk about him. I just . . ."

No anger answered his call—not that he felt a need for it at the moment. Instead, the slithering heaviness he'd lived with for so long moved across his shoulders. Simon braced for it, wondering how long he'd have to carry this weight. As he examined the sensation, though, he could already feel the difference. Being with Brian hurt, but not because he missed him, and not because he was tired of being alone. The pain was for what he'd lost. On Monday, he hadn't been able to imagine remaining friends with a man who'd broken his heart into tiny little pieces before scattering them like bread crumbs.

Today? Right now? Simon thought of Charlie's smile. The warmth of his brown eyes. His exuberance, his every-day joy. And when he glanced over at Brian, he found him somewhat diminished. Smaller. Still sharply outlined, still stupidly important. But no longer at the top of his list.

"We can get coffee after we check the lot sizes and aspects," Simon said.

Brian's answering smile didn't make him any more distinct. In fact, he might have just slipped down the list another notch or two.

CHAPTER 27

Charlie wrote until his butt went numb. The words poured out of him in an incoherent rush, Charlie simply the conduit, his fingers tools of the voices in his head as he dutifully recorded every scene they dictated. Every now and then he'd breathe too deeply, or shift from the worst posture ever, and a twinge would run up and down his spine, lighting the fire of pain he didn't have time to feel.

No rest for the wicked.

No time to be wicked, either, despite the occasional text from Simon.

When he remembered to move, he paced the narrow circumference of his attic den. Scratched Herbert's ears and spoke to whichever cat was pretending to be a couch cushion. Twice, after harried texts from Shelly asking *Where's my book???*, panic sent him downstairs to do something with the porch, stretching his back in healthier ways (maybe) as he pried up steps and cut away the rotting railing.

Then he returned to his desk and resumed the position.

At some point in his timeless present, he leaned away from the keyboard to lace his fingers over his head, turn his hands toward the ceiling, and stretch. Such a bad move. His shoulders crackled like popcorn and something in his back pulled. He couldn't feel his legs. Uncrossing his ankles only worsened the problem. He bent forward, wincing at an uncomfortable twinge, and massaged his calves while swallowing his whimpers, because if he made too much noise, Herbert would join in. Then he'd have to take the dog for a walk, and he didn't have time, he—

Charlie squinted at the screen. Actually, this was probably a good time for a break. Also, if he ever wanted his ankles to work properly again, he should move them a bit.

"Want to go for a walk?"

Herbert was off the couch and pounding down the stairs before Charlie finished speaking. Just as well, as descending staircases with a dog on his way to walkies could be dangerous. Charlie followed, his ankles loosening only slightly by the time he got to the front door. Opening the door with one hand, he leashed Herbert with the other, and then grabbed a sweatshirt from the end of the stair rail. Herbert pushed through the widening gap between door and jamb, and Charlie stumbled out after him, into the chill dusk, blinking, his free hand flying out uselessly as he reached for the missing railing. Before he knew what was happening, he'd dropped the leash and fallen off the side of the porch to land in the untrimmed and mostly leafless rose bushes flanking the steps.

He tried to sit up and swallowed a yell as thorns dug into his palms. Every time he moved, a new barb caught at his skin. This was ridiculous. He should lie back down and roll out, except he was already going to be occupied with pulling thorns out of his ass all night.

Maybe Simon would help him.

Moving slowly in an attempt to limit new contact, Charlie crawled out of the bushes.

Footsteps sounded on the porch above, and Liv called down, "Dad? What are you doing on the lawn?"

Replying with *Oh, Liv, you're home*, wouldn't be his best parenting move ever. It'd taken him this long to put together the fact it was nearly dark outside, and that he should have expected her home hours ago—and hadn't noticed her absence. She'd probably called out and received no answer but the *clack* of his keyboard. It'd happened before. Might have happened on Monday . . . or Tuesday. Whichever day the sandwich had magically appeared on the corner of his desk.

Charlie patted the lawn with his hands. "I'm, umm, checking for grubs."

"You're bleeding!"

Shit, was he? Charlie swiped at his face, his palm coming away wet. From the edge of the driveway, Herbert howled.

Liv jumped over the missing steps and walked over, holding out a hand to help him up. "Did you fall off the porch?"

"Someone took apart the railing."

Liv shook her head.

Getting to his feet, Charlie brushed himself off, smearing blood across his jeans. "What day is it? Have you eaten?"

"Thursday and I was just going to fix myself something. C'mon. We should clean your face and stuff."

"Yeah." He felt a little dazed, as though he'd fallen from a greater height than the porch. "Wait, I need to take Herbert for a walk."

"I'll do it after dinner."

"Sorry. I'd have cooked, but I got all caught up in chapter . . ." What chapter was he up to? Charlie made a whirling motion with his hand. "The 'oh my God we're all going to die' chapter."

"I figured."

Charlie put his arm around his daughter's shoulders. "You're a good kid."

She smiled up at him.

Inside the kitchen, Liv retrieved the first aid kit from under the sink and insisted on swabbing the dirt away from all the scratches on his face and hands before applying liberal smears of Neosporin. He told her he'd get the ones on his ass later. She replied with the well-practiced eye roll. While she put the first aid kit away and washed her hands, Charlie pulled out the stuff to make tuna melts.

"Grab the cheese?" He gestured toward the fridge. "And that bag of mini-carrot things so I can say I gave you a vegetable with your dinner."

"The mini-carrot things are gone."

"Who ate them?"

"You did."

"Huh. Do we have anything else?"

"I'll live without a vegetable, Dad."

And apparently had been doing so for . . . how many days? Charlie knew his parenting skills faded to barely existent when he got toward the end of a book, but he'd always had *his* parents to pick up the slack before. He should reprioritize. "I need to go to the store, don't I?"

"Just finish the book, then we'll do life as usual."

Charlie glanced over at his daughter, who looked oddly pale in the kitchen light. He blinked, thinking it was his vision, but no . . . she had the pallor of someone recovering from the flu. Little circles under her eyes too. He put his hand to her forehead.

Liv ducked. "What are you doing?"

"Checking you haven't turned into a zombie." The joke rang hollowly in his ears. He'd mostly gotten over the fear that every childhood illness might turn into cancer, but only mostly. Charlie pulled out the griddle and set it on top of the stove. "It's only been a few days, right? I didn't miss Thanksgiving?" He wouldn't have been surprised to find this Thursday was actually next Thursday.

"No, Dad. That's next week. School's out Tuesday and Wednesday, by the way." Of course it was. "I was going to stay at Rosalie's and meet you at Uncle Phil's on Thursday."

"Sure. Or Rosalie could stay here." He felt the sudden need to look after his daughter. Put some color into her cheeks.

"I figured if I stayed there, then you and Simon could have the house to yourselves."

Charlie nearly dropped the can of tuna. He got it slotted under the can opener and concentrated on the turning motion while his thoughts jumped up and down, arms waving. The silence stretched as he prepared the sandwiches. When they were cooking, he turned around to find Olivia doodling on the counter with her finger. She looked up and smiled. Charlie's return smile felt . . . wobbly.

He fixed it in place. "We didn't really get much of a chance to talk about . . . last week."

"About Simon?" Liv said.

"Well, that and the whole 'my dad is dating a guy' thing."

"I talked to Rosalie about it, and she wasn't surprised at all."

Not the answer he'd been expecting.

Charlie gripped his nape, which was warm because he was standing with his back to the stove, damn it. "I'm not sure I like the idea of you discussing my dating habits with Rosalie."

"Seriously, Dad. You don't think we've mapped your whole life out for you like a million times?"

"Why?"

"Like I said last week, you shouldn't be alone."

"Cassie lives alone." Yep, that was the best he could come up with.

"Cassie's not lonely."

"I'm not lonely."

Liv gestured toward the stove. "The cheese is dripping on the griddle."

Charlie served up the sandwiches and pushed one across the counter. "What about you, though? Aside from thinking I'm lonely and having Rosie not surprised and whatever else."

Liv contemplated her sandwich for half a minute or so. "Okay, it's weird because I didn't see it, but now I do. You do look at guys. You look at women too, so I never noticed. I just figured you were a people watcher."

"When am I doing all this looking?"

Liv waved a hand. "Then there was the art festival. You were, like, so nervous. Like you were on a date. And you kept watching Simon. You were making sure he was included and having a good time."

"That's the nice thing to do when you invite someone somewhere and they don't know anyone."

"Yeah, but you kept blushing and stuff."

"Huh."

"I'm good with it, Dad. Really. I think it's cute."

"So not cute."

"It is, though! I'm happy for you. You should invite him to Uncle Phil's for Thanksgiving."

Charlie blinked. "You think?"

"Uncle Phil knows what's up with you guys?"

He nodded.

"Then you should. You're dating, right?"

"I got the impression you didn't like Simon so much at the art festival."

Liv shrugged. "I didn't know him then."

"And now you do?"

"He makes you happy, Dad. Anyone can see that. And . . ." Another shrug. "Simon's cool."

Charlie let a grumbly "Okay" escape. She did seem sincere—and still too damned pale. "How about you? What's up that I should know about?"

Liv glanced down at the counter. "Nothing much."

He might currently be running for Bethlehem's Most Inattentive Parent Award, but he'd known his daughter long enough to sense the change in her mood, which meant *nothing much* could be all about the dearth of something or the denial of that same something. Should he ask about The Boy? Or was that affair long dead?

"How's the mural project coming along?"

Liv brightened a little. "Good. We'll start transferring our design to the wall after Thanksgiving." She picked up her sandwich and wrinkled her nose. "Is this tuna okay?"

Charlie sniffed his. "Smells fine to me. Let me smell yours." She passed it across, with an unreadable expression. The half-shrug look was back—though her shoulders were aligned. Her sandwich smelled the same as his. "Smells fine. Want mine instead?"

Liv swallowed. Sweat broke out across her forehead. "Umm, no. I think I'm just going to have an apple or something."

"Are you sure you're okay? You're really pale, Liv."

"I'm tired. It's the end of semester and Rosie and I have been busy with the mural. I probably stayed up too late last night too."

Which he hadn't noticed because he'd been so wrapped up in the book.

"Soon as I'm done with this draft, we're going to spend some time together, okay?"

Liv gave him a tolerant smile. "How about if we go hiking? Maybe we could head out to Hickory Run before the weather gets too bad."

"Friday after Thanksgiving?" Charlie asked.

"Want to bring Simon? I can bring Rosalie."

"No." Appealing as that sounded. "Let's just go you and me."

Liv's smile widened. "Sure, Dad."

CHAPTER 28

Simon opened his door to find Charlie grinning on the front step. He grabbed Charlie's hand and pulled him inside. "How's the book coming? I was waiting for you to text." And the waiting had been stupidly tedious. He'd felt like a teenager all week, checking his phone and gazing wistfully next door.

Charlie pushed him up against the wall. He might have kicked at the door—Simon was aware of it swinging nearly shut and creaking open again as Charlie kissed him. Then his sense of place and time drifted away, replaced by . . . Charlie. Just Charlie. Simon fell into the kisses, letting that teenage feeling come over him. Enjoying the simplicity of standing in a hallway, necking.

When Charlie drew back, panting softly, Simon put his hands on Charlie's shoulders, meaning to hold them apart for long enough for thought to happen.

Because the door *was* open. Yeah, that.

"I finished the book," Charlie said.

Oh thank God. "Congratulations! Feel good?"

"I'm fucking wiped and I still have to revise the damn thing, but, yeah, I feel good. Want to celebrate?" Charlie's eyebrows danced upward.

"I'd love to, but it's Friday. Don't you usually hang out with Phil on Fridays?"

"Not this week. Jen has him cleaning and painting and doing Lord knows what else for next week."

"Next week?"

"Thanksgiving. Want to come?"

All the lightness and brightness inside Simon squinched into a panicked clump. "Where?"

"To Phil's. It's a pretty casual affair, despite all the prep. I think Jen starts getting ready early so that by the time we all get there, her house looks just lived in enough that we don't suspect she cleaned and painted." Charlie rubbed the back of his neck. "I'd like you to come as..." He waved his hand through the air and started down the hall.

Simon wanted him to finish his sentence. Come as *what*? Biting the end of his tongue to keep it from moving, he shut the front door and followed Charlie into the kitchen.

Once there, Charlie leaned a hip against the big island and folded his arms. "Do guys talk about relationship stuff? I mean, I know we talked a lot on our date. We covered our exes and had a sleepover." His eyebrows rose again, a subtle invitation to a shared memory. "I've cooked you breakfast."

Simon returned the smile but said nothing. Charlie needed to get whatever this was out on his own.

After some lip chewing, he did. "Can we have the 'where is this going' talk?"

"We can."

"I... Okay, this feels really weird."

Because Charlie was making it weird, but that was what he did. Simon couldn't find it in himself to be anything other than amused, though, and that in turn had him smiling again. A little more widely.

"Why are you smiling?" Charlie asked.

"Where do you want this to go?" Simon returned.

"I want you to come to Thanksgiving as my boyfriend. Or if that's too stupid a word, maybe as the guy I'm seeing? That sounds so damn casual though, and I guess I wanted you to know this doesn't feel casual to me. Like, I understand we have to see where things go—it's not all, 'Hey, we've had a sleepover, you should move in.' But without sending you to the hills, I wouldn't mind if that was the direction we were heading in." Charlie unfolded his arms and held up his hands. "Let me rephrase. I guess before I get more involved and start introducing you around, I want to make sure we're leaning in the same direction."

The beauty of it, beneath the rambling charm of Charlie's words, was that his request was totally logical. And in giving the question its due—a moment of quiet contemplation—Simon surprised himself by not starting to plan for a trip to the hills.

He wanted this. He'd been thinking in these terms all week, without defining the process, because while the potential of every kiss frightened him on some level, he lived for that small bite of fear. Being with Charlie was like being on a roller coaster. The highs were thrilling, the lows . . . There hadn't been any. Not yet. Undoubtedly there would be. That was life. But—

"You're being all quiet." Charlie stuck his hands into his front pockets and bounced on his toes.

"Sorry. I didn't want to give a flippant answer." Simon stepped forward, put his hands on Charlie's shoulders again, and squashed the urge to take a deep breath. "We're leaning in the same direction."

Charlie gave way slightly beneath his palms, as though settling back down. "Okay." Then he grinned. "Okay. So, we should celebrate me finishing the book."

Simon gave him a quick kiss. "What did you have in mind?"

"This is a good start," Charlie said against his lips.

Time ebbed and flowed again, wrapping them in a cocoon. Simon relearned every contour of Charlie's mouth, though he'd not had the time to truly forget. Couldn't imagine ever letting go of the memory of Charlie's taste, the firmness of his lips, the good-humored tease of his tongue. The way he always lifted his chin in invitation when Simon wandered off track, exploring the shallow dimple on his cheek, the line of his jaw.

Simon ran his tongue along the bristle of stubble, noting the softness. Charlie hadn't shaved in days. He'd showered recently, though. He was all clean skin and muggy warmth with just a hint of November clinging to his hair and clothes. Simon nipped at his chin, kissed his throat. Sighed as the rumble of Charlie's pleasure traveled through his lips.

Charlie was tugging at Simon's shirt, pulling it from a neat tuck and wrestling with the buttons. Simon shoved his hands under Charlie's shirt and lifted it up over his head. Charlie was grinning when his face reappeared.

He turned his attention back to Simon's buttons. "Do you sleep in pajamas? Like all silky with buttons?"

Laughter bubbled in Simon's throat. "As a matter of fact, I do. When it's cool. Summer I mostly just wear boxers."

"Hah, a man who dresses for bed. I knew it."

Charlie had the buttons undone and was pushing the shirt from Simon's shoulders. He bent forward to kiss Simon's chest, then rubbed his cheek against the hair there, as if planning to nest.

Simon ran his hands down Charlie's shoulders, admiring the broad expanse of muscle, warm flesh, occasional freckle. "You sleep in sweats, don't you? Or whatever you were wearing that day."

Charlie laughed. "Pretty much. I did own pajamas once. No idea what happened to them."

"Maybe you could get another pair on one of these regular trips to Target."

Charlie lifted his head, eyes all crinkled at the corners, lips spread in a wide grin. He looked amused and half-mussed from their kisses and just generally good-humored. And . . . just Charlie. So Charlie. Simon quailed slightly as he realized he adored this face, could imagine loving the man attached to it.

Nudging deeper feelings aside, Simon reeled him in for another kiss. Charlie complied, letting their lips blend with languid harmony for a minute or so before pulling back to hook two fingers behind Simon's belt buckle, the skin of his knuckles sending a ripple through Simon's gut. Simon drew in a sharp breath.

Tugging him away from the kitchen, Charlie asked, "Which way to the bedroom?"

Simon pointed and Charlie set off, turning now and again to touch Simon's hip, his shoulder, drop a light kiss to one pec, as though making sure Simon was still there. When they reached the open doorway, he paused to glance around the room before nodding.

"What?" Simon asked.

"Definitely your room. Quiet, uncluttered. Serene. If we do end up living together, I want to move into your house."

Simon wrapped Charlie up in his arms and kissed a few touchpoints of his own. The side of Charlie's neck, his throat, the center of his chest where sparse brown curls tickled Simon's lips. Their fingers collided as they reached for each other's belt at the same time. Simon snorted in amusement and moved his hand down, cupping the bulge at the front of Charlie's jeans. Groaning softly, Charlie pushed into his hand—and attacked his belt. Time ebbed and flowed again, a cozy bubble closing back around them as belts clinked, material swished, lips touched, and breath mingled.

Though Charlie had seemed to be in a hurry earlier, once they landed on the bed, naked, he slowed down. Simon was content to indulge the more thorough loving—the pauses to stroke shoulders and hips, the kisses trailing across skin. Happy sounds and smiles. The odd comment and joke as Charlie explored and discovered.

Then Charlie kissed his way back up Simon's torso, leaving his erection straining for the feel of those fabulous lips, and whispered in his ear, "I want you inside me."

Simon's cock jerked almost painfully.

He shifted so they lay on their sides, facing each other, legs brushing together, hands at hips, and studied Charlie's face. Apparently expecting the scrutiny, Charlie stayed still. Smiled a little. Simon saw the anxiety in his gaze, though, and knew that *Are you sure?* would be the wrong thing to say.

He trailed his fingers along Charlie's jaw. "Honestly, I thought you'd ask if you could top me first."

"I thought about it. I almost asked last weekend. But I want to try this."

"Why?"

"Because I want to know what it feels like, and I trust you."

"Oh, Charlie." Simon traced Charlie's cheekbone with his thumb. Would it be strange to thank him?

He couldn't remember Brian specifically asking—they'd just fallen into a pattern of Simon topping, Brian bottoming. It was what they'd both preferred. They'd switched it up on occasion, but had rarely connected in the same way when they had. It had always been awkward and at some point, they'd simply stopped. Simon had never tortured himself with the idea Brian had left him over his inability to enjoy bottoming, though. If it had been a reason, it had been one of many.

Now, he wondered. He also wondered at the urge to offer himself up to Charlie, even though it wasn't what Charlie wanted tonight.

He pressed a quick kiss to Charlie's lips before murmuring, "Wait here," and then rolled over to check the contents of his nightstand. Lube, he had. Charlie had been in this bed before after all, as a ghost accompanying Simon's hand. Condoms ... He sorted through the disarray of magazines, pens, cuff link boxes, postcards, bookmarks ... Crap and more crap.

Charlie leaned over his shoulder. "Wow. That drawer is full of stuff. I figured your drawers would have like one thing each in them. Centered, you know? All neat."

Simon huffed out an amused breath. "You were supposed to wait over there."

"You took too long. Also, your ass is damn sexy." Charlie rocked forward, pushing his half-erect cock between Simon's butt cheeks. A shiver danced across his skin, hot and cold. He nearly arched, begged Charlie to reconsider tonight's relative positioning.

Charlie's breath touched his neck. "*Would* you ever want to do it the other way 'round? I did some reading and apparently a good portion of gay guys are ... There was a word."

"Versatile?"

"Yeah." Charlie was being quite distracting with his poking and nudging and roaming hands.

Simon held up a condom. "Can you read the expiration date on this?"

Charlie squinted at it. "We're good."

He had half expected Charlie to follow up with some comment about being safe or not having had a partner in some number of months. He'd obviously been doing his research. That he didn't came as an odd sort of relief, and not only because they could have that conversation another time.

As he rolled back over, Simon addressed Charlie's query. "Yes, I would do it the other way around."

Charlie's eyebrows crooked together. "You don't usually, though. Do you?"

"Sex isn't just one thing, Charlie. It's different with different partners. With you? Yes, I'd consider it." Because it would mean something other than top and bottom to Charlie—and Simon. It would mean ...

Charlie was smiling. Simon let go of his thoughts and smiled in return. Then he asked, "Are you sure about this?"

Charlie's smile widened. "Yep."

"If you don't like—"

Charlie silenced him with a quick kiss. "When have you ever known me not to tell you everything that's running through my head?"

To that, Simon could only laugh—and lean in for another kiss.

CHAPTER 29

Charlie wasn't sure. Not at all. But he knew Simon would take care of him. Make it not scary—unless the fact that anal sex was completely and utterly horrific turned out to be the best-kept secret on the planet. The folks on Tumblr certainly didn't seem to think it was. For every video snippet of a man enjoying it, there were about sixteen of women enjoying it.

But when was Simon going to get there? Not that all this kissing and stroking wasn't nice.

Simon pulled away from Charlie's neck, where he seemed to have been working up to leaving a mark to replace the one he'd left last week. "You need to relax."

"I am relaxed."

Simon glanced down at his clenched fists.

Charlie uncurled his fingers and flexed them. "I *am* relaxed. I was just thinking about . . . stuff."

One of Simon's eyebrows quirked upward. "Mm-hmm. I'm going to suck you off."

"I don't want you to suck my dick."

Really, Charlie? What planet are you from?

The I-want-something-in-my-ass planet.

"I mean, normally I'd be all over that," Charlie said. Simon had an amazing mouth and extremely talented tongue. And he did this thing with his teeth— "But it's not what I want tonight."

"Right now, you're so tense, if I touch your ass, you're either going to fly up off the bed and hit your head on the ceiling, or clamp down on my finger so hard we'll have to call a paramedic."

"Wow. Way to kill the mood."

"Charlie." Simon should look exasperated. Instead, he wore a small smile and the deep and clear blue of his eyes sparkled with humor.

"I guess I could use a blowjob."

Simon's smile widened. "C'mere."

He leaned in for another kiss, and Charlie tried to relax into it. Tried not to think about his ass. When Simon wrapped a warm hand around his dick, Charlie stopped thinking entirely. His blood was too busy rushing south, thickening his shaft. He pushed through the circle of fingers, shivering as Simon dropped soft kisses over his chest, tongue flicking out to catch one nipple, the other nipple, and the hollow between his ribs.

At some point during Simon's downward journey, Charlie thought about returning the gentle touches and kisses. The best he could do was put his hands around Simon's shoulders and hold on. Sex couldn't always be a fifty-fifty prospect, right? Sometimes he had to let himself be taken. Literally.

Simon tongued the underside of Charlie's shaft, making his cock jerk. Then he lapped at the crown, humming softly. Okay, maybe a blowjob would be nice. Though *nice* was totally the wrong word for what Simon was doing to his cock. *Oh . . . Oh!*

"Jesus." Charlie gripped whatever he had to hand. A shoulder and something soft—a pillow. He worked at not snapping his hips up. Choking his boyfriend would be bad.

Boyfriend.

The word seemed inadequate somehow.

Simon was nudging his knees farther apart. Charlie wasn't so far gone that he didn't know what was coming next. The grip and slide of Simon's lips, though. The swirl of his tongue. The snap of a plastic bottle cap. More tongue action. Warm, wet suction.

A finger.

He didn't tense. Well, he might have. Charlie had no idea what his ass was doing. The rest of him shivered and trembled. He'd touched himself before. Poked around a bit down there in the shower. It hadn't felt particularly sensual. Maybe he should have done it in bed, on his back like this, knees up and spread, a man tending his cock with thorough and devoted attention.

Another stroke, another shudder.

He lost time after that. Later, he might think about separating the moments, but up until Simon asked if he wanted to stay on his back or roll over, Charlie existed in a place of sharp opposites, each leaning against the other until the myriad sensations were hopelessly entwined. The rudeness of intrusion against a building need to keep Simon's fingers inside him. He'd also been introduced to his prostate and pretty much wanted to spend the next thirty-seven years making up for lost time.

"Charlie?" Simon crawled back up his body to kiss Charlie's lips. He tasted so good that Charlie's brain short-circuited for another few minutes. Then Simon was blurrily close, their foreheads together. "Let's do it this way," he said, "so I can watch your face."

"Okay." Really, he could be hanging from the ceiling. Charlie just wanted Simon's cock where his fingers had been.

A pillow was shoved under his hips, and then his dick was sucked again. His ass lubed up a little more. Then Simon snapped on a condom and knelt between his legs.

Oh God.

"Charlie, look at me."

Charlie opened his eyes. Uncurled his fingers. Entertained, briefly, the thought that he'd gone mad. Most men bought a sports car when they approached forty. He'd asked another man to fuck him. And he was no longer erect. Wonderful.

"You look so good lying there. Your chest is all flushed, and I can see the bruise I left on your neck. Your eyes are all lusty. The way you move for me, I already know this is going to be amazing. Now clench."

Confused by Simon's sudden bout of verbosity, Charlie almost missed the first nudge, thicker and blunter than a finger. He clenched, not sure why, but trusting Simon.

Simon stroked the inside of his thighs, tugged gently on his half-limp cock. Spilled more words. "You're always talking about my eyes, but I wonder if you've ever appreciated your own. So warm. It's like you're always smiling. Just to see you makes people happy."

Another nudge, more stroking and words. Charlie's breath caught in his throat as his ass let go and Simon pushed inside him. It didn't hurt as much as he'd expected. Instead, he simply felt overwhelmed by the compliments and word babble from Simon and the feeling of being stretched. Pressure. A slight burn. More words. The feeling they were doing something so monumental, but entirely personal.

"You feel so good, Charlie. So damn good. I knew you would. I fantasized about you laid out beneath me. On all fours in front of me. My hands on your hips."

Charlie let out a tense breath. "If I'd known you would talk so much in bed, we'd have been doing this the day we met."

"I don't usually." Simon was fully inside him now, and really, they should both be breathless. Charlie was having difficulty drawing air back into his lungs. Simon was only flushed. "You okay?"

Charlie managed a breath. "So very okay."

"Get ready to fly."

Simon drew back a little, then thrust. *Good* didn't begin to describe the sensation. Neither did *flying*. But the potential was there. Beneath the lingering weirdness, the almost too heavy weight of intimacy, the sharp feeling of being in a place he'd never expected to be, and the surprise of it—the anticipation of flight was there. He just needed to strap in and prepare.

It seemed Simon established a rhythm only to ease him into the possibility, and then he changed the pace, the angle. Gripping one of Charlie's knees, pushing it out and up, he rocked forward and hit that magic spot inside.

Oh, hallelujah!

Instinctively, Charlie reached for his cock and found it had plumped again, doing him proud. He stroked idly, the pace of his hand completely out of sync with Simon's thrusts. But that was okay. Every strike against his prostate was worth the mismatched rhythm. Worth everything, really—though he could probably have come from the friction alone.

Who knew his ass could be so pleasurably sensitive?

Everyone on Tumblr, apparently.

Sweat dripped across his stomach. Simon had been reduced to wordless grunts. Eyes wide, eyebrows dark, cheeks flushed with exertion and desire. He was a startlingly handsome man. Even more so poised above Charlie, between his upraised knees.

Charlie put his other hand to the middle of Simon's sweat-dampened chest. Soft curls skimmed across his palm. He kept stroking, Simon kept thrusting, and then it was happening. The low buzz and murmur of *maybe I could come from this* turned into a shout. Three direct strikes to his prostate and a haphazard squeeze of his cock tossed him over the event horizon. His balls let go, his hips thrust uselessly upward. Semen mingled with sweat, splashing across his torso while his dick jerked in his hand.

"Oh fuck, Charlie..."

Through slitted eyes, Charlie could see Simon grimacing. Shuddering. The pace picked up, rocking Charlie into the bed, Simon drilling into him as he shouted and came.

The next few minutes passed in another blur of experience. The white and hazy high of climax—had he come again?—and the wonderful low drag of the after, where all the world might slide into a big warm hole and wallow together, limbs entwined, sweat all mingled with breath. Shaking as they reveled in nothing but pure existence.

The weight of Simon over him was perfect. The squish of spent penis in his ass not as strange as it might be. All that mattered was the fact of Simon being there. Being the one Charlie had done this with.

When Simon pulled away, Charlie whimpered. He didn't care that he sounded like a neglected puppy. The loss of warmth and connection was nearly too much to bear.

"Be right back," Simon murmured, dropping a kiss to his lips.

He returned seconds later with a warm cloth that he used to quickly and efficiently clean up the mess they'd made. And, yeah, it was messy. Charlie grinned as Simon kept discovering other spots to wipe at. Then it was snuggle time. This was the aspect of Simon that Charlie found the most endearing. Well, in this moment, it was the most endearing.

He remembered the stiffness of Simon on the couch after their first handjob in the kitchen. Every time after, Simon had softened. Now they lay facing each other, lower legs entwined, one hand each tucked under a pillow, the other clasping a hip or upper thigh. Simon wore a mellow expression that had him looking done in, but pleasantly so.

Charlie was flying. Still.

Simon nipped at Charlie's lips. "How was it?"

"You were there. How do you think it went?"

Simon's chuckle was low and sonorous. He smiled gently. "You were beautiful."

An image of Simon above him, moving, flashed through Charlie's thoughts. "So were you."

There was no talk after that, though this close, with their gazes somewhat locked, it felt as though words passed between them. An exchange of secrets requiring no language, no acknowledgment. Just more of that space of existence.

Before he drifted off, Charlie's thoughts skipped over a couple of mundane things, such as whether they should eat. Did he need permission to stay? The fact his ass felt kinda sore. The closeness of Simon, his breath as heavy and regular as a satisfied heartbeat, underscored all, carrying him over thought and question until all that mattered was this.

Being here and touching.

Being *with* someone.

Just being.

CHAPTER 30

Simon watched scenery flit past the car window with a mixture of vague curiosity and contentment. Memories of the previous weekend and the intervening days—sex, more sex, laughter, smiles, Charlie being Charlie, and sex—kept his thoughts away from their destination: Thanksgiving dinner.

It was going to be fine.

He liked Charlie. He'd like Charlie's friend Phil, and Phil's family.

Charlie turned onto the next street and slowed. After passing an extended line of cars, he pulled in front of a house with a familiar truck in the driveway and parked against the curb. He killed the engine, but didn't move to exit the car. Instead, he braced both hands against the wheel and took a deep breath. Then he glanced over at Simon. "Ready for this?"

"I *was*. Are all these visitors in that house?" Simon indicated the multitude of cars before sweeping his hand toward a rambling ranch not unlike his place.

"Probably. Phil has a big family. Cousins galore."

"I guess this isn't the time to tell you that crowds make me uncomfortable." Though, being one of many, instead of the only new face at a more intimate table, would have its advantages.

"We'll avoid the living room." Still, Charlie made no move to leave the car.

"Okay."

Charlie showed him an anxious smile. "I keep telling myself that if you were a woman, I'd be bringing you today. So it makes no difference. That sounded fine until this very minute. Now I'm telling myself that I'm not allowed to introduce you as just a friend. Go big or go home, right?"

"I won't be upset if you want to keep things strictly friendly today."

"I would be."

"It's okay to take your time with this."

"I haven't even told my parents yet. I'm sort of torn between 'this is really important, they should know,' and 'it's none of their business.' Then I go back to the whole 'if Simon was a woman' argument." Charlie turned to look at him. "It shouldn't be this complicated. If I wanted to show up with a robot and say we were in love, the only question anyone should ask is whether I've gotten around to installing extra power outlets in my house yet."

"Oh, Charlie." Simon sneaked a hand across the console and gripped Charlie's thigh. For his sanity and Charlie's, he ignored the *in love* comment.

"Phil's good with it," Charlie said. "We've talked. Jen . . . I dunno. She and Merry were pretty close. Phil's mom, though. I should probably prepare you for her."

"Why is that?"

A sudden flush swept across Charlie's face. It hadn't come from his neck this time; it had simply appeared out of nowhere. "I guess I didn't tell you Merry was Phil's sister."

He was meeting *family*? Simon cleared his throat. Panic swelled again. He swallowed it. They couldn't both start gripping steering wheels—the car only had one. "No, you didn't." Now that he had a full appreciation of what today was all about, the situation felt so typically Charlie. Forcing a smile—and resisting the urge to tug at his hair—he said, "You didn't plan out your first book, did you?"

"Huh?"

"You just wrote it, with no thought to the ending."

"Basically."

"So let's get out there and see what happens."

"Why aren't you panicking?" Charlie asked.

"I am, on the inside."

Phil appeared at the top of the driveway, stepping out of the shadow of the front porch. He approached the car slowly, his smile as cautious as his gait; tapped on the window; and wrapped his arms around himself. He wasn't wearing a jacket, and the air had a brittle quality to it.

Charlie pushed the door open, gently nudging Phil a few steps back.

Phil put a hand on top of the door, sending a quick smile in Simon's direction before looking down at Charlie. "What's up?"

"I'm reevaluating all of my life choices up to this point," Charlie said.

Phil glanced over at Simon. "Don't take offense. He does this now and again."

Simon gave what he hoped wasn't too tight a smile in answer.

Turning back to Charlie, who was gripping the wheel again, Phil said nothing for a full cycle of cooling engine ticks and ambient neighborhood sounds. Then, "I've got your back, Charlie. Like always."

Charlie nodded, gaze fixed on something no one else could see. Then he let go of the wheel. "Okay."

Not exactly a war cry, but enough to get them both out of the car.

Phil waited at the bottom of the driveway for Simon to walk up before sticking out a hand. "It's good to finally meet you. This one—" he tipped his head toward Charlie, now standing beside him holding a dish of potato casserole he'd retrieved from the back seat "—has told me a lot about you. You've probably already figured out he talks a lot, but not usually about the same thing. So I'd take it as a compliment."

Phil's grip was firm and friendly. His smile much the same. Simon felt safe in his presence, and it became clear why he was so important to Charlie. Why they were best friends.

Beneath the bright smiles and endless conversation, Charlie had a few more worries than the rest of them. He'd lost someone he loved, and he was raising a daughter on his own. Yet still he flew at life with apparent fearlessness, only taking a pause after he'd already put one foot out over the edge of a cliff. Phil was the man who either hauled him back to land, or jumped beside him.

Unreasonable jealousy needled him as Simon understood something else: he wanted to take Phil's place. He couldn't. He shouldn't. But he did want to find his own niche in Charlie's life.

Be the one to hold him back on occasion, or hold his hand when taking the plunge proved the better option. Drop beside him into the thrill of the unknown.

Live. Truly and fearlessly.

Phil smiled again. "Let's head on in."

"We'll be there in a sec," Charlie said, his voice a little rough around the edges. With a slight nod, Phil walked back up the driveway. Charlie turned to Simon. "I'm sorry."

"For what?"

"For choking on the doorstep."

"Do you want to leave?" Disappointment threaded through Simon. Now that he'd decided to take this plunge with Charlie, the idea they might not left him feeling like an underinflated balloon.

Charlie shook his head. "Hell no. I'd never hear the end of it from Phil, and I am not doing that to you."

"This isn't about me, Charlie."

"For me it is. It's all about you, Simon. Today, and these past couple of months." He lifted his chin. "I'm going to apologize now for—"

Simon leaned over the casserole dish and kissed him. It could have been a mistake. Kissing a man coming to terms with himself—in public—probably wasn't well-advised, so he kept it brief but firm. When he drew back, Charlie was smiling.

"Thanks," he said. "I needed that."

"Now let's get inside before we freeze to death."

Phil's house was much larger than it appeared from the outside. From the varying widths of the doorways leading away from the spacious foyer, it had obviously been added to over the years, turning it into a maze of hallways and rooms. The most obvious destination was immediately to their right—a large gathering of people sitting on and around a pair of sofas. The noise level was comfortable, and the room looked warm and inviting. Simon guessed it was the living room and questioned Charlie's suggestion to avoid it. Surely they could get lost in there somewhere?

A woman approached from the opposite direction, and Charlie turned to greet her, lifting his casserole. "Hey, Jen. I've got scalloped potatoes and Simon."

"And one looks much tastier than the other!" Jen said before clapping a hand over her mouth. "Oh my God. Simon, I'm so sorry. I practiced for this and promised myself I wouldn't say anything weird, then I just did."

Simon had to laugh—there was no other response. "It's okay. I've known Charlie long enough to expect weird."

"Not sure if that's good or bad, but thank you for saying it." Jen hugged Charlie around his dish and kissed his cheek, then offered Simon a warm and happy handshake, emphasis on the happy as she pumped his hand up and down. "It really is lovely to meet you."

"Stop mauling his hand," Charlie said.

Chuckling, Jen let Simon go and tugged the casserole away from Charlie. "C'mon, let's hide out in the kitchen for a while. We can pretend we're cooking stuff that's already cooked."

The kitchen smelled amazing. The whole house smelled good, as any house with a turkey in the oven should, but the kitchen held a variety of other tantalizing odors. The sharp tang of homemade cranberry sauce, the warmer scent of baked pies: cinnamon, nutmeg, and sugar. Instantly, Simon felt at ease, or did until Charlie asked a cryptic question.

"Where is she?"

"In the playroom with the kids," Jen said.

"Who is in the playroom?" Simon asked.

"Our mother-in-law." Jen put Charlie's dish on the counter next to a double oven arrangement that made sense for such a big kitchen and family, then wrapped an arm around Charlie's shoulder. "I've always loved Charlie, but having an enemy in common is terrifically bonding."

"She's not that bad." Charlie wore the expression of an eight-year old who'd told a lie. Disentangling himself from Jen's embrace, he opened the fridge and extracted three bottles of beer. He twisted the cap off one and handed it to Simon. He handed the second to Jen.

The third, he raised in a toast. "To robots."

The beer was cold and refreshing, the company warm and convivial. Simon began to relax. People wandered in and out of the kitchen—guests arriving bearing dishes or looking for something to eat before dinner. Charlie introduced him to everyone as "Simon," no qualifier, and Simon found he liked that. There was no expectation if he was just "Simon." For her part, Jen was the perfect hostess. She made him feel as if he and Charlie had been together forever—and not once did she tell him she had a gay cousin or uncle or friend.

Then Olivia arrived, Rosalie in tow.

They both gifted Charlie and Jen with hugs, and then it was Simon's turn. He was startled when Rosalie squeezed him around the waist. Olivia's hug was swift and sweet.

"I'm so glad you came!" she said.

Simon almost pointed to his chest as though to ask, *Me?*

"Did you girls get any sleep last night?" Charlie was frowning at his daughter.

"A little," Liv said. "But we still have the whole weekend to catch up."

"You look really tired, Liv. Can't this mural planning wait until after the holiday?"

"I'm fine, Dad. Don't worry."

Beside her, Rosalie was glancing back and forth between Simon and Charlie. "Gah, you and Charlie are sooo cute together!"

"Rosie!" Liv elbowed her friend. "You're embarrassing them."

Simon tried unsuccessfully not to blush. Charlie wrapped a hand around the back of his neck, indicating he fought the same battle. Their eyes met, and they exchanged a secret smile that, while small, was suddenly everything. Charlie's expression was far from embarrassed. Instead, he seemed pleased and happy.

Simon was therefore also pleased and happy.

Or he was until a cool, stern voice spoke from the other side of the kitchen.

"There you are."

CHAPTER 31

Charlie tried not to wince and knew, instantly, that he'd been unsuccessful.

How could he have imagined his mother-in-law might stay on the other side of the house, surrounded by grandchildren? Because denial was an art he'd mastered about eighteen years ago.

"Beatrice, I'd like you to meet—"

"I know exactly who he is. How *could* you?"

"What?"

"You know what I mean." Beatrice folded her arms, and the worst of it was that he could see Merry in the pose, except that Merry had never hated him for getting her pregnant and ruining her "prospects." Or if she had, she'd never said.

Nope, not going to do this now. "Do we have to do this today? We're supposed to be relaxing and having a good time."

Phil chose that moment to enter the kitchen. "Mom, Jake and Kara are here—"

"Not now, Philip."

"If now stops you from harassing Charlie, then, yes. Now."

She turned to him, lip curling. Who looked at their son like that? "Did you know he would be bringing his . . ." She untucked a hand so she could flick her fingers in Simon's direction.

"Boyfriend?" Phil's voice had a slight edge to it. "Yes, I did."

Charlie glanced at Simon to see if he was getting ready to bolt. Glancing up from studying the label on his beer bottle, Simon lifted an eyebrow. Charlie shook his head, not entirely sure what he meant, but relieved when Simon didn't interpret the gesture as *go*.

"And you didn't think to let me know? I had to hear this from my grandchildren! From the mouths of babes!" Beatrice drew in a trembling breath. "He ruined Merry's life now he aims to do the same to Olivia."

Liv gasped. Rosalie's eyes rounded impossibly. Cousins began to gather in doorways.

Charlie ground his teeth together until the urge to swear turned to dust. "How is me being in a relationship ruining Olivia's life?"

"What you write in those books of yours is bad enough! But to expose Olivia to—"

"That's enough!" Phil waved his arms like a fire marshal. "This is my house, and Charlie and Simon are my guests."

Beatrice's attitude was already upsetting. Watching Phil defend him? That sliced right through Charlie's torso. Not that Phil had felt the need to step up, but that he always did and always would. Even after all of it.

Putting his beer bottle on the counter, Charlie backed toward Simon. "Listen, Phil, we can just go. I don't want to spoil the day."

"It's a little late for that, isn't it?" Beatrice hissed.

"No, it's not." Liv put her hands on her hips. "Simon is the best thing to happen to my dad in the last five years. If you can't handle that, then maybe you're the one who should leave."

"Liv!" Charlie choked out.

"Well, I never!" Beatrice clutched her chest.

Jen and Phil's younger kids pressed into the kitchen then, bringing with them shrill questions and requests for food.

Feeling as though his legs might give up on him at any moment, Charlie groped for Simon's hand. He didn't complicate the gesture with thought. It could have been a need for support or a show of defiance or simply a primal reaction to being hunted by a dozen stares. "Thanks for the beer, Jen. You can keep the casserole."

"What?" Jen said. "You're not leaving."

"Dad, no!" Color flushed Liv's cheeks.

"Damn straight," Phil put in.

"Oh, let him go. We certainly don't need any more drama."

"Mom!" Phil snapped.

"No. This isn't happening. Dad is staying." Liv reached for him... and missed. Her hand dropped about six inches short of Charlie's arm. He couldn't figure out what was going on until Rosalie shrieked. Then Liv was crumpled at his feet.

His knees hit the ground beside her before he made the conscious decision to move. "Liv?" He touched her pale face, which felt cool and clammy, then grasped her hands. "Liv!"

Jen appeared next to him. "Phil? Get a damp cloth."

Liv's eyes fluttered open. "Wha—"

"Liv. Oh my God, are you okay?"

"Dad?" She turned her head. "Why am I on the floor?"

Charlie looked helplessly at Jen.

"I think you fainted, sweetheart," Jen said. "Did you two eat breakfast this morning?"

Charlie got his arms beneath his daughter. He tried to lift her up and quickly realized that standing from a kneel wasn't going to happen. He got one leg unfolded, and then Simon and Phil were pushing in on the other side, one with the requested damp cloth, the other tucking a hand under Liv's shoulder.

"Let's get to a couch where you can put your feet up," Charlie said. "Can you walk?"

Jen stood with them, pressing the cloth to Liv's forehead. "Rosie, can you grab a bottle of water from the fridge? And tell me about breakfast."

"Well, if this is the best—" Beatrice began.

Jen and Phil turned in unison. "Not now!"

Charlie followed Jen to the small sunroom off the dining room and encouraged Liv to sit on the wicker couch before pulling her feet off the floor so she'd turn and lie down.

"I'm fine, Dad."

"Just lie down for a minute, okay?"

Sighing dramatically, she pressed the cloth to her forehead and allowed herself to be arranged to Charlie's satisfaction. The pressure against his own head and throat was so great, Charlie turned to ask if they could have some room, only to find it was just them, Jen, Phil, Rosalie, and Simon.

"Apparently she didn't eat this morning." Jen sat at the end of the couch by Liv's feet. "Her blood sugar probably dropped. Used to happen to me all the time at her age. She's well otherwise, isn't she?"

"Yes." The word tasted oddly like a lie, though. Every time he blinked, Charlie traveled back in time. He pictured Liv after Merry's death. The pale ghost she'd become. How he'd worried he might lose her too, and how hard it had been to make himself present enough to be her anchor. He saw her over the past year, how she'd stopped smiling. The serious little frown line between her eyebrows. More recently, her skin winter-bleached before winter had even arrived. Her moods. The thing with The Boy.

He clutched at Liv's cool and clammy hands. "You'd tell me if something was wrong, wouldn't you?"

Liv chewed on bloodless lips. "I—"

"She just needs some food." Rosie jumped up. "I'll go fix her a plate."

Charlie grabbed on to Simon's hand for support as he pulled himself up. Then he stood for a second, waiting for his blood to stop rushing and tingling around, and thinking about the warm space Simon would make for him against his chest if he asked. A hug would feel pretty good right about now.

Except that now wasn't the time to demonstrate what a shitty parent he was. "Where'd you park your car?" he asked Liv.

"Why?"

"Because I want to make sure you're not blocking anyone until I can come back and get it."

"What? No, I don't want to go home. I'm fine, Dad."

"You're not fine. I'm taking you home."

Obviously sensing Charlie's mind was made up, Olivia turned an appeal toward Jen. "I'm fine, really. It's not a big deal."

"I've got some popsicles in the freezer. Want to try one of those? The sugar might do you good."

Liv glanced up at Charlie. "I'll eat a popsicle, okay? I just need some sugar."

Charlie glanced at Jen, hoping her expression would give him the answer he needed. Had he been home, he'd have been silently ranting at Merry right now, all the while acknowledging that as much as he missed having a partner when it came to discipline, he hadn't had one for long before she'd died. Merry had been too sick.

That was what frightened him now. Olivia pale and flushed at the same time. Laid out on the couch, just as Merry had been those past few Thanksgivings.

Jen gave him a small nod.

"Okay." He couldn't say more. His throat was too tight. Backing away, Charlie ducked down the hall to the kitchen, passing Rosalie with the promised plate. "Hold up," he called. He grabbed a popsicle from the freezer and handed that over as well. "Make sure she eats, okay?"

Rosalie gave a quick nod and hurried off.

Charlie turned back to the kitchen and went looking for his abandoned beer. When he couldn't find it, he pulled another two bottles from the fridge.

"One of those for me?"

Charlie glanced up at Simon, startled. Then he held out the other bottle. "Sure."

Simon took it and twisted the cap off. It was weird watching him put the neck of the bottle to his lips. He should be drinking from a glass. Or not drinking beer at all. Simon was a fancy-scotch kind of man. Or maybe a wine drinker. Would he prefer cider?

"What can I do?" Simon asked.

"About what?"

"You're obviously not okay, so tell me what I can do. Should I go? Should I carry Liv to your car for you so we can all leave? Should I grab a six-pack from the fridge and set you up with a bottle opener and a bucket?"

"I'm not going to get drunk."

"You look like you want to."

"It's been a pretty shitty afternoon so far."

Simon didn't smile, but his expression softened as if he might. "From where I'm standing, it hasn't been too bad."

"Really? My mother-in-law has gone from hating me to wishing I'd never been born— No, you know what? She already wished that. Now she's probably figuring out ways for me to have an accident. And Liv is being Liv."

"Sounds like a normal day to me."

Charlie opened his mouth to say . . . well, he didn't know. Might never know, because suddenly he was laughing. Only he felt more like crying. He put the back of his hand to his mouth to squash his chuckles. "Fuck, if anyone looks over now, they're going to think I'm insane."

Simon glanced behind them, then rubbed the back of Charlie's shoulder. "No more than the rest of us."

"How can you be so calm?"

"Oh, Charlie." Normally when Simon said his name that way, it was like a sympathetic sigh tinged with amusement. This time, Simon simply sounded sad. "I'm forty-six years old. I've met my share of disapproving parents and shitty parents. Your mother-in-law has nothing on my family. And you? You're a good father."

"You're forty-six?"

"That's what you took from that?"

"You don't look it, that's all. I mean, you've got the whole mature, I've-totally-got-my-life-together thing going, but I never guessed you were ten years older than me." And it didn't matter, really. Charlie's brain simply wanted something to rest against for a while. A pocket of shade on an otherwise too bright day.

Charlie pointed his bottle toward the stools lined up on the other side of the kitchen island. "Let's sit a bit, yeah?" He inspected the platters of munchies laid out across the counter. "Maybe grab a snack in case we have to leave in a hurry. Then I can at least say I fed you on Thanksgiving."

"Dinner after the show?"

Charlie scoffed. "Just going to make sure Liv is eating her popsicle. I'll be right back."

CHAPTER 32

Simon set one hip against the tall stool and gripped the counter as it tried to slide out from beneath him. So not cool or together or however Charlie might imagine forty-six to be. Simon steadied the stool and sat on it, then took a moment to just breathe. To collect his thoughts and prepare for whatever else the afternoon and evening might toss his way.

A shuffle and hiss pulled his attention to a door on the other side of the kitchen. When he glanced over, two heads withdrew to the sound of retreating giggles.

Charlie returned to the kitchen and grabbed another couple of bottles from the fridge before levering himself onto one of the stools.

"I think we're being spied on by children," Simon said.

Charlie checked the other doorway. "Looks like they've got all they need for now. They'll reconvene for gossip in one of the bedrooms."

"Nice."

Charlie shrugged. "As you're apparently used to disapproving parents, I'm used to being the subject of gossip. Shotgun wedding, sick wife, and single dad. Now I've added *hot new boyfriend* to the list. Oh, and *lets his daughter faint on Thanksgiving*." He took a swig of his beer, nearly emptying the first bottle. "And doesn't know how to make her listen."

"And drinks himself into a stupor in the kitchen?"

"It'd take more than light beer to get that far. Phil buys crap beer."

"What are we doing here?"

Charlie glanced over at him. "I needed a moment, and you're like . . . my space of calm. If that's okay."

Simon nodded. Sipped his crap beer.

"You're only nine years older than me, by the way," Charlie pointed out.

"Good to know."

"I don't have a problem with it. You could be fifty, and I'd still think you were..." Charlie sighed softly. "Did you ever want kids?"

Simon considered the subject change for a couple of seconds before answering, "I never stopped to think about it."

"Really?"

He shrugged. "I suppose there might have been an idle thought here and there, when I was feeling settled. But then Brian would do his thing and I'd spend the next few months figuring out if he really was sorry and if I was being an idiot for believing him, and then I was mostly busy believing I was happy."

Charlie offered him a sympathetic look before asking, "What makes you think I'm a good father?"

"You care and Liv knows you care. She knows your days begin and end with her."

Charlie rocked back a little, apparently surprised. "Did I tell you that?"

"Anyone can see it. That's probably what annoys your mother-in-law so much. The fact that you're obviously doing a good job."

"Are you still in touch with your parents?"

"No."

"Are they..."

"They're alive and well in New Jersey. Well, I assume they are. I haven't spoken to them in over twenty-five years."

"Wow. I'm sorry."

"Don't be. It all happened a long time ago." He knew he sounded far calmer than the situation might warrant for some. But it *had* been a long time ago. Learning to let go of certain expectations had been one of his earliest lessons in accepting the fact he was gay, and it had been surprisingly easy. He'd only really missed his family until he'd realized he wouldn't have to sit through another Thanksgiving and lie about who he was dating and about what he wanted to do with his life. He didn't want to be a doctor, and he didn't want to marry a woman. "I'm one of six, and I honestly wonder if they even noticed the empty spot at the table one night. Knowing my mother, she probably didn't even set out a place."

"Did they kick you out?"

"I left before they could."

"How old were you?"

"Nineteen, and already a disappointment because I'd won a scholarship to study architecture, which my father just didn't get. Apparently designing houses or buildings isn't a real career." Simon picked at the label on his beer bottle and wondered, idly, where the bottles they'd been drinking before had ended up. He glanced over at Charlie. "So I figured I might as well seal the deal by telling him I was gay as well."

"Ouch."

"Then I went upstairs, packed my bags, and left."

"You were okay?"

Simon found a smile for the earnest expression on Charlie's face. "Yes, I was okay. I had a place to live on campus, I got a part-time job to supplement my scholarship, and I lived out loud for the first time in my life. Made some good friends, got myself a boyfriend, then another one. Got my degree and kept on living."

"Okay, so in maturity, you're actually like thirty years older than me."

"I doubt it."

"There were times when I figured I'd get kicked out, even before the business with Merry. I did some stupid things. Then I had to tell my dad I'd gotten a girl pregnant. I could tell he didn't want to believe me at first. Then he just shook his head, like he could tick another box on the list of stupid that Charlie would do before he died. I think my mom cried for a week. But then they stepped up, you know?" Charlie looked off into the distance. "If I'm a good dad, it's because of them. I couldn't have done any of it without them. We lived with my folks for about two years after Liv was born, then moved back in with them when Merry got sick again."

"Again?"

Darkness rippled across Charlie's features. "It was the pregnancy that did it. She developed choriocarcinoma. It's a pretty rare cancer.

That's why we only have one kid, even though they were able to treat her the first time. It just felt like too much risk."

Right there was the source of all of Charlie's pain. Simon could see it. The wound was so deep, it might never heal. His heart ached at the thought and the realization there was nothing he could do.

"Then when Liv was nine, it came back. In her liver. She never did well with the drugs and therapy, even the first time. They made her so weak and sick. So we moved back in with my folks, and they helped me keep it together. Especially after she died. If anything, they're the reason Liv turned out okay."

"You should give them a call."

"Tell them how they're been gone less than a year and I'm fucking it all up?"

"No. Call them because you can, Charlie," Simon said.

Phil stepped into the kitchen, his forehead wrinkled into a serious frown. Simon didn't know whether to duck for cover or leap to Charlie's defense. He stood in preparation for either.

"Hey, listen, Liv isn't doing too great," Phil said.

Charlie stood so fast he spilled his beer. "What happened?"

"Apparently the popsicle didn't agree with her. According to Rosie, she fainted in the bathroom and knocked her head pretty good on the side of the tub."

Charlie swayed. Phil caught one arm, Simon the other. A second later, Charlie had shaken them off to run out of the kitchen.

"This way," Phil said, grabbing Charlie's arm and redirecting him to the other hallway. The house was a complete warren.

"What can I do?" Simon asked, knowing now was not the time to get in the way.

"I'm going to drive them to emergency. Can you take Rosie home and then drop Liv's car back at Charlie's place?"

He'd rather go to the hospital, but sensed Charlie would need Phil more right now. In this, Phil had seniority.

Simon nodded. "Consider it done. Charlie has my number if you guys need anything." He'd even offer to run interference with Beatrice Kinney, though his preference would be to support Charlie directly. Thankfully, Phil's mother didn't pass the kitchen on her way to the commotion brewing on the other side of the house.

Simon retreated to the now-empty living room to wait until Rosie was ready to go. It was a while before she appeared, and he spent the time pondering the difference between the emptiness of this one, large room and the quiet solitude he'd spent the past twenty-seven years telling himself he was okay with.

CHAPTER 33

Liv complained the entire way to the hospital, her main argument being the fact she was lucid enough to complain, which seemed rather circular to Charlie. He responded with silence. He might be a shit parent, but he'd learned how to deal with a whining child. He could barely hear her anyway. The voices of recrimination and panic were having a loud argument inside his head. A quieter voice chimed in when the others took a breath, but seeing as its argument was the same as Liv's—she was walking (sitting, presently) and talking (whining) and obviously not dying right at this moment—he ignored it.

Thank God he wasn't driving.

Phil dropped them off at the emergency entrance. "I'll park and come back in."

"You don't have to wait; we could be a while." Charlie checked the time on his phone. Already the day seemed ageless. "I can call you later, or we can just cab it home."

Phil shook his head. "I'll come in for a bit, see what's what."

The noise inside the hospital competed with Charlie's slowly slipping sanity. Thankfully, the lump in the center of Liv's forehead convinced the desk staff she should be seen fairly quickly—lucidity notwithstanding.

She objected to the wheelchair. "I'm fine, really." In the unforgiving light of the hospital, she did not look fine, though. Her skin was so pale that she might have been living underground, and her hands were shaking.

"Liv, be reasonable. You've got a lump the size of Mars on your head and you've been pale for days."

"I don't want you in there with me."

The nurse gave Charlie a sympathetic smile. "We'll just be checking her reflexes first, getting a general history, while we wait for a spot to open up in one of the X-ray suites." Her reasonable tone was about as practiced as Olivia's whine. "There are some chairs in the hall outside both areas if you'd like to wait."

"I can help with the general history," Charlie insisted.

Liv moved in front of the wheelchair and sat heavily, as though her legs had only just gotten her that far. "I'll sit, okay?"

Charlie looked from her to the chairs in the hall and back again, aware he was holding up proceedings. "Fine."

He stalked toward the chairs and sat so hard the plastic creaked.

Phil found him a few minutes later. "What's the word?"

"Olivia is the most stubborn child ever born."

"So far, so good, then."

Phil creaked down next to him, and they spent the next five minutes in what might be a companionable silence—discounting the constant fuzz of noise in the ER, and the fact that Charlie wasn't feeling all that companionable. He had too many memories of sitting in hospital corridors waiting for tests, and many of them included a solid and quiet Phil sitting to his left, just as he was now. It should be a comfort, having him there. Instead, his bulk served more as a reminder.

Charlie got up to pace, and Phil caught him on the first loop back. He stood, put a hand on each of Charlie's shoulders, and pulled him to a halt. "Whatever it is, we'll figure it out, okay?"

The words Charlie had been trying not to say seared a path up the back of his throat. "What if it's cancer? That's not something we can figure out."

"Liv has been healthy her whole life. Cancer doesn't just happen."

"Yeah, it does. All the time."

"Fuck, Charlie. Let's think positive here. Jen said she used to faint when she was a teenager. Not eating properly and all that? And didn't Liv break up with her boyfriend? So she's probably been feeling off for a while. You know how it is."

"No, I don't, because I never broke up with anyone." He'd never had a chance, because Merry had gotten pregnant and then died.

Feeling bitter and small, Charlie twisted out of Phil's grip and paced the corridor again. He'd gotten to his turning point when another pair of arms came out of nowhere to wrap him up. The familiar scent of wet clay and patchouli enveloped him.

"How are you doing?" Cassie asked.

"What are you doing here?"

"Simon told me what was happening. I saw him dropping off Olivia's car. Why didn't you call?"

"Did he come with you?"

Cassie shook her head, and a mixture of relief and sorrow wound through Charlie. Combined with all the other emotions swirling around inside him, his psyche was starting to resemble a cheap breakfast buffet.

He wriggled free of Cassie's grasp and continued pacing. Cassie's and Phil's voices in quiet conversation marked the end of every loop. Vaguely, he wondered what they were talking about. Him, he supposed. Probably not his failures—more like what they'd do with him once Liv had been checked out.

Speaking of which, where were all the nurses?

Before he could pester the desk staff, Liv came around the corner, followed by a nurse with an encouraging smile. "So far everything looks good, Mr. King. We're waiting on a couple of blood tests."

"The X-ray?"

"We're holding off on that, pending the results of the blood tests." Was that usual? "If we had any serious concerns, we'd be looking for a bed for the night. Might just be a bump on the head."

The nurse retreated, leaving Liv, who was looking limp and lackluster.

"How're you feeling?" Charlie asked.

"I'm fine. Bringing me here was a waste of time." She slumped into one of the plastic waiting-area chairs.

"Olivia!" Cassie chastised. "If your father had an egg on his head like that, you'd want him to get checked out, wouldn't you?"

Liv hesitated, and Charlie imagined her weighing the pros and cons of letting him slip into a coma from which he might never awaken. Then she shrugged. "I suppose. I'm just tired. It's been a kind of stressful day."

No kidding.

Another nurse arrived in the hallway, scanning the collected faces. When she saw Olivia, she came over. "Can I have a moment alone with Miss King, please?"

Charlie's heart punched forward, nearly tipping him toward the floor. "What is it?"

"I believe it will be up to Miss King to share the results."

Results?

Phil was standing now too, and the nurse seemed a little cowed with three adults looming toward her, even though Cassie's presence added more width than height.

Charlie moved toward Olivia, but Cassie caught him by the arm. "Give her a minute, Charlie."

He glanced down at her. "Why? If she's sick, I've got a right to know."

Cassie shook his head. "Trust me on this one, okay?"

What did she mean?

Phil was darting quizzical looks back and forth, but Charlie allowed Cassie to lead him to the other side of the waiting area.

When Liv burst into tears, Charlie pulled away from Cassie and skidded to a halt in front of her chair, dropping to his knees to take his daughter's hands. "What is it? Liv, please. Tell me what they said."

"Oh, Dad..."

"What?" The word echoed over and over in his head, squashing and stretching toward eternity.

Liv fell forward into him, her cheek wet against his. She sobbed and shook. "I'm sorry. Dad, I'm so sorry."

It could only be the worst news. The absolute worst. Charlie felt the world opening up to swallow them. Then Liv said something and the hole beneath him shut with a clang. The single word in his head fell over, and a new phrase danced around his brain, bright like a Fourth of July sparkler and just as deceptive.

Another echo, one that threw him back eighteen years.

"I'm pregnant."

"How?"

It was the most basic question with the most obvious answer, but it had bounced between Charlie's ears the entire way home. Thank fuck Phil had been driving. Charlie couldn't have operated a car. Here, standing in his kitchen, surrounded by people—Phil, Jen, Cassie, Olivia—he could barely remember how his hands worked. He had a glass in one and a bottle of water in the other. Had he been trying to get a drink?

He put both down on the counter and asked again. "How?"

Liv adjusted the bag of frozen peas clutched to her forehead. Her expression suggested she was considering a flippant response. Then she simply started crying again. More like leaking. She'd been a sniveling, wet mess since the hospital.

Charlie ached to hold her, but his parental duty came first. He had to establish the how and the why before he worked out what to do next. Could you punish a child for getting pregnant? Seemed like something beyond a grounding offense.

And Liv wasn't really a child anymore.

One of those stupid home movies played through his head, a grainy film reel of this exact conversation. Had his parents yelled or gone silent? Probably both. His mother was the yeller. His dad the strong, silent type. He could remember Merry's mother screeching. Cursing him from sunup to sundown. *"You've ruined her! Ruined her!"*

Charlie rubbed his forehead. "I'm trying to understand how this happened."

"We were careful. Always. But one time the condom just kind of got lost." Liv's lips trembled. "I guess it broke? I dunno. It wasn't there that one time." And she was crying again.

Jen put a hand to Liv's shoulder. "Liv, honey, they have pills for when that happens. But we're going to figure it out, okay?"

"What's to figure! I slept with my boyfriend and the worst thing ever happened," Liv said. She might have taken the words right out of Charlie's mouth. "Now I'm going to have a baby, and all you all want to know is how it happened. I had sex, okay! I had sex."

Charlie pushed through the kitchen door and out into the yard. Phil followed him and then stood back as Charlie took out his frustration on the half-constructed chicken coop, kicking it until his toes hurt, then picking up one corner and tossing it against the wall of the house. The frame split in half, the *crack* almost satisfying.

"Feel better?" Phil asked.

"No." His immediate anger had faded, but he still felt drained and confused and completely unprepared for the curveball life had just tossed across the field.

"Charlie—"

"Where did I go wrong?"

"You didn't. These things happen."

"No, they don't. It's because I'm such a fuckup, isn't it?"

Phil shook his head.

"Your mother is going to kill me," Charlie said. "She's going to hire a steamroller and squash me flat in my own driveway."

"That's—"

"My little girl had sex, Phil. I feel so stupid for not realizing that's what was going on. Not that I could have done anything. I know she's not seven. But . . . God, she's going to be a mother at eighteen, and by the time she gets to actually do anything other than raise a kid, she's going to be so fucking tired and completely out of touch with how the world works. And too old to make a proper go of shit."

"Are you talking about yourself or her?"

Charlie stumbled back a step and shook his head. He opened his mouth to say *Of course I'm talking about Liv*, then closed his lips tightly over what would be at least half a lie. Frustration returning, he balled his fists and changed course. "What if she gets the same cancer Merry did?"

"Highly unlikely."

"So was getting pregnant."

Phil heaved a sigh. "Not really."

Charlie sucked in a sharp breath.

Phil shrugged. "Look, it's not like she did it on purpose, and this doesn't need to be the worst thing in the world. It happens. Yeah, it's kind of a coincidence that it happened with you and Merry and it happened with your daughter. But the how and the why? No surprise at all. Liv was in love. Just like you and Merry. You saw it. I saw it. And, hell, we both know what being seventeen is like."

"How am I going to do this again?" As he said the words, Charlie again felt the slap of Phil's previous comment: *"Are you talking about yourself or her?"* He had to focus on Liv here. On being a better fucking parent and giving her the support she needed. Scrubbing his hands over his face, he said, "I'm so unprepared for this. I'm not the calm and rational one. That was Merry's job. How am I going to do this without her?"

"Same way you do everything else." Phil gripped his shoulder. "It's going to be okay."

But Charlie was shaking his head. "Doesn't feel like it."

"C'mon. Let's head back inside. Catching our death isn't going to help anyone."

With a weary sigh, Charlie pushed back through the kitchen door. Jen, Liv, and Cassie looked up, the three of them wearing cautious expressions. Was he really that frightening?

"Did you know you were pregnant? Before today?" Charlie asked.

"I . . ." Liv hiccupped. "I suspected."

"Does Justin know?"

Liv shook her head. "No."

"Then why did you break up with him?"

"Because the condom broke and I got scared."

"I don't understand."

"I knew you'd be upset if I made a mistake, any mistake, and it didn't matter because it happened anyway."

The entire planet hit him square in the face. "Wait. What?" Silence rang through the kitchen, followed by the echo of his voice, the *crack* of timber, the icemaker dumping a load into the bin. At a distance he couldn't reach, he recognized the fact his fears had become Liv's, and that that wasn't right. But he couldn't get close enough to rational thought to work it out right then. Instead, he could only grit his teeth and ball his fists.

Before he could explode, Phil had him wrapped up in a stifling embrace. Charlie twisted once, figured out he wasn't going to break Phil's hold without injuring them both, and leaned into his friend instead.

The rest of the evening blew away on a storm of emotion. Charlie managed another rant, and Liv cried enough to fill the pond out back.

Jen and Cassie and Phil picked up sodden tissues, rinsed out glasses and mugs, and generally stood on alert until Charlie couldn't do much more than slump into one corner of the couch. Liv was upstairs, presumably in bed. Even if she was packing a suitcase and plotting a midnight escape, Charlie wouldn't blame her. On the one hand, she might be better off without him. On the other, his life might be less stressful without her.

When he contemplated those hands, though—thoughts bouncing back and forth between them—he decided that both of those eventualities rested in the same palm like a hot and burning ember that he was too afraid to grip. Liv would always be a part of him. She'd always be his daughter. The other hand, the empty one... Well, it was empty. Because he didn't know what to think and feel. He'd moved beyond anger and into sadness.

That hand was grief—for all he'd wanted, for all he'd lost. For the bright young spark he'd been at eighteen, for the wife he'd loved. For his baby girl, who'd been a bright spark on her own.

For the fact he'd never really considered his life with Merry and Liv a sacrifice.

But now he was alone, and while it had been five years, tonight his grief felt as big and insurmountable as it had in those first weeks. And, not for the first time, he wondered if he had the strength to get past it.

CHAPTER 34

When Charlie's driveway filled with cars on Thursday evening, Simon knew well enough to stay away, despite the fact that none of his text messages had been answered. He could hear the yelling from his side of the hedge. Hopefully, yelling meant Liv was well enough to participate in whatever it was stirring the hive of family and friends gathered next door. He sent a final text of support, not expecting a response—and felt unreasonably hurt when he didn't get one.

Friday inched past at the pace of a blue whale's heartbeat. Charlie still wasn't taking calls or answering texts. Simon could quite easily imagine his phone lying in a crushed pile of metal and glass somewhere, but preferred to believe Charlie was just too involved with Olivia to even respond with a simple text. Being excluded stung. The worst part, though, beyond his worry over Olivia's health, was the ache behind his sternum.

He didn't know if it was still unreasonable.

For a while, he buried himself in work. He'd set his drafting table in the best possible position to take advantage of natural light, and November continued to surprise him with sunshine. Working there was nice—until it wasn't. Until he remembered he was working at home because it was a long weekend, and that he'd expected to wake up beside Charlie this morning and perhaps spend the day being lazy and cozy and *with* someone.

The ache returned with a vengeful pulse. Berating himself for being selfish, Simon massaged his chest. Next door, Charlie was dealing with Lord knew what, and here he was feeling dejected.

When he thought back over their conversation the previous Friday, however, the pulse became a stab. Something sharper.

Charlie had wanted to know if they were thinking and moving in the same direction. Hadn't they established that they both wanted more? The *boyfriend* word had been tested and tossed around. Charlie had taken him to meet his friends and family.

And now Simon sat alone.

"This isn't how it's supposed to work."

Simon put his pen down and pushed back from the table. His lower back was stiff from sitting for so long, proving he'd lost time, productively or otherwise. Pacing his studio soothed that ache, but not the insistent combination of stabs in the chest—the feeling that climbed toward a climactic peak as he followed his determined feet through the house, out the door, and toward the gate in the hedge.

Sometime over the past couple of hours, clouds had blanketed the sun. The air smelled like snow. Simon patted his pocket, checking for his phone. Should he text before he knocked on Charlie's door? He fumbled with the screen, pulling up his list of recent calls and thumbed Frank's name by mistake. He cut the connection before Frank answered and shoved the phone back into his pocket. Charlie wouldn't answer anyway. Taking a deep breath, he pushed through the gate and approached the kitchen door.

The lovely old house stood quiet and almost sad, the gray of the siding and chimney solemn in their silence. Herbert was missing from his usual spot, his stack of plastic chairs neglected. Next to his pad, the chicken hutch, or whatever Charlie had been building, lay in a pile of oversized splinters. At the sight of the destruction, Simon took a step back, surprised. A house like this should be surrounded by projects. It was a family home. But this... When had Charlie done this, and why hadn't Simon heard it happening?

What the hell was going on over here?

Simon had to knock twice before he heard footsteps. Liv answered the door, looking sylphlike—her hair a wild tangle, her eyes large against her pale skin. A bruise in the middle of her forehead. She had a blanket wrapped around her shoulders.

"Liv, are you okay?"

Shaking her head, she retreated into the kitchen and called for Charlie. Simon stepped into the kitchen after her, but she'd disappeared. Listening to the slow beat of Charlie's footsteps on the stairs, then in the hall, he actually considered leaving. Sneaking back next door.

Coward.

Charlie was as washed out as Liv, his perpetual tan sucked from his skin by tragedy. Hair sticking up, eyes heavily shadowed, cheeks almost hollow. He moved with a shoulder-slumped walk, as though struggling beneath a great, invisible weight.

Simon started forward. "Hey, how is everything?"

Charlie didn't answer, and Simon wasn't even sure he was all there. He seemed to be staring at nothing.

"I tried to call," Simon said. "I've left messages."

"Sorry."

A single word. He could work with that. "Okay. I just wanted to check you were all right. I was worried. Is— Can you . . .? What did the doctors say?"

Simon knew Charlie's greatest fear must be losing Liv to cancer, and while he waited for Charlie to find an answer to his question, he prayed. His parents' god thought he was irredeemable, but Simon had always wanted to believe there was another one out there, the one who was supposed to be all about love.

"She's pregnant," Charlie said.

His silent prayer cut off midsentence. "What?"

If possible, Charlie's shoulders seemed to dip lower. He was being crushed by something Simon couldn't see. But he could guess what it was.

"Charlie . . ."

"I can't." Charlie shook his head, backing away. "I need to deal with this, and that means this is all I can do right now. I can't be with you, Simon. We can't get involved. I'm sorry. I know . . ."

Over the roar of his blood, Simon wasn't sure if Charlie kept talking or not. All he could hear was: *"I can't be with you."* Rationality tried to raise a hand. Simon shook his head. He didn't want to hear what that little prick had to say. Courage poked him in the ribs, insisting he fight for what he wanted. Stop Charlie from leaving him on another empty doorstep.

He didn't want to hear from Courage, either. Or the voice suggesting Charlie didn't really know what he was saying. That he was hurt—hurting. That he had too much going on at the moment. That he needed time.

The voice he did hear was small. A whining echo. *"I can't be with you."*

Aware his head was bobbing nonsensically, Simon backed up until he nearly fell through the kitchen door. The gate hinges rang eerily. A cat darted out from beneath the hedge and disappeared behind a tree. Then he was inside his own house, not remembering having crossed his yard. And his phone was ringing.

Simon pulled it out, hoping it was Charlie calling to say he was sorry. Implore him to come back. Tell him he needed him.

It was Frank.

Simon raised the phone to his ear—if he hung up without saying anything, Frank would only call him back. "Sorry, I called by mistake."

"That's okay. I wanted to catch up with you anyway. How'd Thanksgiving go?"

Oh God.

"It didn't work out."

"I can't be with you."

"The dinner or Charlie?"

"Both. Frank, can I call you back later?"

"You don't sound good. What happened?"

Simon looked around his empty house, taking in the pale walls and quiet furniture. He'd known he wouldn't be here forever, but he'd tried to make it comfortable, peaceful. It was to have been his haven. Now, it seemed bare. Stark. Lacking in personality. He could hear his thoughts echoing from the uncluttered surfaces. He could hear Charlie.

He didn't want to hear Charlie.

"Simon?"

"You were right."

"About what?"

"Everything."

CHAPTER 35

Charlie stared after Simon, knowing he'd just done something terrible. His legs wouldn't move to follow, though, and his mouth remained resolutely shut, his lips glued together by the same force that kept his feet pinned to the floor. The great weight of responsibility. The voice that said he didn't have time to play. He was supposed to be an adult, a father.

"Dad?"

Liv hovered half in, half out of the kitchen, the shadows of the hall reaching out to swallow her. Her pinched expression felt like a razor blade to his heart.

"Did you break up with Simon?"

He shrugged and shook his head. He didn't know if he had or hadn't. He'd meant to ask for time, but he'd also meant to cut things off at the ankles—almost relishing the pain it would bring, because he'd needed to punish himself for all that had gone wrong over the past year. He'd missed so many deadlines, he might have killed his career, he'd let his daughter get pregnant, and he'd fallen in love.

"Dad?"

He opened his mouth and Liv flinched. Charlie rubbed the side of his face in an attempt to rearrange what might have been a snarl. Liv crept across the kitchen toward him—her posture anxious, but maybe she was also drawn to him by the same force that pulled his arms out and put them around her. He tugged his daughter in against his chest, hugging her tight.

"I don't want to yell anymore, Liv. I'm too tired."

She sniffled into his shoulder.

"I'm sorry, Duck," he croaked. "I'm so sorry."

"No, I am."

"We're going to figure this out."

"Not much to figure. It's done. I can't get un-pregnant."

Not a conversation he wanted to have with a seventeen-year-old. Another seventeen-year-old. He could hear his father's voice, as clear now as it had been then: *"Do not ask her if she wants to keep it. Ask her what she plans to do."* Charlie hadn't understood the distinction then, and he'd fumbled the words, drawing an expression of horror across Merry's face. Today, he wouldn't fumble.

Pulling out of the sticky embrace—when had they last done anything like have a shower, or just wash their faces?—Charlie pulled a sigh from his gut and pushed it out. As the breath left him, he actually felt a little better. Sort of.

"We need to eat and get clean and then talk. Did you get any sleep last night?"

Liv nodded.

Charlie turned her around and propelled her toward the hall. "Go have a bath while I fix us something to eat." He tried for a smile, almost wincing at the crackly feel of his skin. "No tuna, right?"

"And no cheese or lunch meat. Nothing hot or spicy."

Oh boy. "So soup is out?"

"Soup is cool."

Apparently eggs worked too, salad was a go, and she wanted fruit juice. She'd been craving fruit juice.

While Liv bathed, Charlie put together a buffet of snacks, then started a list.

OB/Gyn.

Vitamins.

School/college—future plans.

The Boy.

He was tempted to put Simon on the list, but figured he needed a second sheet, one he could title: *Shit Charlie needs to sort (for himself).* He had a damn book to revise and should have been securing at least one technical contract for January. Then there was his convention schedule for next summer, and...

Simon.

Charlie swallowed. His list would have to wait. For now, Liv had to come first. And the number-one item on the Liv List, not written down, was the delicate question of pregnant vs. un-pregnant.

Liv took the question right out of his hands, arriving back in the kitchen in a cloud of bubble bath vapor, lotion, and the words: "I want to keep the baby."

Gripping the edge of the counter, Charlie looked down and watched the plates of food swim and spread as tears filled his eyes. The emotions punching through him had no name. He was simply overwhelmed. And there was nothing simple about it, really.

Liv touched his hand. "Is that okay?"

"Whatever you want, Liv."

"I can go to Florida. Live with Gran if you—"

"No. We can do this. You and me." He glanced over at his daughter. "That's if you want to stay."

"Of course I do. I thought maybe you wouldn't want me to."

Charlie shook his head. "I know I've done nothing but yell for about three months. Three years? Probably your whole life. It's not you, Duck. I just get frustrated and angry and scared. But I'll always love you, okay? You're my best girl, and I will always love you and want you close to me."

"Oh, Dad."

More hugging and crying ensued. Liv cried. Charlie sucked his tears back into his manly well of grief. Then they sat down to pick at his buffet and go through the list. By the time they got to *School/college*, Charlie was exhausted.

"What day is it?" He glanced out the window to see night had fallen. Again. "What time is it?" He checked the display on the microwave.

"It's Friday night."

Charlie jotted down the date. "When is the baby due?"

"We won't know the exact date until I visit a doctor, but I think around June."

"How are you doing to cope with school?" he asked, making another note.

"The same way Mom did."

Charlie nodded. Liv was a smart kid. She could finish out the second semester early if she had to. She was also her mother's daughter. She'd make sure it happened.

"How's your head?" he asked.

She had a colorful bruise and was still way too pale.

"I'm okay. Tired, mostly."

"Tummy?"

"Settled."

Charlie looked back down at his list. He felt Olivia's gaze join his, both of them staring at the last item. *The Boy.* "Are you going to tell him?"

Liv made a soft sound, something between a sob and a sniff. "I don't know how. I was going to talk to him about the possibility the day I broke up with him, and then I was just ending it and I didn't know why."

God, that sounded so familiar.

"How did Mom tell you?" she asked.

"She didn't. Her mom figured it out and called my mom. Apparently that was after her dad talked her mom out of calling the police."

"Was Grandpa okay with it?" Liv had never really met her maternal grandfather. He'd suffered a fatal heart attack about six weeks after she'd been born. Beatrice blamed Charlie for that as well.

"He never said. He was a quiet man. He didn't come after me with a gun, though." Charlie sucked on his lower lip for a while before continuing. "I think you need to tell Justin, but do it when you're ready and maybe without expectation. Like, if he wants to be involved or you want him involved, we'll work something out. But if he walks away, then we'll deal with that too."

"Do you think we should get married and stuff?"

"Nope. At least, not right away. If that's what you want. Eventually."

"But—"

"No one made me marry your mom, Liv. It was the number-one suggestion and it seemed like the right thing to do at the time, but I did it because I loved her, and once I got over freaking out, and realized the police weren't going to arrest me for having sex with my girlfriend, and that God wasn't going to strike me down, and that the

Earth didn't plan to—" Charlie cleared his throat. "I was excited to meet you. I was scared, and I had no idea how I was going to make it all work. But the thought of having made a little person was kind of amazing and entrancing." He smiled. "I could wish I'd waited a few years, but I don't regret having you."

Liv's lips were trembling. Her reddened eyes full of tears again. "Thanks, Dad."

"We should call my mom before Beatrice does."

"Can we do it tomorrow? I'm tired and I don't think I can do the talk right now."

"I hear you." Charlie lifted his chin. "Go get some sleep."

"Okay." Liv rushed around the kitchen counter and fell into his arms. "I love you."

"Love you too, Duck."

After cleaning up the leftovers, Charlie pulled on a few more shabby layers and took Herbert for a walk. The neighborhood looked different, and not just because it had finally decided to snow. Small flakes floated down from the dark sky, visible in that instant before they touched his face. Licking one from his top lip, Charlie glanced around at the familiar strangeness. He felt as though he'd been away for a hundred years. But, really, nothing had changed. He'd simply been somewhere else for a few days or weeks, what with the book and—

He paused outside Simon's house. Sometimes when he walked past, he could hear Simon playing the piano. The music was never loud enough for him to identify the tune—not that he was up with his symphonies and whatever—but he liked the quiet melodies that floated across the night breeze. Tonight, Simon's house was quiet and dark.

His feet wanted to trace the path to the front door. His fingers curled in anticipation of knocking. Even Herbert seemed keen to visit, straining at his leash.

But, like Simon's house, Charlie's heart felt quiet and dark. Or maybe his most vital organ was simply taking a break. Letting him get on with shit without squeezing and leaping and generally being distracting.

It hurt to turn away. It was a sharp pain, but he had to do it. He was in danger of failing at the most basic job on the planet. Complicating that would just . . .

Adjusting his grip on Herbert's leash, Charlie pulled the dog away. "Can't go there, boy," he murmured. "We've got other paths to walk right now."

CHAPTER 36

Where are you?

Simon blinked at the text, trying to make sense of it. Why did Frank want to know where he was? Dazedly, Simon put the same question to himself. Where was he, and how had he not noticed Frank's previous three texts?

He sat at a table, paper fanned out in front of him. Drawings covered most of the pages. Plans and elevations, a couple of vague landscapes, and a sketched portrait. Not ready to deal with why he'd drawn that particular face, Simon tucked the page under the others. Then he turned the whole packet over. He didn't need to see that kitchen, either. He picked up his phone, stood, and stretched. Took proper note of his surroundings. He was in the conference room of the architectural office. They had desks and a drafting table in another room, but the bright light splashing into the conference room made it a more inviting space. Not quite as comfortable as the studio he'd set up at home, but he'd needed distance from the house next door. From Charlie.

Apparently that was his thing: distance. He'd moved across a state line to put distance between himself and Brian. And Brian had followed. Simon didn't imagine Charlie would come knocking at his office door anytime soon, though. Charlie would be pretty busy for the next twenty years—assuming Liv kept the baby.

The phone buzzed in his hand. A call this time. Frank obviously starting to wonder if he'd fallen off the edge of the world.

"Hey," Simon answered.

"Where are you? I've been texting you for half an hour."

"I'm at the office."

"On a Sunday?"

"It's quiet."

"Your house is quiet." When Simon made no response, Frank continued with, "Planning on coming home anytime soon?"

"Are you at my house?"

"Yes. I've tried all of your windows and doors and I've been loitering on the front step for about fifteen minutes. I'm assuming the fact I haven't been arrested yet means your neighbors are either all away, or unaware there is a crime rate."

"It's a quiet street."

"Mm-hmm."

"What are you doing here?"

"Do you really have to ask?"

"I'm fine."

"You're working on a Sunday. That is so not fine."

"I've never kept regular hours."

"Simon."

Simon glanced at the facedown pile of plans and sketches, none of which represented a current project. "I'm not working. I was . . ." He didn't know what he was doing.

"Oh, hon."

"Don't do that."

"Want me to meet you at your office? I've got wine and yummies. Also, if I don't seek shelter soon, I'm going to lose about six toes and maybe three fingers."

Pacing the conference room, Simon toyed with different answers to the simple question. Did he want Frank to come here, or did he want to go home? More questions popped up. Frank had arrived with a care package. Would uncorking a bottle of wine mean it was over? That he was ready to give up on Charlie—perhaps on Pennsylvania? "You better come here. If I come to the house, I might start packing boxes."

Frank knocked on the street door fifteen minutes later. Simon let him into the office and took the bags so Frank could stamp his feet and rub his hands together in an effort to return circulation to his extremities. God forbid he actually dress for the weather. Then again, he'd probably expected to leap from the warmth of his car to the warmth of Simon's house.

Simon led the way to the conference room, where Frank started sifting through the papers on the table while Simon unpacked wine, crackers, cheese, and whatnot from the bags. "There's enough food to keep us through a blizzard here," he said.

"I figured you probably hadn't eaten since Friday."

Grunting softly, Simon went to retrieve glasses, plates, and hopefully a corkscrew from the office kitchen. When he returned, Frank was holding up one of the pages, examining it closely. He glanced up, a curious look on his face.

Oh no.

Snatching the sheet out of his hand would be childish and would make the sketch seem more important than it was. Instead, Simon concentrated on setting down the glasses and plates without breaking anything.

"Is he really this gorgeous, or only beautiful in memory?"

"Don't."

"Did you ever draw Brian?"

"Plenty of times."

"But not like this."

"It's just a sketch, Frank. A doodle."

"No, it's not." Frank put the page down and rounded the table to stand beside him. "I'm sorry things didn't work out with him, hon. I really am."

Shrugging, Simon handed over the corkscrew. "Here."

Frank picked up one of the wine bottles. "Want to talk about it?"

"No. I said all I needed to on Friday afternoon."

"You said next to nothing on Friday afternoon."

"I told you that you were right. Wasn't that enough?"

"As much as my ego requires occasional stroking, no, it wasn't. What happened?" Frank waved the corkscrew toward the sketch. "Why are you skulking about your office instead of knocking on Charlie's door?"

Wearily, Simon sat. "Because his daughter is pregnant, and as a single dad, that's got to be his focus at the moment. Taking care of his family. He doesn't have time for me."

Frank poured the wine, nudged a glass toward Simon, and sat next to him. "Is that what he said?"

"Basically."

"Which means he said something else, and you interpreted it that way."

"Not this time. His situation is pretty clear, Frank."

"Situation with Brian was pretty clear for about ten years and you chose to interp—"

"Don't."

"Okay, I won't." Frank checked his watch. "For the next hour, our conversation will be confined to idle gossip and speculation of people not related to us by blood or semen. Then we'll return to the subject at hand for reassessment."

"Or we could just get drunk and forget how to talk."

"I only brought two bottles of wine, darling."

"I'm sure Arthur has a bottle of something stashed somewhere."

True to his word, Frank played the part of *TMZ* until they'd finished the first bottle of wine. Simon even found himself chuckling at one particular story, engaged enough to ask, "Wait. Hold up. He did what with the pool float?"

"Sunscreen and slippery plastic. I'd experiment the next time I go somewhere tropical, but a man my age shouldn't frolic in a public place."

Simon waved vaguely. "They have those resorts. For older men. Any men, really. Brochures full of hard, glossy bodies. It's probably all guys like us. Boring enough to be turned on by pool floats."

"We should plan a trip."

For half a second the thought appealed. Oh, to get away. Then the great balloon of depression that Frank's presence had managed to deflect for the past hour bobbed back into the room. And it wasn't light, like a balloon was supposed to be. It was heavy and insistent and wanted to knock the side of his head.

Or maybe he'd just had too much wine.

Simon gripped his nape, the motion reminding him of Charlie. "If I pack a single bag, I might never come back."

"I don't believe that." Frank reached over to touch his knee. Simon stiffened slightly, half expecting his friend to make another pass at him, but Frank merely patted his pant leg and withdrew. "I didn't see your move to Pennsylvania as running away. I know I might have conveyed that impression at the time, but honestly—I think the move was the best thing you could have done. This office, the projects you're working on. You've been happier here than you have been in a long, long while."

Question was—and why did Frank's presence come with so many damn questions?—did Simon's happiness over the past few months have more to do with the business or Charlie? "You know what I keep asking myself?"

Frank shook his head.

"Why I stuck it out with Brian for so long."

"Because you're not a quitter, Simon. Then there was the whole matter of you two being in business together." Frank drained his wineglass and set it aside. His attention remained fixed on the glass as he continued. "And I don't know if you've ever really given yourself enough credit. Seen the guy the rest of us see."

Pushing air out of his nose in what was supposed to be a snort, but sounded more like a weary exhale, Simon put his glass down and reached for the cheese platter. His appetite had returned after the first glass of wine, but this handful of crackers served a different purpose: avoiding Frank's statement. Or the subject of himself entirely.

After a moment, Frank picked up the corkscrew. "Okay, I can see that's as much *you* as we're going to talk about in this intermission. Time for the second bottle?"

The street door banged open, letting a blast of cold air into the office. Simon got to his feet and arrived at the conference room door in time to see Arthur stamping and rubbing his hands. Rather than express surprise at finding Simon in the office on a Sunday afternoon—over a holiday weekend—Arthur simply smiled. "Ah, there you are. Oh, and with wine, I see. Excellent. Excellent."

Simon glanced down at the empty glass in his hand. "We were just about to open a new bottle."

"Wonderful."

Arthur followed him into the conference room. His smile widened. "Frank. Nice to see you again."

Frank had stood and extended a hand. "You too. How was your Thanksgiving?"

While the two exchanged pleasantries, Simon retrieved another glass and plate from the kitchen. When he got back to the conference room, Frank and Arthur were chatting like old friends. Thankfully, they weren't discussing sunscreen and pool floats.

Then Arthur said, "But the King house is certainly special." He turned to smile at Simon. "Charles is a good man. Terrible shame about his wife. Tragedy like that would bury some."

Looking down—or anywhere that wasn't Arthur's kindly face and Frank's unreadable expression—Simon saw the sketch of Charlie. He briefly closed his eyes and sighed. Wasn't the point of Frank's visit not to talk about Charlie? To help him move forward and make a new plan? Something that didn't involve packing and running. Or just packing.

Frank broke the awkward silence by pouring Arthur a glass of wine.

"Thank you." Arthur put the glass down and shrugged out of his overcoat, draping it over the back of a chair. Then he pulled a phone out of his pocket. "Simon. I had a project to discuss with you. I planned to print out the material and show it to you tomorrow or Tuesday, but seeing as you're here..."

"What sort of project?"

"A local developer has acquired land north of 22. Up past Bath."

Another development. Another collection of houses that were merely variations on a theme. Simon could already picture the neighborhood. Maybe this one would appeal to him on the same level as Burnside Province. Maybe it would have some sort of historical significance. But even if it wasn't fair for him to assume so, sight unseen, Simon had a feeling it wouldn't. That accepting another contract for a development—*now*—would be the start of a slippery slope. In another year he'd be doing exactly what he'd left behind in New Jersey: building soulless houses he didn't care about and telling himself he didn't care because he was making good money. Then half of those houses would remain vacant as the market shifted once again and his name would be attached to emptiness and neglect.

This wasn't what he'd moved across the river for. Not what he wanted.

A quiet roar sounded in Simon's ears. Not his imaginary balloon of depression bouncing off his skull again. Something else. Something deeper. "No."

"We can look at it later, then."

"I mean, no, I don't want to do it."

"But Burnside is eighty percent sold already," Arthur pointed out. "The buyers love your plans."

Simon shook his head. The effects of the wine surged through his bloodstream, making his head spin and his blood hum, but his thoughts were clear. He didn't want this, any of it. He didn't want to build pretty houses on a hill. And he didn't want to be heartbroken and thinking about running away. He didn't want to spend another ten years ignoring a situation of his own making, and he certainly didn't want to escape to some sad resort in the Bahamas or drink more wine with Frank in an effort to forget the house he loved and wanted to care for... and the man who lived inside it.

Simon put his glass down. "I'm enjoying working with you, Arthur. We make a great team, and if you're not ready to retire yet, that's okay. I get it. This isn't just a business, it's a craft. I'm all right with keeping a partner, with us continuing as we are until you decide you're done.

"But I had a very specific plan when I came into this agreement. I'm done building houses that have little meaning. I want to leave something other than featureless neighborhoods behind. I've enjoyed working on Burnside Province, but it's not where my heart lies. I want to care for houses like Charlie's."

Simon reached for the stack of drawings at the end of the table and fanned them out. "This is what I want to do." He picked up a hastily sketched plan of Charlie's ground floor with the kitchen extended in a way that would fit with the outline of the house, the period and the general tacked-on nature of other extensions. Begin to bring harmony to the many-wise shape. "I want to work with history. It's houses like this that inspire me. I want to preserve them. Love them."

"Sounds to me like you want to preserve something more than a farmhouse," Frank said.

Yes, he did, and that *want* was louder, messier and altogether needier than anything architectural. It beat in his chest, where the ache had resided for the past few days, increasing in tempo until Simon had to put the papers down. "I need to go."

"Wait." Frank moved in front of him, put a restraining hand on his arm. "It's late Sunday afternoon, and you look like you haven't slept in two days. You haven't shaved, you probably haven't showered, and you've had too much wine to drive just now."

"I'll take a walk."

"Listen to me. What you're thinking is absolutely the right thing." Frank glanced at Arthur and the older man gave a gentle nod. Frank squeezed Simon's arm. "Let's take a walk together, then I'll follow you home. Make sure you get all clean and shiny for your grand gesture."

"My what?"

"Honestly, Simon, it's like you've never been in a relationship before."

Arthur hadn't lost his smile throughout the entire exchange, but his expression now had a more wistful cast to it. He poured himself another glass of wine. "Don't mind me," he said. "I'll clean up here."

"The project..."

"I won't say I'm not disappointed, but if there's one thing I've learned in all my years, it's never say never. We can tuck this one away for another time—maybe after you've restored that lovely house." Arthur's eyebrows jumped up suggestively.

Simon found a laugh. It was short and felt a little prickly, but the essence of it was there. Lightness. Something other than depression swelled inside him. Now he really wanted to fly out the door. Skip the walk, collect nothing, and arrive right outside Charlie's place.

Frank still had a hold of his arm, though. "So, that walk?"

"Let's go."

Frank had been right. Simon had needed a walk, a shower, and a few hours of sleep, because it was the next morning before he found himself in front of Charlie's house—wondering if *another* walk might bolster his courage. With the porch in pieces—disemboweled steps and missing rails—the house didn't look very inviting. The windows were dark, and Herbert wasn't howling in the backyard. Liv's car was missing from the driveway. Maybe everyone was out?

Instead of retreating as his inner coward suggested, Simon hopped up over the missing steps and pushed the bell. Nothing happened.

Charlie still hadn't fixed it. Shuffling the collection of plastic bags that were cutting welts into the fingers of his right hand over to the other side so he could acquire a matching set on his left, Simon knocked on the door.

Nothing stirred but the November wind searing a frozen path across the back of his neck.

Simon raised his hand to knock again and stopped as the door shuddered and creaked open to reveal Charlie. He looked awful. Sleep-deprived but wired. Hair sticking up every which way, glasses hiding a dull and listless gaze. His sweats hung from his hips, and the mysterious stain front and center on his T-shirt resembled the cellular structure of the Ebola virus.

"I didn't know you wore glasses." *Nice opening, Simon. Just perfect.*

Shrugging, Charlie turned away from the open door and disappeared into the gloom of the house. Simon took it as an encouraging sign—Charlie hadn't asked him to leave or simply shut the door in his face. He stepped into the hall, turning when Charlie did, following him into the living room. The wreckage of a living room.

Charlie wasn't the best housekeeper, but his house had always been comfortably messy, not strewn with empty casserole dishes and coffee mugs, stacked cereal bowls, and a dazzling array of beer and soda cans. An old quilt swallowed half the couch. The TV showed frozen carnage—a game paused halfway through a failing mission, apparently.

Herbert poked his nose out of the quilt, and a cat jumped up onto a table to inspect the contents of Mt. Cereal Bowl.

"Jesus."

"I thought you might be Shelly." Charlie flopped onto the slice of couch not inhabited by dog or quilt. "Just in case you're her eager recruit—no, I'm not in the mood to finish the fucking book."

"I thought it was finished."

"Drafted. Far from finished."

"Charlie, what's going on here?"

"You're the one making house calls, maybe you could tell me."

This wasn't the Charlie he'd fallen for. This man was sullen and bitter—and probably hadn't taken a shower since Friday. This man wasn't the cheerful and engaged father Simon had enjoyed getting to know. In fact . . .

Oh God.

Simon dropped his bags and approached the couch on a floor suddenly made of eggshells. "Is Liv . . . Where's Olivia? Is she okay?" If something happened to that girl, something beyond what now seemed like the minor inconvenience of being pregnant, Charlie would fall apart just like this. Simon's heart started breaking for him, and he was mad too. Furious that Charlie had kicked him out of his life right when he needed someone. "Tell me what happened!"

Charlie gave him a curious look. "She's at Rosalie's."

Simon stopped breathing. "She's okay, though?"

"She's still pregnant, if that's what you're asking. But obviously dealing with it a lot better than I am."

With his fear nudged aside—somewhat indifferently—all Simon had left was anger. "Then what the hell, Charlie? Why does your living room look like a street corner and you the bum who has taken up residence on it? For Christ's sake, I thought something terrible had happened."

"Something terrible has happened! I nearly messed up the most important job I've ever had. I'm a sorry excuse for an adult." Grumbling, Charlie searched his side of the couch and produced an Xbox controller. He unpaused the catastrophe on the television and started hammering buttons. "What are you doing here, anyway?"

Simon rocked back on his heels, confused now, as well as aggravated. This was a side of Charlie he didn't know—a side he didn't much like. And for as tired and messed up as Charlie was, Simon felt worse. A sudden weight had dropped onto his shoulders. Maybe it was the pieces of his heart. The memories of the weeks he'd spent falling in love with a man who'd up and disappeared.

"I'm gonna go, okay?" Simon backed away from the couch. God, he was stupid. As if being kicked out once wasn't enough, he'd come back for more. He paused in the doorway. "Take care of yourself, Charlie. Please. Can you . . . just take care of yourself? Olivia needs you."

Charlie scowled at his game.

The hallway was long and dark and perfectly funereal.

And long. And dark.

Simon had his hand on the front door when Charlie called out, "Wait. Simon, wait."

Don't turn around.
You need to leave already.
Don't look back.

Simon pulled the door open.

"Simon, please." Charlie had moved into the hall, his steps punctuated by an odd rattling. Simon turned around. Charlie held up a box. "What's this?"

Even though he couldn't see it clearly, Simon knew what it was. He'd bought it, after all. "A Resistance X-Wing Fighter."

"Why?"

Kneading his forehead, Simon once more considered slipping away. Disappearing. Heading back next door, packing his boxes, and leaving another dead end behind. Surely that would be easier than explaining what he wanted.

Why he'd bought Charlie a toy for ages eight to fourteen.

Then the *fuck it* button got flipped. Maybe it was the wind pushing through the open door, curling around his ankles with sharply cold fingers. Or simply that he'd run out of anger. He'd never been particularly good at sustaining a vigorous rage. Brooding always suited him better.

"Because I care about you," he said.

"You bought me Legos because you care?"

After pushing the door shut, Simon moved toward Charlie, feeling like a mouse approaching a tiger. "Yes. I hate seeing you like this. It hurts. I get it, okay? Your world has just been turned upside down. But Liv's pregnancy isn't the apocalypse, and this isn't you. This isn't the man I met however many months ago. The guy who convinced me we might have something. Who made me want again."

"You have no idea what you're saying."

"Actually, yeah, I do. I stayed up half the night practicing it with a friend."

"You— What?"

"I don't want to let go. I refuse to be collateral damage. What we had, what we could have, is too good. I don't want to let it go."

Charlie opened his mouth and Simon put a hand up.

"Let me finish saying my piece. I'm tired of letting things I want slip through my fingers. Of sitting back and just letting life do whatever it wants. I moved to Bethlehem to start again. On the one hand, I figured I was kidding myself. That I was too old to start a new business partnership and truly do anything useful. You know what's really sad, though? I was okay with the thought of failure. I was a state away from anyone who knew me, so if everything went south, I could just fade into obscurity.

"Then I met you, Charlie. You were so full of life! Like purpose personified. You were everything I'm not. Fading away was no longer an option. Being here, with you, the projects I've been working on . . . This is what I've wanted my whole life. A partnership that works on the most basic level. A man I'm friends with, someone I respect and admire. Someone who knows how to give as well as take. That's you, Charlie. Or it was until four days ago."

Charlie rocked back as if he'd been punched, covering his stomach with his free hand, and huffed. His chin dipped, taking his gorgeously expressive face out of view—which might have been a good thing. Simon hadn't thought he had any heart left to break, what with all the pieces sitting heavily on his shoulders.

Clutching the Lego box to his chest, Charlie continued backing away. Said something that sounded like "I tried" and "lists" and "can't."

He disappeared back into the living room. Simon hesitated only a second before following and found Charlie hiding behind the door, facing the wall. Still clutching his box of Legos. Simon touched his back, putting his open palm to Charlie's shoulder blade, and winced as Charlie stiffened and shuddered.

"Hey."

Charlie shook his head, pressed closer to the wall.

"Charlie."

"I'm not all that."

"Oh yes, you are," Simon said.

"I used to be. I used to . . . I can't."

"Can't what?"

"I can't do this. I barely managed the first time. I only got through it because . . . But she's not with me anymore. She's gone. Merry's gone, and I'm fucking up the only thing I have left."

"Oh, Charlie."

"I'm spinning in place and going everywhere at the same time because I don't know which way to go. I'm all alone here. No one is telling me what to do, and I'm afraid I'm going to mess it up, because that's what I do. I mess everything up. I wish ... I wish ..."

Charlie seemed to break then, the rigidity of his spine giving out so that Simon's hand was all that held him up. Disregarding his own heart, Simon slipped his arms around the man trying to fall headfirst through a wall, and hugged him. Charlie struggled for a second before sagging.

Simon could probably count on one hand the number of times he'd seen an adult cry, and it wasn't something he'd ever pictured Charlie doing. From the very first, he'd been drawn to Charlie's strength and inner light. So when he felt the telltale shudder of sobs moving through Charlie's frame, bone-deep and wracking, Simon held on more closely. Fuck his own heart and his needs and his wants. Charlie needed him. Now.

He turned Charlie around and pulled him close, fitting Charlie's head to his shoulder so that his glasses smooshed to one side, and wrapped him up tight. Charlie hung on through a tsunami of emotion, the storm fierce but short. When he tried to back away, face still downturned, Simon let him take one step. No farther.

"Don't shut me out," he said.

Charlie shook his head.

"Look at me."

Fiddling with his glasses, Charlie continued shaking his head. "I'm so sorry, Simon."

"If you're apologizing for kicking me to the curb, apology accepted. If you're apologizing for this—" Simon gestured between them "—no need."

"I'm such a—"

"You're overwhelmed, that's all. Let me help you."

Charlie took his glasses off, folded the arms in, and slipped them into his pocket. The act seemed overly thoughtful and precise, though his hands shook throughout. Then he looked up, his face a mess. Eyes red rimmed, nose red.

"How can I miss her so much, but still want ... need ..."

A lump formed in Simon's throat. It was becoming clear that Charlie's state had less to do with Liv's pregnancy and more to do with the loss of his wife. Charlie had obviously loved her richly and deeply. He couldn't do life any other way.

Thinking on that, Simon wavered, regretting his speech about not wanting to let go. He would never try to replace Merry. Simon felt he could exist beside her memory, though. That he could be who Charlie needed now.

"It's okay to need someone, Charlie. To want to be with someone. Some of us are lucky to find just one person who suits us for our whole lives. And some of us find more than one. You don't have to be alone."

"I'll bring you bad luck. Merry died because of me, and I'm failing Liv," Charlie whispered. But he didn't back away.

Sensing Charlie needed to be told a truth he so desperately wanted to believe, Simon said gently, "You have to stop blaming yourself for your wife's illness."

"I . . . I'm sorry."

"I know you are. Now forgive yourself."

Charlie stiffened and his eyes squeezed shut as he struggled with the concept. He wouldn't be able to do it all at once, but if he could make a start—Charlie had been holding on to his guilt for too long. But maybe he'd been waiting for someone to give him permission for that too. To let go.

Then Charlie breathed out a sigh, opened his eyes, and stepped in, arms circling Simon's torso. He tucked himself against Simon's chest, turned his head back into Simon's shoulder, and *leaned*. Fell into Simon as though giving him half his weight. He'd made his start.

Oh, thank God.

Dotting small kisses along his hairline, Simon held him close. "It's going to be okay, Charlie. I've got you. Everything's going to be okay."

CHAPTER 37

Charlie opened his eyes and blinked at the slightly blurry squares of light across the ceiling. He was in bed, and it was sometime in the afternoon, judging by the angle of the sun. When had it stopped snowing? Had it been snowing this morning? Was it Sunday or Monday?

Given the weight of his limbs, he'd been asleep for a while. Days could have passed. He stretched languidly beneath the cozy layers of blanket, inhaled the intoxicating scent of sleep and soap, and contemplated letting himself fall back under.

Next to him, someone snuffled. Charlie glanced over, and the memory of that morning broke through his lassitude. Simon! The name echoed across Charlie's mental landscape a few times, stirring feelings of warmth, shame, more warmth, and deep gratitude.

Simon lay curled on his side, on top of the quilt, with his face half buried in the extra pillow. He'd insisted Charlie take a nap, after encouraging him to shower and change his sheets. Firmly encouraging. Apparently Charlie had smelled like socks and old pizza boxes.

"If you ever want to sleep with me again, you'll take a shower."

"Yes, sir," Charlie had answered before doing as advised. Grateful for the instruction.

Had Charlie ever actually told Simon how gorgeous he was? How utterly beautiful? His nearly black hair, the way it curled at his nape—and over his forehead when he wasn't in neatly pressed business mode. The contrast to his pale skin, red lips, and celestial eyes—the clear and boundless blue Charlie could picture even while he slept.

Simon looked far sexier than any angel should, and with a new bout of neediness, Charlie couldn't imagine moving forward without him, let alone leaving the bed. He'd cried in front of this man, and instead of asking him if he had something in his eye, Simon had held him. Then had started on the inadvisable scheme of trying to sort out Charlie's life.

Charlie reached out to caress Simon's cheek and decided to brush the hair away from his forehead instead. Simon's skin was warm beneath his fingers. Not soft and smooth, but not like sandpaper, either. Just . . . his. Charlie couldn't think of any other way to describe it. Simon so often felt like such a unique being. Wondrous in his difference from expectation. Singular and self-sustaining. Charlie had never really paused to compare him to Merry, or the experience of being with him to that of being with a woman. He was . . . Simon.

Eyelids fluttering, Simon curled a little tighter before breathing out. He woke, blinked, and smiled. "Hey."

"I love you."

Simon's smile widened lazily. He didn't look surprised, which was good. Nor did he say it back, which was okay.

"I'm not saying it because you came to rescue me. It's *you*. Everything about you. You let me cry—I had no idea how much I needed to cry. And you made me take a shower and clean up my room. I needed someone to do that too. That thing you said? Before, when you were telling me why I couldn't toss you away? The bit about wanting a partner. I . . ."

Simon caught his fingers and threaded his through so they were holding hands. "I love you too."

The smile spreading over Charlie's face corresponded directly with the warmth unfurling in the middle of his chest. "Is that why you came back?"

"Yes."

"Can it be this easy?"

Simon scoffed. "This has been easy?"

"I mean falling. Feeling this way."

Simon moved his head against the pillow, and Charlie couldn't figure out if it was a nod or a shake. The fact that Simon remained next to him seemed more important.

"Thank you for coming back." Charlie kissed Simon's fingers where they intersected with his.

"I think it was the hardest thing I've ever done in my life."

"Didn't feel that way from my end. You were all you, clean and pressed. Speech prepared. Bags of supplies."

"Battle prep." Though his tone was quietly humorous, Simon looked thoughtful and a little weary. Had he really stayed up all night practicing what he would say?

"I'm sorry I told you to leave the other day. I was so overwhelmed."

"Every relationship has its hiccups."

"Do you have to be so perfect?"

"Oh, Charlie." Every time Simon said his name that way, Charlie shivered from the intimate caress of it. "I'm not perfect. For days I disliked you intensely. I was hurt and I felt stupid. I even started planning my flight from Pennsylvania. Pathetic, I know. I figured it was my fault because I'd let *you* happen, even though I thought it was a bad idea."

"You thought getting involved with me was a bad idea?"

"Fire burns." When Charlie offered up nothing but a frown in response, Simon continued, "You're so bright. So alive." His voice turned husky. "Hot." He pulled their joined hands to his lips and kissed the back of Charlie's knuckles.

"I'll try not to burn you again."

Simon's smile turned inward. "You will, and I'll hurt you. We're people, not ideas. I'm ready for it, though. For you, for something I'm willing to fight for."

"What changed your mind?" The question Charlie really wanted to ask was *Why now, why me?*

Simon's expression flattened, his smile disappearing. He tried to roll away, onto his back, but Charlie still held his hand. It was oddly comforting, in a way, to witness this small attempt to shut down, to see Simon's humanity. Charlie didn't want to cause him pain, hadn't intended to. But Simon's reaction felt like a gift.

"Hey." Charlie let go when Simon tugged at his fingers. Simon didn't leave the bed, though. He pushed up to a sitting position, his back crushing a pillow against the wall. Charlie bunched up another pillow and sat beside him.

Simon glanced over at him. "You make me feel worthwhile."

Charlie had nearly forgotten the question. But the beat of silence between accepting Simon's answer and matching it to what he'd asked, and what he'd wanted to ask, worked in his favor. Simon deserved much more than a flippant response.

What to say, though? How could a man like Simon not know his own worth?

It would be easy to fling anger at the ex who'd apparently broken Simon's heart so slowly, he hadn't felt it happening. Or to take Simon for task for not seeing it. For not believing in himself. Charlie didn't like the idea that he might be a hypocrite, though. Nor did he want to state the obvious. Simon knew all of this and had acknowledged it in his reserved way.

"Your quietness does the same for me," Charlie finally said.

Simon arched an eyebrow.

"I know you're listening to me, even when I ramble. And that makes me feel worthwhile," Charlie explained.

Simon smiled before demonstrating the quiet thoughtfulness Charlie liked so much. "One of the questions I asked myself, after Friday, was if you might be having issues with your sexuality."

"No. Not really. I mean, this has been kind of surprising, but not so much as it could have been. I told you I figured out I was bisexual a long time ago, but it wasn't something I put a lot of thought into."

"Why?"

"I've been so busy doing everything else, it seemed like exploring my sexuality was just one of those things I wouldn't ever get to." Charlie felt the corners of his mouth turn down. "Sometimes when I write, the line between fantasy and reality gets blurred, and there have been a few times when I worried that my desires weren't mine, or that what I was doing with Kaze was too much a reflection of what I wanted. But being with you has always felt too natural for me to discount my feelings."

Simon touched his hand.

"It's mostly what's going on with Liv that's thrown me, which is equal parts embarrassing and annoying. It's not only the fact she's going to have a baby at eighteen, or that her future plans are going to be very different to what we'd imagined—or that I'm going to be taking care of yet another kid who happened because sex happens and condoms aren't one hundred percent effective—but the messed-up feelings I have about Merry's death. Like, rationally, I know it wasn't my fault, but it was so easy to take that on. Sometimes I was only accepting what everyone else thought anyway, and sometimes I felt like I deserved it. That. The guilt."

"I can't tell you how to feel, or even qualify your thoughts, but you had to know on some level that it wasn't you."

Charlie sighed. "I think I just got really good at using my guilt as an excuse not to move on, which wasn't working out for me because you know what else I was thinking, underneath it all?" When he'd been yelling at Phil and Liv and Jen and just generally being obnoxious. "I was thinking, 'What about me?' I wanted you, Simon. A lot. I'd just started to explore a side of myself that suddenly felt important. And then I had to give it up."

"You don't have to."

"I know that now. I don't know why I didn't know that then. Maybe I was too upset to think clearly."

Simon squeezed his hand. Charlie returned the squeeze. It was a simple thing, a conspiratorial gesture.

"So Liv is keeping the baby?" Simon asked.

"I think so."

"I thought she might."

"Why?"

"Because when I look at your daughter, I see you. And neither of you really wants the world to come to an end."

"For a while, there, I thought I could make it all come crashing down. Just wait for the roof to fall in and crush me. I figured that would be less painful than pretending to be an adult again."

"I wouldn't have let that happen."

Quietly spoken, but so sincerely. Behind the beautiful blue of Simon's eyes, a fire burned. Not hotly, but perpetually, like a thing of myth. It was Simon's core of strength. Did he know it was there?

"I love that you were ready to fight for me," Charlie said, then perhaps ruined the sentiment by adding, "It's fucking sexy."

Simon arched a dark eyebrow. Same one as before. "Yeah?"

Charlie tried for a grin and found it came quickly and naturally, and that he had no trouble lifting one eyebrow to match Simon's. "Yeah."

CHAPTER 38

Raising Charlie's hand to his lips, Simon kissed each knuckle in turn. Charlie's skin tasted sleepy. The scent of laundry detergent and soap drifted up around him, surrounded by the warmth of Charlie's skin. The essence of him—strength and sunshine combined with his now-bright smile. He'd heard the term *his heart swelled* and always thought it an odd phrase. Why would anyone want their heart to feel bigger, and wouldn't it be uncomfortable? It was, in a way. A squeezing sensation had wrapped his chest, and the pressure behind his breastbone threatened to invoke panic.

He'd told Charlie he loved him, and it was the truth. He did. In this sharply tender moment, however, he finally understood what those words meant. They weren't for Charlie, they were for him. They named a feeling inside, foreign and familiar both: a song in his heart, the words causing the ache, the swelling. And it was a gift from Charlie, the man who'd allowed Simon to step in and save him. To be there, even quietly.

He pressed a last kiss to Charlie's thumb, then lowered their hands so he could lean forward, kiss Charlie's mouth. Touch the plumpness of his lips, enjoy the way they cushioned his own. Never quiet, Charlie made soft sounds as they kissed—shuddering breaths and little moans. He put his hands to Simon's face, thumbs grazing over the shadow of his cheeks, and the crisp scrape against stubble echoed in Simon's ears—a part of their kiss. A part of them.

Charlie's face was smooth. He'd shaved after his shower. Simon kissed a cheekbone, an eyelid. Sucked on the lobe of one ear, nipped. Smiled as a groan chased Charlie's shudder, as fingers plucked at Simon's shirt buttons, gave up with an impatient flap and pushed inside to touch his chest.

Leaning away, Simon pulled at the same buttons, undoing them with a practiced flick, and shrugged his shirt from his shoulders. Charlie drew his own T-shirt over his head and tossed it aside. Simon covered the bared chest with his hands, smoothing his palms over soft brown hair, stiff nipples, and warm, wonderful skin.

"God, you're beautiful."

Charlie blushed, his neck reddening first in that endearing way, before the color spread up and down. "I could say the same of you. I think it all the time. I never say it because I didn't know if you could say that to a guy, but why not, right? Men can be beautiful, can't they?"

"They can."

With the breadth of his shoulders and torso, Charlie might well become solid one day instead of defined. Simon hoped he would. That he'd slide into middle age comfortably and gracefully, a man built not only to carry heavy things, but to give broad hugs, the sort that pulled everything into a tight and reassuring embrace.

It was his usually sunny aspect that made him beautiful, though. The way he rambled when he talked. The brightness of his eyes. The generosity of his heart.

Charlie reached for his hand, and Simon pulled away, gently. "Let me love you," he said, spreading his palms over Charlie's chest again. He leaned forward to nip at Charlie's lips.

"But your shirt's all off. I wanna play too." Charlie skated his fingers across Simon's bare chest, up toward his shoulders.

"If you can move after I'm done with you, you can have your way with me."

"Deal."

"Now put your hands over your head and hold on."

Charlie did as he was told, eyebrows raised, a playful smile on his lips. He gripped the top of his pillow and jerked his hips up invitingly. "Love me."

Chuckling, Simon traced the trail from Charlie's navel to the waistband of his sweats. Plucked at the elastic and let it flip back. He smoothed his palm over Charlie's stomach, tickled his hips, and flicked his waistband again, joy sparking within him at every twitch of skin, every hissed breath from Charlie. He sensed more than saw

Charlie readjusting his grip, felt the tightness of expectation string through his body, pulling taut.

He slid his fingers beneath the waistband to explore the constrained length of Charlie's erection, folded sideways and trapped by the warm cotton of his underwear.

Arching beneath him, Charlie let out a breathy groan. "Oh. God, yes. I love it when you touch me. I don't know why another hand always feels so good, but it does."

"Maybe because you can't direct my hand. You don't know exactly what I'm going to do next."

Simon tugged Charlie's cock, using the fabric of his underwear to provide friction. Beneath him, Charlie shuddered and hissed. He closed his eyes and pushed his head back into the pillow, willingly giving himself up to Simon's care. Simon leaned down to flick a nipple with his tongue, bite and tug, grinning as Charlie's chest rose to meet him, the sparse hair around the nipple tickling his lips. Simon licked that too, and worked his way across to the other nipple.

"It's like there's an electric current running from my chest to my cock. How does that work?" Charlie bucked upward, apparently following the current again, his chest and hips almost undulating as Simon continued licking and fondling.

Simon slipped his hand inside Charlie's underpants and wrapped his fingers around the firm length of Charlie's dick. "If you're turned on enough, I should be able to kiss your shoulder and have you feel it here." He squeezed and moved to kiss Charlie's shoulder. Planted a trail of soft kisses toward his neck, grazed his teeth over the corded tendons there, kept caressing and squeezing the pulsing length in his hand.

Charlie breathed and writhed and moaned. He moved one hand from his pillow to grip Simon's shoulder, fingers digging in hard enough to leave bruises. "Best. Handjob. Ever. Don't stop. Please."

Simon stopped.

Charlie growled.

Simon loosened his fingers so he only just held Charlie's cock. He breathed across Charlie's neck. Flicked the nearby earlobe with the tip of his tongue.

Whining, Charlie pushed his hips up and to the side in a clear effort to reengage Simon's hand. "More. Please."

"Patience . . ." Simon let go of warm, wonderfully hard things to tug at Charlie's sweatpants and underwear, exposing his hips and bobbing erection. He licked his palm and took hold again, delivering one stroke.

Charlie whined.

Simon tightened his hand around Charlie's cock, below the glans, and twisted slightly. Charlie's hips jerked upward. Simon slid his fingers over the crown, collecting the generous slick of pre-come spilling from the slit, and stroked back downward. Just once.

"So fucking cruel."

Charlie didn't seem much put out by the torture. Eyes heavy lidded, lips parted in a smile, he had a deliciously needy look to him. Simon teased Charlie's lips with his tongue, and Charlie gasped and jerked again.

For a while, Simon jerked him and kissed him in tandem, pushing his tongue into Charlie's mouth. He rode the waves of Charlie's body, sliding his hand down into the up and up away from the down, establishing a steady and predictable rhythm. When he felt Charlie approach his climax—the tiny twinges and quickening gasps, he stopped again.

Charlie complained. Babbled. Pleaded. "I won't play with you if you keep torturing me."

Simon held still, letting nothing but his breath whisper across Charlie's skin, right at the base of his throat.

"Okay, I will. Just move your hand. God, please, move your hand." Twice more, up and down, and he came—yelling, body jerking upward. "Fuck, fuck, yeah . . . Oh God, yeeesss . . ." He fell into groans and finally lay still, trembling and breathing. Obviously trying to smile, and failing.

Simon bent down to lick at the pearly droplets sprayed across Charlie's chest. Charlie put a hand to his face, encouraging him up, and kissed him. "That was the absolute best."

Oh, Charlie. He had no idea what Simon had in store for him. None. Smiling, Simon kissed him back, playing with his tongue. "Up for round two?"

"Only if it means I get to love you. I'm cooked."

"Wuss."

"I can't believe you just called me a wuss."

"I'm nine years older than you. Any failure on your part to recover from my attentions enough for more than one fuck a night is up for ridicule."

"So what you're saying is that you're Superman."

"No. But really turned on by you and sure I can make it happen as often as we need it to."

Laughing, Charlie pushed up off his nest of pillows, hands to Simon's shoulders, and rolled him back. When he tried to climb over Simon's hips, he discovered his sweatpants and underpants, and grumbled—which was entirely too cute—as he tried to pull them off without changing position.

Simon nudged him away. "I need to take my pants off too." If he didn't let his dick stretch out soon, he'd do himself a permanent injury.

"Who says you get to take your pants off?"

"Charlie..."

"I might just bite your nipples for three hours as payback."

"You loved it."

Charlie smiled. "Yeah, I did. Okay, let's get undressed."

A task they accomplished in less than thirty seconds before bouncing back onto the bed. Charlie quickly pinned him again, climbing over his thighs so he sat right beneath Simon's erect cock. Semen glistened against his chest like dewdrops. Simon thought to point out it would be harder to wipe away once it dried, then forgot how to speak as Charlie bent and licked his lips, kissed him and nuzzled, the scent of him—warm and sexy—moving in, the heat of him delicious against the perpetual chill of the old farmhouse. And it was just Charlie. Having Charlie sit astride him.

Simon's heart filled again. "Love me," he said on a sigh.

"First, I get to tell you you're beautiful. Gorgeous."

Beneath his breastbone, Simon's heart beat furiously. Largely.

"And that I love you." Charlie kissed him a final time before beginning the journey downward, stopping at each nipple, closing his lips over the bump of each rib, the warm tickle sending flushed shivers across Simon's skin. Charlie took his time, but didn't dally, marking points as though traveling a map. Every kiss made Simon feel beautiful and cherished and loved. Charlie's delight in him translated into every touch.

He shivered when Charlie breathed across the head of his cock. His thighs twitched as Charlie traced a line toward center from his hip bones—moving quickly to the rigid point at his groin. Charlie planted his hands there, at the tops of Simon's thighs, and used his tongue, somehow wrapping it around the head of Simon's cock.

He looked up with a smile and licked his lips. "You taste so good."

No hesitation, no questions in his eyes. When it came to sex, Charlie seemed to possess an innate confidence. He simply appreciated the body before him, regardless of gender. For Charlie, this wasn't about being with a man, it was about being with *Simon*.

Charlie's lips closed around him, drawing all thought from his mind. Simon flung his arms up and back, imitating the pose he'd asked Charlie to take, and gripped the pillow behind his head. Humming in pleasure, he gave himself over to the wet heat of Charlie's mouth.

It was hard to hold his hips still as Charlie tended him—sucking rhythmically, tonguing the vein on the underside of his cock, licking, teasing, tasting, and moaning. He bucked once, feeling the barrier at the back of Charlie's throat, and huffed in surprise as Charlie dug a hand beneath his hip and encouraged him upward again.

Simon lost all sense of time. His world narrowed to sensation, to the ripples coasting across his skin, and the exquisite need building down low. Charlie fondled his sac, squeezed between. Nudged a finger backward, beneath his balls, the motion almost careless. Simon keened and squeezed his pillow. Parted his thighs, inviting more.

He wanted to ask Charlie to fuck him—but was too far gone to form words. *Next time*, he promised himself, knowing that if he forgot, he'd find himself here again, with Charlie loving him, stroking him, curiously touching where he most needed to be touched.

His climax seemed to come upon him suddenly, even though he'd felt the pull for a while. A stack of tightly packed blocks trembled and fell, and he tumbled with them. He shouted, surprising himself with the volume, and lost the ability to form words. He was babbling and coming, and Charlie was still sucking, swallowing him down.

By the time he returned to reality, Simon's lungs burned. His skin tingled. His legs were numb. The ceiling over Charlie's bed showed long shadows instead of squares of sunlight, and the scent of sex pushed at his nostrils—warm and humid.

Charlie lay next to him, humming softly. He smiled when Simon turned to him, and whispered, "Welcome back." Kissed him with lips that tasted of salt and wind and sunshine.

"Fuck," Simon murmured. Charlie had proved he was a fast learner before Thanksgiving, but this blowjob eclipsed all others. "Fuck." He'd come up with some other words soon. Next year, maybe.

Grinning, Charlie bumped their noses together.

Then the thump of the front door closing echoed through the walls, and a familiar voice called out, "Dad?"

Oh God, not again.

Charlie started laughing.

CHAPTER 39

Charlie called downstairs that he'd be there in a bit, and dragged Simon out into the hall, naked and laughing—actually laughing—and into the bathroom. He turned on the shower and shoved him into the stall, laughing louder as Simon swallowed a yell.

"Cold." Simon tried to push back out.

Charlie stepped in with him. "I'll warm you up."

And he did, soaping, stroking, and making Simon come again. He'd never tire of making Simon come. Ever.

The day had all but disappeared by the time they got downstairs, whiled away with showers, naps, and sex. Another shower. Charlie felt as though he'd been on vacation. His skin buzzed with satisfaction, and his hands and feet were all toasty. What that meant—the hands and feet part—was beyond him, but he noticed it, nonetheless. A glance toward the living room as they passed showed Simon had been busy before his nap. The quilt was folded and most of the detritus of Charlie's funk cleared away.

The dishes were in the kitchen, stacked around the sink, and Justin was doing them.

The Boy was in his house.

"Why are you doing my dishes?"

Justin flinched and blushed and pulled his hands from the pile of soap bubbles in the sink. "Mr. King."

Not an adequate reply, but the fact he was here answered a slew of other questions. Charlie glanced over at Liv, who had been digging around in the fridge. She shrugged.

Rosalie put away the plate she'd been drying and grinned. "Are you two back together? So awesome."

Swallowing, Charlie glanced at Simon, who seemed to be taking Rosalie's enthusiasm in stride.

Liv looked between Charlie and Simon and smiled. "I caught you two in bed again, didn't I?"

Charlie answered with a soft choking sound.

"Good thing you can't get each other pregnant."

Oh, hell no. Charlie held up a hand. "Too soon, Liv. Way too soon." A smile was tugging at his mouth, though. Girl had his sense of humor—and his sense of timing.

And Justin appeared about ready to drown himself in the sink.

Charlie studied his daughter. The dark circles beneath her eyes were gone and the bruise on her forehead was fading. Even the general air of doom and gloom that seemed to have followed her for months had dissipated. She looked something like he felt. Renewed, or just refreshed.

"How are you feeling?" he asked.

She smiled again. "Good."

"You manage to eat today?"

"Yeah, Rosalie's mom had soup and that was just perfect." She picked up Charlie's abandoned list and waved it. "I've jotted down some numbers for us." She nibbled on her lower lip. "Aunt Jen texted me the number of her obstetrician and the name of another one she's heard good things about." She pointed to the second and third lines of new scrawl. "And this is a clinic we can go to for tests. These are websites for resources for teenage mothers."

She glanced over at Justin, who shuffled in place.

Throat suddenly tight, Charlie took the list from her. He couldn't see the names and numbers; his vision was all blurry for some stupid reason. Not the blurry that required glasses, either. He was crying again. Not sobbing or wailing, just doing some ridiculous weeping thing.

Because he wasn't doing this alone and couldn't figure out why he'd ever thought he'd have to. It wasn't his baby, it was Liv's, and she was stepping up. Apparently Justin was too.

And Simon was a warm tower of strength behind him, fingers lightly touching the back of Charlie's shoulder. Even Rosalie was ready to get involved. A single day with her had restored the color to Liv's cheeks and the light to her eyes. Rosie's mother had made soup.

"C'mere." He beckoned Liv into his arms. "God, I'm so sorry I fell off the rails, Duck."

"It's okay." Liv burrowed in and hugged him tight. "It's not going to be as easy as making this list, is it?"

She'd thought making the list was easy? "No. But we'll get through it."

Over Liv's shoulder, he watched Justin continue to fidget. The guy looked as though he would happily die, right then, right there. Charlie let go of his daughter and approached him slowly, aware of the sudden silence that fell over the kitchen. He knew everyone expected him to start yelling and breaking things. Justin probably expected it too.

He stuck out his hand. Justin studied it for nearly thirty seconds before slipping his palm carefully into Charlie's. "Welcome to the family," Charlie said.

"I—"

"Just be good to her. That's all I ask. Do that and you're always welcome in my home."

"Thank you, sir."

"Call me Charlie."

He could feel Justin trembling, and had to squash the absurd urge to pull him into a hug. It was too soon. He still sort of wanted to kill this young man, but he also wanted to adopt him. Tell him that life as he knew it wasn't necessarily over.

"So." Charlie cleared his throat. "Is everyone staying for dinner? We've got a ton of Thanksgiving leftovers and pie and—"

"And soup!" Liv said. "We brought some back with us."

"Awesome."

There was a brief knock at the kitchen door before it opened, letting in a gust of wind, a swirl of leaves and . . .

His mother.

Charlie gaped. "Mom!" His father followed after, shouldering two bags and hauling another. "Dad! What are you guys doing here?"

"Hello to you too!" His mom said before looking for someone to hug. She found Rosalie first. "Oh, Rosie, you're more beautiful every time I see you." She tugged on a braid. "Love what you've done with your hair." Then she advanced on Liv, pulling her granddaughter into a fast embrace. "Livie." She patted Liv's hair and cheeks and shoulders, eyes shining. "You're okay. Thank goodness."

Charlie prickled. Did she think he couldn't look after his own daughter?

Actually . . .

He was next to be swept up, his mother hugging him so tightly that his ribs creaked. "I know we didn't need to come, but we wanted to. You sounded so upset on the phone. So here we are." She stroked his cheek before patting it in a wonderfully maternal gesture that nearly brought his tears back.

"Thanks, Mom. We are okay, but it's good to see you."

It was. It really, really was.

"And who's this young man?"

Poor Justin was all but wilting under her curious scrutiny.

"Gran, this is Justin," Liv said. "Um, he's . . . you know, my boyfriend."

At that pronouncement, color finally returned to Justin's cheeks. Stepping up, he offered his hand and a polite "Ma'am."

"Well, hello, Justin. It's lovely to meet you."

Then his mother turned her gaze on Simon, the last unidentified person in the room.

Charlie managed to speak without clearing his throat first. "Mom, this is Simon. *My* boyfriend." Not friend, not neighbor or guy-I'm-seeing. Definitely not lover, because, wow, this was his mom. And not the-man-I-love because that was something he wanted to keep to himself for now. Hold it as private and precious and special.

His mom's eyes widened. Behind her, his dad dropped a bag.

Should he share the love part?

Then his mom smiled, took Simon's hand, and pulled him into a gentle hug. "It's wonderful to meet you, Simon. I'm Heather."

"Good to meet you, Heather," Simon murmured with one of his calm but confident smiles. Simon turned to the elder Mr. King, his expression quietly expectant, and Charlie wondered if this would be the moment when he discovered his dad wasn't the most chill man on Earth.

His dad's greeting was more subdued, but he managed a smile as he took Simon's hand and introduced himself. "Richard King." Then he looked at Charlie, over at Simon, back at Charlie again. Shook his head and said something that might have been, "Well I'll be damned."

His mom, meanwhile, was examining the state of the kitchen. "Did you have a party?"

"No, I . . . I just forgot to clean up for a while."

"I meant to get to it while you were napping," Simon put in, his expression sweetly earnest.

His mom smiled. "Oh, he's a keeper." She clapped her hands together. "Okay, I can see dishes are being done. Richard, bags upstairs, please. Are there sheets on the bed in your old room, Charlie?"

"You can have . . ." Oh shit. No, they could not have their room, the room he'd come all over half an hour ago. "I'll go check."

"I'll help," Simon said.

"Justin, are you staying for dinner?"

"Yes, ma'am."

"You are something else, aren't you? When you finish the dishes, can you set the table? Liv, Rosie, what do we have to eat?"

With that, they were dispatched. Then served leftovers and soup, and it was perfect. Dinner was a noisy affair with much laughter. His mother peppered Justin with friendly questions, learning more about him over the course of an hour than Charlie had figured out in several months. His father kept darting looks at Simon, but seemed more curious than anything else, and when they finally started talking, they quickly discovered a number of shared interests.

All in all, it was a better Thanksgiving than the one Charlie had been doing his best to forget.

His mother cornered him in the kitchen when they were clearing dishes. "So, Simon."

"Wouldn't you rather talk about Liv and Justin?"

"Plenty of time for that." She tilted her head. "I wondered about you, you know. When you were younger."

"What do you mean?"

She gestured toward the dining room.

"Oh." Charlie didn't know what else to say. He wasn't going to ask if she was okay with it. His life was his. Who he slept with was his own business.

"I was almost relieved when you got Merry pregnant."

"Ah..."

"Because I didn't know what I'd do if you brought a boy home."

Charlie swallowed.

His mom smiled. "He's lovely, Charlie. Really, he is. It's none of my business, but I wanted you to know that. That I like him." She squeezed his arm. "And you look so happy with him and . . ." She sniffed, her eyes filling. "That makes me happy. You've been alone for far too long."

"I was fine."

"There's a world of difference between 'fine' and 'good.' Now you're good."

"You think Dad's okay with it?"

"Oh, honey. Of course he is. He's very open-minded, you know. Quiet about it, but he's not going to object to you being with someone who makes so much sense for you."

A heavy breath gusted out of him, a weight lifting. "Can I bring Simon down to Florida for Christmas?"

"I'd be disappointed if you didn't."

CHAPTER 40

Charlie wanted to sit on the roof.

"It's like thirty degrees out there," Simon said.

"But it's not snowing!" Charlie's smile suggested Simon should celebrate this fact with him. "I used to go up there a lot when Liv was young."

"Really?"

"It was about the only place I could get some peace and quiet sometimes."

"Isn't your basement quiet?"

"Not when Liv's down there with Rosie. And tonight The Boy is down there too."

Simon smiled at Charlie's continued insistence on calling Justin *The Boy*. "How about the attic?"

"Everyone knows where to find me up there."

"Your bedroom door has a lock on it."

"I don't want to have sex with you. Not right now, anyway. I want to show you the view from the roof."

"In November."

"We'll do it again in the summer, I promise."

"Okay."

They took the quilt from the couch downstairs and went up to the attic den where Charlie propped open a window and climbed out. Shivering, Simon followed, sure he'd either slide and fall to his death or leave his fingers and toes stuck to the slate.

The night air wasn't exactly arctic. Though even snuggled next to Charlie with the quilt wrapped around their shoulders, their situation couldn't exactly be described as cozy, either. But it was warm enough, and the chill breeze tickling the back of his neck was refreshing after the hours of eating and drinking with Charlie's family. The view proved worth the visit as well. Streetlights traced the roads, and the college and town were visible in the distance, like a map viewed from space.

Not that any of it mattered, really. He was here, doing this thing, for Charlie.

I'd do anything for him, Simon realized with a soft start. Behind that thought came the quiet and somewhat wry acknowledgment that it hadn't been like this with Brian. He'd loved Brian—that much wasn't an illusion. They'd spent a decade building a business together, and in many ways they'd been a good match. What he had with Charlie, though, what he wanted to share with Charlie, was different. Sharper, more meaningful, and in only a couple of months, perhaps deeper than any relationship he'd had before.

Maybe it was the difference between loving someone and being in love with them.

Having apparently decided three minutes of silence was all he could manage, Charlie said, "I used to come up here a lot when Merry was sick. Sometimes it was like the roof was trying to fall on my head or the walls were pressing close, and I needed space, you know?"

Simon nodded.

"I'd come up here and watch the sun set, even in winter when the wind wanted to blow me off the roof."

"I bet it's spectacular from up here."

"It is and we're going to do that too." Charlie leaned into Simon's side and drew the quilt a little closer around their shoulders. "I figured out the name of my first book up here."

"During a particularly windy sunset?" Charlie's first book was called *Ride the Wind*, after all.

"Yep. The name came to me first, then the rest of the book. Kaze, being tossed around by gravitational forces and popping out into the unknown. Becoming an adventurer, even though that wasn't how he'd started or what he wanted."

Just like Charlie.

Simon tucked his arm around Charlie's shoulders, under the quilt, and pressed a kiss to the side of Charlie's head. "I can't wait to read the last book."

"I figured out the third book up here too. The one where Jory happened."

"That's obviously my favorite one."

Charlie laughed softly. "Have you really read them all?"

"Yep."

"You're, like, a most excellent boyfriend." He sighed then, which took a little plumpness from his praise. "If I don't get it organized soon, Shelly is going to drop me."

"I'll help."

"You can't—"

"Not with the writing or editing or whatever. With Liv. First job will be to put your porch back together before someone kills themselves."

"Probably a good idea."

"I drew up a couple of plans for the kitchen too, for when you're ready for a new project."

"Yeah?"

"Some quick sketches."

"Will you come to Florida with us, for Christmas?"

Wow. Um . . . Simon's thoughts stuttered to a halt, tugged from kitchen plans to something he hadn't yet contemplated. The sky overhead pulsed, the cold stars throbbing, the lights of Bethlehem dancing beneath. "Are you sure?"

"My mom really likes you. I think my dad does too."

That had been a moment, watching Charlie's parents process the fact their son was seeing a man. When it came down to it, though, their reaction scored a perfect ten. No one could be hit with news like that and not take a minute to think about it.

Simon had the feeling that had they been less than thrilled, they'd still have been polite about it. Invited him to dinner, and talked to Charlie afterward. The hug from Heather, though—that had been a true welcome.

"Yeah. Okay, I'll come." Thank God Charlie couldn't see his goofy smile in the dark.

Charlie shifted next to him. "I love it when you smile like that."

Trying not to smile had the opposite effect. "You're like a piece of candy, Charlie King. Too damn sweet, always tempting, and just happy-making."

"You have a high opinion of candy."

"Yes, I do."

"I've got another proposition for you."

"Yeah?"

"I want you to think about moving in with me."

Simon sucked in a very cold breath and shivered. The sky pulsed again. The stars wheeled a little.

"I know it's soon, but I feel like you need this house. I know you love it as much as I do. And . . ." Charlie bit his lips.

"What?"

"I want you to feel like you have a home. Your house is nice, and I could use some of your clutter-less decorating, but when you're here, you're more relaxed. More you. This house needs you. I need you."

Charlie lifted his chin so their lips could meet, and delivered a soft kiss. Simon deepened it, untucking a hand from the quilt so he could frame Charlie's face. Claim him. It was a beautiful kiss, given to him by a beautiful man. A gift on top of so many others. Yes, he'd been the one to sweep in and offer his help. Save Charlie from himself. But he'd only been able to do it because he'd wanted this. Wanted it enough to fight for it.

He needed the house. Oh yeah. But he needed Charlie more. "I'll think about it."

Charlie pressed a quick kiss to his lips. "Good enough." Another kiss. "You'll be saying yes, just so you know. But take your time and do your thinking."

Simon laughed. "When am I going to say yes?"

"Probably next week. I'm pretty irresistible. Like a cheesy little cracker."

Laughing again, Simon pulled him close. "Yes, Charlie. That's exactly what you are."

CHAPTER 41

June

Charlie shifted in his seat, his jeans squawking against the plastic. Why were these chairs so uncomfortable? And why would they use upholstery that turned every fidget into something that sounded like a fart?

Next to him, Simon was absorbed in a book. Though Charlie had seen the cover a thousand times, the sight of it still made his stomach flip, and the title made his eyes roll around in their sockets. It was so damned corny. *The Wind Never Dies*. The last Kaze Rider book with the hero and his lover riding off into a (windy) sunset. Sometimes he couldn't believe he'd finished the damn thing. Others, he was just so relieved to be done, and glad that in the two weeks it'd been out, the book had already performed well enough to smooth any feathers ruffled by his missed deadlines.

And his most ardent fan was a quiet architect from New Jersey. When not dispensing with clutter and keeping them on a regular laundry schedule, Simon liked to recline on the couch in their newly decorated living room and read.

Charlie tugged the book from Simon's hands. "Stop. You've already read it three times. It's embarrassing."

Simon snatched it back. "Kaze and Jory are about to get discovered by Perseun drones."

"Which you already know. How can it be a surprise? And how can you read right now?" Charlie bounced up out of his seat and paced across the narrow lounge with Justin.

"Because there's only room for two people to pace," Simon answered. "I'm waiting my turn."

"I'm after you, man," said Phil, who'd been sitting on the other side of Charlie.

"Take it out to the hall," Charlie's dad said. "I'm next."

His mom looked up from her huddle with Jen and Cassie. "You all know you're ridiculous, right? Justin, sit down, you're making me nervous. And Charlie, be a dear and go get us all some coffee."

"But what if I miss—"

A nurse appeared in the doorway and surveyed the room with a frown. It was crowded in there. All of Phil's kids were clumped in one corner, forming a circle around Beatrice. His mom, Jen, and Cassie had the other side. Charlie, his dad, Simon, and Phil formed the men's station by the door. The Beckers, Justin's parents, had the final two seats in the small lounge. Justin floated in the middle, looking alternately ill and dazed.

"Would the father like to come with me?" the nurse asked.

As one, the entire room seemed to gather behind Justin and push him forward. The young man braced a hand on the doorway, stopping the tide from carrying him through, and asked, "Is everything okay?"

Charlie leaned over him. "Is Liv okay? Is it done? Do—"

The nurse held up a single hand. "I'm going to assume there's only one father, and that's the lucky guy who gets to come with me right now. As for the rest of you, everything's fine. Olivia and baby are doing well."

Charlie's knees trembled. "Boy or girl?" Liv hadn't wanted to know the gender, which had been thoroughly annoying . . . and so like her.

The nurse smiled. "A girl."

His little girl had had a little girl. Charlie's vision misted, and he turned to find something other than his shirt to wipe his eyes with. His dad and Simon offered him handkerchiefs. He took both, pressing one to each eye. Behind him, the surge of family had finally knocked Justin through the door. Charlie watched his lanky frame disappear down the hall with a mixture of jealousy, respect, admiration, and jealousy.

He wanted to be the first, aside from Liv and Rosie, to see his granddaughter. *Oh, my God. I have a granddaughter.* But he also remembered what that first glimpse would mean to Justin...and Justin was a good kid. A decent young man. Not every guy would weather the storm of Liv's need to breakup and makeup three times over the course of nine months. In fact, the last time, Justin had refused to leave the kitchen, saying only, *"How about if I just stay here and save you the phone call tomorrow?"*

Had to love him, and Charlie did. Justin was the son he'd never had, and even if he and Liv never did make it official, he would always be a part of their lives. Therefore, Justin deserved this moment, and this moment was truly his.

There was nothing like meeting your child for the first time.

Nothing.

Swallowing, Charlie turned back to Simon and handed him the wadded-up rag that had been a pristine square of cotton only a minute before. His dad already had another hanky in hand, thank goodness, because Charlie had inherited the messy crying from him. His dad's face was red and wet and creased.

"You okay?" Simon murmured, putting an arm around his shoulders.

Charlie leaned into his side. "Yeah. Maybe. No? I really don't know."

Simon kissed the side of his head, precipitating a wave of hugs and kisses that rippled through the lounge with everyone sniffling and laughing and celebrating. Charlie found himself face-to-face with Beatrice at one point and tried to just give her a nod.

She took his hand and squeezed it. No smile, no return nod, no speech about how she'd been wrong about him and they could start over. But she'd touched him willingly. Had to mean something, right?

A long, long while later, it was his turn to meet the baby. Charlie grabbed Simon's arm. "Come on."

"But—"

"And leave the book here."

Simon handed his book to Phil and followed Charlie down the hall. They entered Liv's room together. Liv was propped up in bed, flushed and exhausted, but obviously happy. Radiant, in fact. Rosalie sat in a chair next to the bed, and in her arms was a wrapped bundle of joy.

How could he think of a baby as anything else?

Charlie kissed his daughter's cheek. "Hey, Duck."

"Hey, Dad."

"How was it?"

"Scary."

He gripped her shoulder. "But look what you did!"

She turned to her baby and smiled. "Yeah."

Charlie gazed at his granddaughter's face, and his heart knocked painfully in his chest. "She's perfect, Liv. She looks just like you."

"Doesn't she?" Rosalie said, smiling proudly down at her best friend's daughter.

"She looks a bit like you too, Dad," Liv said. "She's got our eyes."

"And your mouth," said Charlie.

Rosie grinned. "Maybe Justin's nose?"

Simon leaned in, squinting. "Definitely Justin's nose."

"I want to name her after Mom," Liv said.

Charlie simply nodded. If he opened his mouth, he'd start sobbing.

Liv nodded toward the baby. "Want to hold her?"

No. Yes. Maybe?

Definitely.

Charlie eased his arms under his granddaughter, under *Merry*, and lifted her out of Rosie's arms. "Hey, you."

He turned to show the baby to Simon and found his fabulous eyes shining with tears. He shouldn't have been surprised. Simon was a quiet guy, staid in some ways, but more loving than anyone Charlie had ever known. When they were together, Simon always held his hand, touched his shoulder or arm, kissed his temple.

Charlie knew Simon needed the small touches as much as he did, that he'd been waiting for this, for what they had, all his life.

So had Charlie.

When Simon looked down at Merry, his expression shifted from one emotion to another. Surprise, delight, anxiety, and that wonderful warmth that always rested beneath, whatever he did. The essence of Simon.

"She's beautiful." Leaning over, Simon said it again to Liv. Louder. "She's beautiful."

"You ready for this?" Charlie murmured.

Simon arched a single eyebrow. "You've got it handled, Charlie. I'm the background guy. Besides, this isn't our baby." He hadn't taken his eyes off her, though.

"You decorated her room," Charlie said.

"I'm aware of where my strengths lie."

"You're going to love her. I can already see it in your face."

Simon smiled. "I loved her before she was even born."

"Are you guys plotting to steal my baby?" Liv asked.

Rosalie giggled.

Charlie turned back around. "Nope, we're just getting ready to be grandads." He grinned at Simon. "Right?"

"Is this one of those questions where you tell me the answer before I get to think about it?"

"You already love her. You said it yourself."

Simon put an arm around Charlie's shoulders and squeezed.

Charlie leaned into the man he slept next to every night and woke to every morning. The man who'd helped him turn his house into the home he'd always wanted it to be. The man who sometimes seemed to be a more capable father than Charlie was. The most wonderful addition to his family since Olivia.

The man who'd made his life *right* again.

"We're ready for this, aren't we?"

Simon kissed his temple. "We're ready."

RP

Explore more of the *This Time Forever* series:
riptidepublishing.com/titles/universe/this-time-forever

Dear Reader,

Thank you for reading Kelly Jensen's *Building Forever*!

We know your time is precious and you have many, many entertainment options, so it means a lot that you've chosen to spend your time reading. We really hope you enjoyed it.

We'd be honored if you'd consider posting a review—good or bad—on sites like **Amazon, Barnes & Noble, Kobo, Goodreads, Twitter, Facebook**, **Tumblr**, and your blog or website. We'd also be honored if you told your friends and family about this book. Word of mouth is a book's lifeblood!

For more information on upcoming releases, author interviews, blog tours, contests, giveaways, and more, please sign up for our weekly, spam-free newsletter and visit us around the web:

Newsletter: riptidepublishing.com/newsletter
Twitter: twitter.com/RiptideBooks
Facebook: facebook.com/RiptidePublishing
Goodreads: tinyurl.com/RiptideOnGoodreads
Tumblr: riptidepublishing.tumblr.com

Thank you so much for Reading the Rainbow!

RiptidePublishing.com

Acknowledgments

This book was easy to write and difficult to edit because Charlie's journey became so personal. Often, he represented my thoughts on a page, and having some of those thoughts marked as possibly inappropriate or alienating was a humbling experience. Parenting is the hardest job I've ever attempted—and a parent can only ever try to get it right. Writing is so much the same. In the end, we do our best, which means remaining open to new ways of thinking and doing—many of which will be taught to us by our children, whether they're flesh and blood or words on a page.

I had a lot of first-, second-, and third-round readers for this project, and all of them had valuable feedback. Thank you, Eileen, for being the first person to meet Charlie and tell me I had to keep writing him. That was the easy part. Thanks to the man who inspired Simon and made him special. (Yes, I'm being deliberately vague.) Thanks to Jenn, Laura, and Rain for guiding me through the second round. Your suggestions made this book stronger. More thanks to Kris and my editor, Caz, for handling the third round. I've taken your lessons to heart.

Thanks to the Fort and my Lady Writers for the feedback on various scenes. And for listening. And simply for being there.

Thank you to the readers who keep buying my books! You inspire me to continue writing.

As always, thanks to my family, particularly my daughter, for teaching me to be a better human.

Finally, thanks to the team at Riptide for helping to shape the best possible version of this story, from concept to cover art to completion.

ALSO BY
Kelly Jensen

This Time Forever series (coming soon)
Renewing Forever
Chasing Forever

To See the Sun
Out in the Blue
Wrong Direction
When Was the Last Time
Best in Show
Block and Strike

The Counting series
Counting Fence Posts
Counting Down
Counting on You

The Chaos Station series, with Jenn Burke
Chaos Station
Lonely Shore
Skip Trace
Inversion Point
Phase Shift

The Aliens in New York series
Uncommon Ground
Purple Haze

ABOUT THE *Author*

If aliens ever do land on Earth, Kelly will not be prepared, despite having read over a hundred stories of the apocalypse. Still, she will pack her precious books into a box and carry them with her as she strives to survive. It's what bibliophiles do.

Kelly is the author of a number of novels, novellas, and short stories, including the Chaos Station series, cowritten with Jenn Burke. Some of what she writes is speculative in nature, but mostly it's just about a guy losing his socks and/or burning dinner. Because life isn't all conquering aliens and mountain peaks. Sometimes finding a happy ever after is all the adventure we need.

Connect with Kelly:
Newsletter: eepurl.com/czGhYz
Website: kellyjensenwrites.com
Facebook: facebook.com/kellyjensenwrites
Twitter: twitter.com/kmkjensen

Enjoy more stories like *Building Forever* at RiptidePublishing.com!

Midlife Crisis

With a little faith—and a lot of love—he may finally be able to live as himself.

ISBN: 978-1-62649-668-2

Until September

Come September, will he want the family he never asked for?

ISBN: 978-1-62649-356-8

RIPTIDE PUBLISHING